THE MALLEE GIRL

JENNIFER SCOULLAR

PILYARA PRESS

ALSO BY JENNIFER SCOULLAR

THE WILD AUSTRALIA STORIES

Brumby's Run (The Wild Australia Stories - Book 1)

Currawong Creek (The Wild Australia Stories - Book 2)

Billabong Bend (The Wild Australia Stories - Book 3)

Turtle Reef (The Wild Australia Stories - Book 4

Journey's End (The Wild Australia Stories - Book 5)

Wasp Season (The Wild Australia Stories - Book 6)

Paradise Valley (The Wild Australia Stories - Book 8)

THE TASMANIAN TALES

Fortune's Son (The Tasmanian Tales - Book 1)

The Lost Valley (The Tasmanian Tales - Book 2)

The Memory Tree (The Tasmanian Tales - Book 3)

Copyright © 2023 Jennifer Scoullar
All rights reserved.
No part of this book may be reproduced in any form or by any electronic or mechanical means, including information storage and retrieval systems, without written permission from the author, except for the use of brief quotations in a book review.

This is a work of fiction. Names, characters, organisations, places and incidents are either the product of the author's imagination or are used fictitiously, and any resemblance to actual persons, living or dead, business establishments, events or locales is entirely coincidental.

Version 1
Print ISBN 978-1-925827-46-0
Pilyara Press
Melbourne

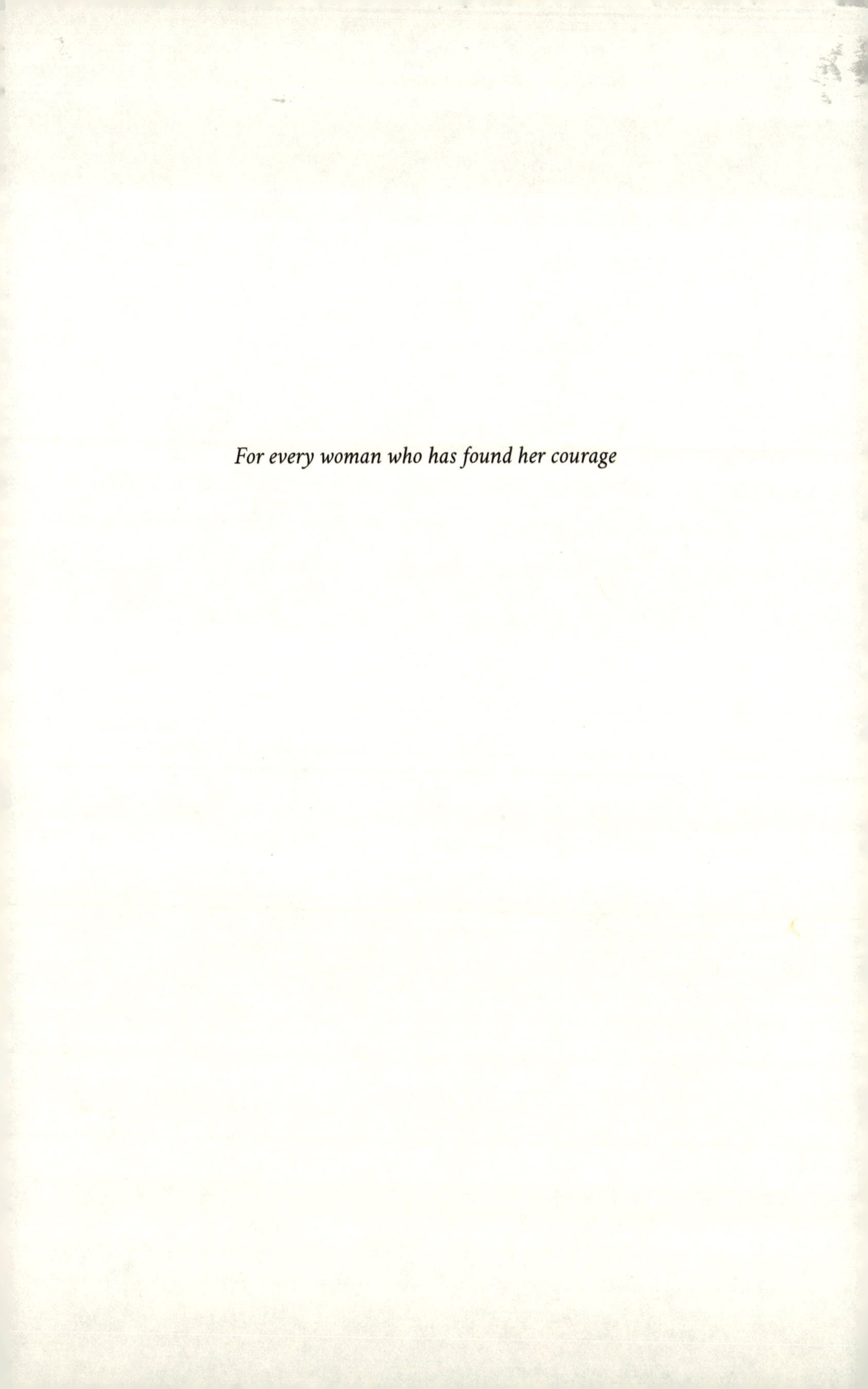

For every woman who has found her courage

CHAPTER 1

Pippa Black stared out the kitchen window at the dusty sun-beaten paddocks beyond. How could it be this hot at eight o'clock on a mid-September morning? Such early heat didn't bode well for the coming summer. She used a cup to bail some washing-up water from the sink for her collection of potted plants on the sill. Basil, parsley, rosemary and thyme. African violets for colour and aloe vera for soothing bruises and sunburn. The only green things in sight.

The tiny town of Kilpa had recorded its lowest winter rainfall on record and, so far, the spring rains had failed too. Cade, Pippa's husband, had given up on harvesting what was left of the wheat crop, and had turned their starving sheep into the paddocks. They were dirty brown blobs surrounded by dirty brown stubble. Even the few stunted mallee trees were brown, their customary grey-green foliage layered with topsoil from last week's monster dust storm.

Their farm, ironically enough, was named Fairview. But there was nothing but sheep and dust and more sheep for as far as the eye could see. Even Pippa's friends, the magpies, had fled. She missed their dawn chorus. Now she awoke to the cawing of scavenging crows. Dying sheep were easy pickings.

Pippa opened the window wider, hoping for the hint of a breeze.

Sweat trickled down between her breasts, making her shirt cling uncomfortably. The house would be an oven by the afternoon. She wiped plastered strands of fair hair from her face. Pippa wanted to cut it short for summer – it would be so much cooler – but Cade liked it long. She sighed in resignation. There was no arguing with Cade.

Pippa slapped a ball of dough onto a floured board, working it with the heels of her hands. Drought meant Cade had slashed their household budget, insisting they could save money by baking their own bread. It was all right for him – Cade didn't have to fire up the range in sweltering heat. And he wouldn't even buy her a little fan for the kitchen.

Pippa fanned herself with a *Women's Weekly* kept on the bench for that purpose. Her mother, Ruby, passed the magazines on when she'd finished with them. She loved their fashion and beauty tips, but Pippa couldn't relate to the glamorous women gracing their pages. She was tall, blonde and thin, but there the resemblance ended. The models dripped with style and confidence. Pippa wore Salvation Army clothes, was shy as a mouse and her chin was too long.

She switched on the pocket radio sitting on the sill and kneaded the dough in time to *Not Pretty Enough* by Kasey Chambers, waiting for it to become smooth and elastic the way Mum had taught her. She winced as she worked; her wrist still ached where Cade had grabbed it. Pippa paused to rest her hand, worries churning through her head on repeat. She was her own worst critic. Blaming herself for the mess of her marriage. Wishing for the millionth time that she'd made different choices, better choices. What was it they said about hindsight? Always twenty-twenty.

Cade had found employment in the sand mine at Millburn, an hour's drive away. There'd been no choice but for him to take outside work – the farm was running at a loss. Pippa had offered to help by resuming her old job at the Kilpa general store where she'd worked before they were married. The humble position that she'd once looked down her nose at now seemed like the height of fun. But Cade didn't want his wife to work outside the home. It would be a humiliation, he said, so they were making do on his small wage and by selling off the odd pen of skinny sheep.

Duke, their clever red kelpie, scratched at the back door then opened the flyscreen with his paw. 'You're getting spoilt,' she said as he trotted in. 'Don't get used to sleeping on the bed. Cade will be home for dinner.'

Cade had stayed overnight in Millburn to have a Friday night out with the boys. It had happened a few times lately. Pippa didn't mind. It meant she could sleep curled up beside Duke's warm, protective form. She could relax and dream. She could sleep late instead of rising at five to cook Cade's breakfast and pack his lunch. He didn't want her making sandwiches the night before and leaving them in the fridge. He said they had to be fresh. Yes, Pippa liked it when Cade didn't come home.

The sound of a car in the distance interrupted Pippa's reflections. She looked out the window to see a plume of dust billowing up the long, straight driveway towards the house. It was Cade, and he was in a hurry. What on earth was he doing home at this time? He normally slept in until lunchtime on Saturday mornings after a big night out. Duke began his loud guard barking. The big dog, who'd been a wedding present from her mother, always warned of Cade's arrival as if he were a stranger. The habit had earned Duke plenty of clouts during the past four years.

The black Ford ute screeched to a halt in front of the house, spraying gravel and nearly slamming into a verandah post. Cade threw himself from the cab, mounted the porch steps in a single bound and burst inside. Pippa stared, wiping floury hands on her apron and taking in his filthy face, dishevelled clothes and dusty hair. Cobwebs clung to one ear.

He fixed wild eyes on her and grabbed her arm. 'We have to get out of here, babe – right now.' His voice was low and urgent.

Pippa pulled away. 'Cade, you're frightening me.'

He scrubbed one grimy hand over his face while holding her tight with the other. 'There's no time to explain. Trust me, we have to go this very minute.'

Pippa started to protest, but Cade's brow furrowed menacingly, and she went quiet. He was too upset to reason with, that much was clear. She took off her apron. 'I'll just wrap the dough to prove and get my bag from the bedroom.'

'There's no time!' He was shouting now. Duke began barking in a high-pitched frenzy until a vicious kick silenced him.

Fear rose in Pippa's throat as Cade half-pulled, half-carried her from the house and bundled her into the ute. He slammed the door shut, climbed behind the wheel, then swore and punched the dash. Pippa knew better than to ask what was wrong. She cowered as he leaped out and dashed back into the house. Moments later he came sprinting back and hurled his precious laptop onto the rear seat. The Ford roared to life, spun in a tight circle and tore down the laneway that led to the back gate.

Their farm bordered Hattah-Kulkyne, a vast, semi-arid national park known for its red dirt, native pine woodlands and mallee scrub. The park was popular with tourists, nature lovers and campers, which was something Pippa couldn't understand. Cade and the drought had killed her childhood love of this harsh, ancient land. What was the attraction of poor sandy soil, sad stunted trees and searing hot summers? And why was Cade driving straight into that godforsaken wilderness like a madman?

'Look out!' called Pippa. A flock of startled emus raced ahead of them. The huge birds barely managed to dodge off the track in time.

Cade put his foot down harder and drove on with gritted teeth, heading who knew where. The old ute had next to no suspension, so each pothole and corrugation made Pippa's teeth rattle. The kilometres flew past. When she finally plucked up the courage to ask Cade what was wrong, he didn't answer. He didn't even seem to hear, so lost was he in some private madness.

Pippa sank back in her seat. She wore shorts and her bare skin clung to the hot vinyl. Bulldust streamed in through the half-open windows, choking her and leaving an ever-thickening film of dust on the dash. She tried closing her window, but that was equally unbearable. Within minutes the cabin became a furnace.

The ute wasn't in good shape. It had a lot of dings and Cade was too miserly to re-gas the air conditioning. When he'd sideswiped a gatepost, denting a front panel and cracking the headlight, he'd repaired it with gaffer tape. This small act of stinginess was a constant annoyance for Pippa. Her family were proud of their cars. However old, they were always well maintained. On top of that, Cade said they couldn't afford to fix her twenty-year-old Honda Civic, which meant she no longer had her own car to drive. She suspected that he liked it that way.

Pippa glanced at her husband, alarmed by his wide eyes, by his fixed staring at the road ahead. Frightened by how far he'd moved beyond her reach. Whatever had happened last night? Pippa coughed and gazed out the window. Nothing for it but to wait Cade out.

The nightmare drive seemed to last forever. How long had it been? One hour? Two? Hard to tell. The dash clock didn't work. Pippa didn't have her phone, and she couldn't get her bearings in the featureless, flat monotony of red dust and mallee scrub.

At last a low line of trees appeared on their right – the Murray River. Cade headed for it and found a place to park near the river-bank, his frenzy apparently spent. Pippa glanced around. She knew this place – a remote branch of the Murray that was one of her father's favourite fishing spots. He'd camped out here with Cade more than once.

Pippa looked across to where her husband was slumped over the wheel, head sagged on crossed arms. She eased the door open and climbed out of the baking cab, half-expecting Cade to give chase. When he didn't move, she walked down to the boggy water's edge to splash her face.

The once mighty Murray River that marked the park's eastern boundary had been laid low by thirsty irrigators and years of drought. It flowed like a sluggish brown snake between dying red gums, imparting a sense of desolation and despair. Pippa closed her eyes and sank down in the shade with her back against a tree trunk, fanning herself with a switch of leaves. She felt naked without a scarf around her neck. She always wore a scarf.

A few minutes later Pippa felt a tap on her shoulder and jumped like a startled deer. Cade stood over her, offering a canteen. She gulped the warm water down greedily. When she'd had her fill, she stood up and inspected Cade's broad face. His manic expression had been replaced by one of apprehension.

'What now?' she asked. 'Can we go home?'

'No,' he snapped. 'Now we wait.'

'Wait for what?' She kicked at the tree in frustration. 'What's happened, Cade? Tell me.'

To her utter astonishment he wrapped her in a great hug. He wasn't a physically affectionate man. And were those tears?

'I've done something, Pip.' He let her go and moved restlessly from foot to foot.

'Done what? Come on Cade, tell me.'

His expression soured. 'The less you know the better.'

The sound of approaching vehicles made Cade stiffen. He ran to the ute and grabbed a rifle from the tray.

Pippa's breath came in shallow gasps as she stared at the weapon. Her husband had lost his mind. Her first instinct was to flee, but to where? And anyway, she couldn't outrun a bullet. So instead she huddled on the ground beneath a tree and made herself as small a target as possible.

<h1 style="text-align:center">CHAPTER 2</h1>

A beat-up blue station wagon drove into view on the other side of the river, followed by a white Hilux ute. Cade lowered his weapon and shouted. The drivers got out and waved before inflating a dinghy and launching it into the water. Then the stouter of the two rowed across the muddy brown ditch and scrambled up the riverbank towards them.

Pippa recognised the man's Mohawk and the Iron Cross tattoo on his bull neck. Dylan, one of Cade's new friends from the mine. He'd been to the house a few times, joining in on the mysterious computer sessions in the spare room. Drinking too much. Murmuring obscenities to her when no one else was listening.

He marched up to Cade, grinning, and clapped him on the shoulder. 'You did it, mate. Didn't think you had the guts, but I have to hand it to you.'

Cade shrugged his friend's arm away, eyes blazing, and shoved him hard. Something must have happened between them. Had Cade found out about those lewd suggestions made behind his back? Pippa hoped not – she and Dylan would both be in trouble then. Her husband was a jealous man. But no, that couldn't be it; Cade would do a great deal more than shove Dylan if he knew.

The two men moved aside a few metres, talking low as if not wanting to be overheard. Pippa pricked up her ears, trying to catch their words. Whispers soon turned into raised voices.

'You said nobody would be there.' Cade shoved Dylan again. 'Now you've dumped me right in it. And what's this shit about CCTV footage? You said you'd seen to that.'

Pippa drew in a quick breath. CCTV footage? She should have guessed Dylan was a crook. Had Cade committed some sort of robbery? It was possible. Their financial problems might have made him that desperate. She stood up and edged closer to the men.

Dylan spat on the dusty earth. 'Relax. I disabled the main camera myself. If they've picked you up somehow it will just be the car, and you had dummy plates on, right?' He pointed to Pippa. 'Why'd you bring her for? She'll just slow you down.'

Cade glanced at Pippa, then dragged Dylan further away so that she could no longer hear them. After a few more minutes of heated arguing, the men returned. Cade stood hard-faced. Dylan looked smug. He leered and lit a cigarette, taking in Pippa's tangled hair, sweaty shirt and short shorts. His gaze lingered on her bare thighs. She sat on the ground again and moved her legs behind the tree, burning with embarrassment, trying to hide the bruises.

'Tell you what, mate.' Dylan kicked at a stick, raising a tiny cloud of dust. 'I'll do you a favour and take her back home.'

Pippa shivered, despite the heat. Much as she longed to go home, she didn't fancy being alone on a long car ride with that creep.

Cade glared at Dylan, his face like thunder. He seemed strung tight enough to snap. 'My wife stays with me.' Pippa flinched as the muscles in his sinewy arms tightened, ready to throw a punch. Dylan saw it too and backed off.

'Okay, no sweat. I guess she might be useful.'

'Get up, babe,' said Cade. Cautiously, she climbed to her feet, wiping her dusty hands on her shorts. 'Take everything out of the ute. We're changing cars.'

'Why?' She knew she shouldn't ask but couldn't help herself. She was desperate to know what was going on.

Dylan shot Cade a questioning look. 'She doesn't know?'

Cade frowned and gave the slightest shake of his head.

'What don't I know?' said Pippa. Cade shifted uneasily. 'Tell me!' Silence. Rising anger made her abandon caution. 'Suit yourself. Stay here if you like, Cade, but I'm going home.' She held out an unsteady hand. 'Give me the keys.'

He slowly withdrew a keyring from his pocket and twirled it. 'So you want these? You want to leave me?'

Pippa lunged for them.

Cade struck her a vicious backhander, hurling her to the dust. 'I said, we're not going home.' She tasted blood on her lip. 'See what you made me do?' he roared.

'Steady on, mate.' Dylan reached down and pulled Pippa to her feet.

She shrank away, rubbing her hand where he'd held it and eyeing Cade warily. He was battling to keep control. The struggle showed on his face: in his eyebrows drawn low and close, in the curl of his lip and the stiff set of his jaw.

Cade's wild eyes found hers. 'Everything will be fine, babe,' he managed, roughly stroking her burning cheek. 'Now clear out the car like I said.'

Pippa nodded dully, touching her aching nose. She waved away the persistent little bush flies landing on her split lip. She wouldn't argue any more – not now, not when he was like this.

Pippa began pulling stuff out of the ute. She heaved a jerry can full of petrol from the tray. She dropped two ammo boxes in the dust, the searing hot metal casings scorching her fingers. Then, after checking to see whether Cade was watching, she dragged the boxes behind a stump. Him and his guns. It would serve him right if the ammo was left behind.

She set his laptop carefully on a broad mallee root, along with his wallet. She pulled out a pile of fencing tools and his filthy clothes from the mine. Toothpaste and deodorant in a plastic bag. Two empty water canteens. Thirsty as she was, she didn't fancy filling them from the muddy Murray. There wasn't much more in the ute.

Of course there wasn't – Cade had stopped her from packing them a bag.

He came over, rummaged through what was left in the tray and swore. 'There's bugger all I can use here.' He picked up a pair of bolt cutters. 'Oi, Dylan, help me move this stuff.' He spotted the ammo boxes behind the stump and yelled at Pippa. 'Why'd you put them way over there for? I might have missed them.'

The men carted the contents of the ute down to the river and ferried it all across to the other vehicles. Pippa watched them with dead eyes, then glanced over to the ute, a flicker of hope in her heart. Maybe …

She'd often thought about leaving Cade. The problem was that she was gutless. Everybody knew it. When Pippa was a child she hid from the Sunday lunch church ladies. Her mother, Ruby, excused this rudeness, saying, 'Don't mind Phillipa. She's always been shy – timid as a mouse, that girl.' When Pippa fled from their belligerent gander her brothers fell about laughing, saying, 'Pippa won't say boo to a goose.' When she saw a tiger snake in the chook pen and was too frightened to collect the eggs for weeks, Dad had called her spineless. He was right. She didn't have a brave bone in her body. For as long as Pippa could remember she'd been a coward, jumping at shadows. Scared of the dark. Scared of hell. Scared of her evangelical preacher father. Even scared of God, which was probably a sin.

Pippa was a grown woman now. She'd conquered many of her fears. Church ladies, geese and snakes no longer frightened her. But her husband? Cade filled her with dread. She glanced over to where he was loading the ammo boxes into the dinghy. Cade was far more dangerous than a tiger snake. How would she ever find the courage to leave him? There was nowhere to run where he wouldn't find her. Going home to her family wouldn't help. Even now, she could hear her father shouting from the homemade pulpit of his tiny country church.

'Wives, submit to your husbands as to the Lord. For the husband is head of the wife as Christ is head of the church …'

She'd never admitted to her parents how bad things were in her marriage. She was far too embarrassed and, anyway, what was the point? According to Pastor Jay Sullivan it was her duty to endure whatever Cade dished out. Secretly, Pippa thought that it didn't sound like something Jesus would say. She'd read the Bible. Jesus talked about loving each other. He was kind to prostitutes and adulteresses. He said to do unto others as you'd have them do unto you. Nowhere did Jesus say that particular teaching only applied to men.

She'd tentatively raised this inconsistency with her father. He'd accused her of defying him and unleashed a torrent of biblical quotations about children honouring their parents and daughters obeying their fathers. He hadn't mentioned Jesus once. But then Dad had always preferred the Old Testament. At times Pippa harboured the suspicion that Dad wouldn't much like Jesus if he met him.

Mum would be quietly sympathetic if Pippa left her husband, but she wouldn't go against Dad – and Dad would send her straight home to Cade. There was nobody else she could turn to. Having been home-schooled her whole life meant that she'd made no real friends. The fifty-strong members of their church were mainly relatives, and all were in thrall to her father. The notion of escaping her marriage had always seemed like an impossible dream.

But now? Cade's crazed flight into the bush could be the terrifying catalyst she needed. If she could somehow get away, she'd worry about the rest later. If the spare keys were in the car … Pippa opened the driver's door and looked under the floor mat where Cade sometimes kept them. No such luck.

She collapsed in the dust beneath the poor shade of a half-dead red gum, head resting on skinny knees. She was chilled, shaken and had no idea where Cade was taking her or what he'd do next. Today had started out like any other Saturday morning, yet now she was completely lost, her world upended in the blink of an eye.

'Well, so what?' she said aloud, finding a fresh switch of leaves to fan herself with. Her world consisted of little more than misery and loneliness anyway. No great loss. But she was reminded of something her mother would say – better the devil you know. And this new, madder Cade was not the devil she knew. He was worse, much worse. What had he done, she wondered – the thing he wouldn't tell her? What was her husband capable of?

Pippa gulped but couldn't swallow. Her throat was like sandpaper. She tried not to think of Duke, abandoned at the farm; tried not to think of what would happen to him if she didn't get back. The place could go for weeks without visitors. Pippa licked her bloody lip, but no spit would come. Her swollen tongue dragged painfully across the broken skin, rasping like a cat's. She twisted a gum leaf between her fingers. It crumbled to dust.

The men rowed back across the river with buckets, spades … and were those fire extinguishers? The only things left by the ute were Cade's laptop, wallet, and the jerry can of petrol. To Pippa's astonishment, Cade opened all the ute's windows and hurled his laptop into the cab, along with his wallet and phone. Then something else – the car keys. He picked up the jerry can, flipped the lid and took a box of matches from his pocket.

Pippa stood and squinted into the sun, unsteady on her feet, trying to make sense of the scene playing before her.

Cade looked grim. 'Babe, get down to the river.'

She hesitated.

'I said move!' He shoved her towards the bank. Pippa stumbled to the water's edge then turned, staring in disbelief as Cade poured petrol over the ute. He tossed a lit match. Dylan leaped back and hooted with excitement as the vehicle erupted in flames.

Pippa gasped and looked to Cade, but he seemed unperturbed, unmoved. Even from a distance the radiant heat scorched her skin. She closed her eyes and shielded her face with her arms. Could this day get any stranger?

CHAPTER 3

Cade swore beneath his breath as his vehicle burnt. No going back now. When the fire was almost out, they rowed across the Murray towards the waiting vehicles. Pippa sat in the dinghy among the assorted tools, staring blankly at the burnt-out hulk of their car. When they reached the other side, Cade told her to get out and wait by the water.

Pippa didn't argue. She just kept staring back across the river.

He and Dylan carted the dinghy and tools up the bank. Dylan pointed to the dark-blue station wagon and tossed something to Cade – car keys and a burner phone. 'There's some clothes in the back.'

'I'll need a bloody lot more than that now someone's dead,' he snapped. 'The story's all over the news. It won't just be a matter of lying low for a week or two like we expected.'

'I told you, we're working on it.' Streams of sweat ran down Dylan's jowly face. 'A word of warning. That old Holden's a bugger to change gears,' he said. 'And she slips into neutral sometimes. But her tank's full and the rego's in your new name.'

Cade cast the car a contemptuous glance. 'You could have stolen me something better.'

'It's not nicked,' said Dylan. 'The car's clean.' He handed over a wallet containing a driver's licence in the name of Nathan John Jones, bearing Cade's photograph.

Cade examined it. 'According to this I'm fifty years old.'

Dylan grinned. 'So you've aged well.'

Cade shot him a murderous look.

'Quit complaining. I drove a three-hour round trip for that. Luckily, they had some off-the-shelf licences on hand in Swan Hill.'

'Who's Nathan John Jones?'

'A hobo living under the old Murray River Road bridge,' said Dylan. 'We pay off homeless guys and use their identities.'

'Oi,' yelled the man sitting in the Hilux ute. 'We don't have all day.'

'Is this who I'll be from now on then – fifty-year-old Nathan Jones?' Cade turned the licence sideways. 'Where's the hologram?'

The other man honked his horn.

'It was the best they could do at such short notice,' said Dylan. 'The Melbourne boys are working on a whole new identity for you, and they really know what they're doing. You should see their licences. All the security features just like VicRoads. Embossed date of birth under your photo, green strip, holograms – the works. But until then, that card you've got there? It should do for a random traffic stop.'

Cade looked at the fake licence doubtfully, then flipped through the wallet: two hundred dollars and a prepaid debit card.

'Relax,' said Dylan. 'By tomorrow night you'll be at the safe house.' He glanced at Pippa, standing huddled by the river. 'Will she be a problem?'

Cade stuffed the wallet into his pocket. 'Pippa's as loyal as they come,' he said. 'She won't cross me.' She wouldn't dare, he thought, and thank Christ for that.

'You're all good then,' said Dylan. 'Now go on, leg it. And by the way, the boys have set up a national fundraiser for you. You're a bloody legend, mate. You've put our little cell on the map.'

Dylan's flattering words calmed Cade down. A flush of pride suffused his tired body. It may have taken thirty-four years, but he was finally receiving the respect he deserved.

Cade called for Pippa and she stumbled up the bank. He pointed to the blue station wagon. 'Get in.' Pippa climbed into the front passenger seat. She found a half-empty bottle of water inside the door and drained it in two great gulps.

Cade stared at her. Even when half-dead from the heat she was beautiful. 'We'll stop for drinks once we're down the road away,' he said, more softly.

She nodded, face impassive. Dylan was right – he shouldn't have brought her. But being without his wife was unthinkable. Nobody made him feel powerful and important the way Pippa did. Nobody else could soothe him when he was angry and build him up when he was down. Nobody else could satisfy him in bed. There'd been other women, but they'd been a waste of time. It was Pippa's body that he craved in the dark. With the magic of her soft, slim form and willing ways, she transformed him into a king. Other women were demanding and opinionated, but not his Pippa. She knew what he liked and always delivered.

Of course, sometimes she pushed his buttons. She was a woman, after all. But when he lost his temper and hit or kicked her, she made allowances. He was sorry afterwards and she knew it. But not everyone might be so forgiving; Pippa was one in a million. And if he left her behind she'd find someone else. It wouldn't be hard for a gorgeous girl like her. He'd rather die than let that happen.

The thought of Pippa with another man made his knuckles show white as he gripped the steering wheel. He glanced across at her sweet face, strands of sandy-blonde hair whipping against her cheek as she leaned out the window into the breeze. Leave her behind? Not a chance. A fresh start would mean nothing without his true love by his side.

Cade briefly rested his hand on Pippa's knee, hoping for a smile, but she kept staring out the window. What was she thinking, he wondered? He needed to come up with some sort of an explanation for their frantic flight. He'd tell her the truth soon, but not yet. She'd need time adjusting to the reality of their new life first.

Cade wiped the sweat from his eyes, lit a cigarette and wound his window all the way down. Not that it helped much. The air outside was as baking hot as the air inside. Dylan could at least have given him a car with air conditioning. Still, it felt good to be on the open road with his girl, putting the miles between him and his problems. Paddocks and trees and towns slipped by. For the first time in days he felt tension slide from his muscles. He would have whistled if his lips weren't so dry.

Pippa reached for the radio in the dash. Cade's newfound peace vanished, and he slapped her hand away. She didn't argue or ask him why. What was going on inside her head? Dammit! This was no time to be distracted. He needed to think, needed to keep his wits about him. Needed to make sure Pippa didn't hear any news bulletins.

Cade's stomach lurched alarmingly. Could she somehow sense the magnitude of what he'd done? He suddenly wanted to confess his crime. He wanted to tell her about the Renegades and how the patriot group had provided him with the kind of friendship and approval that he craved. Tell her about the emptiness that had been with him since childhood and explain why the two of them must start afresh. But he'd never been good at expressing his feelings, so he kept quiet and drove on, pondering the many unfairnesses of life.

Cade's mother had died when he was ten. He sometimes still heard her voice as she kissed him and his big brother, Brodie, goodnight.

'You boys can be anything you want to be. Follow your dreams and don't let anyone tell you otherwise.'

Cade had believed her – believed that he was special and destined for greatness. Then Mum lost her battle with cancer, abandoning him and Brodie to the tender mercies of their father. Cade had never forgiven her.

His father eked out a living growing wheat. He was a hopeless farmer, too lazy to fertilise the soil and too mean to hire help. More often than not he kept Cade and Brodie home from school to use as cheap labour. Sending them out on foot to spray hectares of thistles in the sweltering sun. Working them from dawn to dusk at harvest time. Using them as punching bags when he got drunk. Their mother wasn't there to protect them any more or take the brunt of Dad's anger in their place.

Brodie escaped the misery of home life when he and his mate went joyriding in a stolen car. Cade had begged to go along that night. The car hit a tree, killing both boys, breaking Cade's heart. He wished he'd died too, and he added Brodie to the list of people who'd abandoned him, alongside their mother.

Cade left the farm straight after the funeral without saying good-bye. He found work as a roustabout with a mob of shearing contractors. As the kid of the group at fifteen, he never felt like he belonged. He dreamed of being a gun shearer, but it wasn't to be. Shearing was back-breaking work. He earned the ire of the other men for being slow. He earned the ire of the station owners for being clumsy, leaving too many nicks and cuts on their sheep. His so-called mates laughed and named him The Ripper. Cade still felt a quiver of rage to think of it.

But he'd showed them. One night he burnt down the woolshed where they were all bunking. Some men suffered serious burns – served the bastards right. Suspicion never fell on him. The police blamed the blaze on drunken men and discarded cigarette butts, leaving Cade in the clear – but not with his fellow shearers. They knew. They ran him out of town.

Years of itinerant labouring followed. He was always the outsider, envious of others' good fortune. When his father died, Cade inherited Fairview and married Pippa. He found God and joined Jay's church, but it didn't last. All that praying? He couldn't keep it up. Sundays became like any other day. Pippa wasn't happy. She missed her family, but she was his wife and would do as he said. And Cade was happiest when he had her to himself. Then the drought hit, turning his land into a dust bowl.

Cade's luck changed for the better when he found work in the sand mine at Millburn. A steady salary eased his money worries and growing friendships at the mine eased his isolation. Dylan wasn't some God-botherer sermonising about sin. He was an everyday bloke who echoed Cade's own bitter dissatisfaction with the world.

'We're second-class citizens in our own country,' Dylan said one smoko as he read a newspaper article about refugees. 'Bloody foreigners coming here and taking our jobs. Muslims and all – damned terrorists, the lot of them.'

Not only were Cade's own resentments reflected back to him daily, but he also picked up some new grievances.

'All these bushfires lately?' said another man. 'It's not climate change causing them, like those damned greenies say. It's space lasers financed by the Rothschilds. Then they buy up the land of bankrupt farmers for a song and sell it off to China.'

'Space lasers?' asked Cade, intrigued.

'My oath. My wife says her hairdresser read about them on some science website.'

Cade hadn't known about this outrage. He added Jews to his hate list. They were joined by socialists, communists, the government and feminists, to name a few. In the beginning he didn't understand what all these groups stood for, but his new friends quickly educated him.

'Feminists?' said Dylan. 'I ain't holding nothing against women.' He dug Cade in the ribs and chortled. 'More's the pity! But once they get these uppity ideas in their heads that they can do a man's job – that they're equal in every way? Well, it turns them into ball-breakers.'

Cade glared at him.

'I don't mean your missus,' Dylan added. 'Pretty as a picture, cooks a damn fine roast and she's happy for you to be head of the house. That's the kind of woman a man needs. But not everyone's so lucky. My old lady found another feller, ran off with my kid, and yet I'm the one whose being hounded for child support. I bust my gut every day in that mine so that my ex can shack up with another man. Now I ask you, is that fair?'

A sheep strayed across the road ahead, interrupting his musings. Cade blared the horn, and bile burnt his throat as he recalled the story of Dylan's wife. *My old lady found another feller.* Faithless bitch! He regarded his friend with a kind of pity mixed with contempt. How could a man let his woman get away with that?

Rage welled up from deep in his stomach. Cade pulled off the road and retched out the door. A hot wind from the north whipped his face. He felt like he'd vomited up the last drops of moisture from his body.

'Are you all right?' Pippa rubbed his back. 'It's probably heatstroke. We need to find a shop, Cade, get some drinks. This sort of heat is a killer.'

Her presence soothed him. Pippa was a treasure. Loyal and caring. Making a home for them on a shoestring in the middle of this terrible drought. He loved her for it, he really did – but if she ever pulled something like Dylan's wife? If she ever even thought about it …?

Cade fought to relax his tightening fists.

CHAPTER 4

Pippa leaned back in her seat as Cade started up the car again, a smear of vomit still clinging to his chin. She had no idea where they were, or where they were going. She knew so little of what lay beyond Kilpa. From childhood she'd been taught to fear the outside world, a world filled with all kinds of wickedness. She knew they were heading north, though. The sun told her that.

Half an hour of silent driving brought them to the small town of Dixon's Creek. She didn't recognise the name. Why would she? Apart from a week-long honeymoon in Noosa, she'd never been farther than Mildura, and that had just been to get her driver's licence. Pippa made a mental note of the town's name anyway. If she managed to escape from Cade, this knowledge could help her retrace her journey.

Dixon's Creek wasn't much more than a service station, church and war memorial, but there was a licensed general store. Cade slowed the car and angle-parked in the main street. Thank God. She was dizzy and nauseous, with a raspy throat and a thumping headache. If she didn't get a drink soon she'd faint.

'Wait here.' Cade got out and marched into the store.

He took the keys with him, but Pippa didn't have the energy to be disappointed. She was too sick to take advantage of any mistakes

Cade might make. A few people passed by in the street or gossiped on the corner, aimless and free. She stared at a tall grain silo with a giant mural of a soaring eagle painted on its side. How had the artist managed it? The silo must have been thirty-five metres high. Pippa envied that beautiful bird, so brave and powerful. To her surprise, tears tracked down her dusty cheeks. She'd thought she was too dried up for crying.

Cade returned with cold bottles of Coke, hot sausage rolls and a litre bottle of whisky. Pippa couldn't eat, but she guzzled the cola in great swallows, burping at the bubbles. With each gulp she could feel strength seep back into her dehydrated body.

He thrust a sausage roll at her. 'Eat.' She shook her head. 'Eat!' This time she took the offered food, nibbling at the soggy pastry as Cade nodded in satisfaction, trying not to gag. He started the car.

'Honey, where are we going?' she ventured, hoping his mood had improved with the food and drink.

'I'll tell you when we get there,' he said. 'It's still a long drive. Hours. Why not get some sleep?'

She was suddenly overwhelmingly tired. Yes, sleep. That was what she needed. Pippa laid her seat back as far as it would go and drifted off.

When she woke it was dark, and Cade was shaking her shoulder. 'Out you come, sleepy-head.' He stank of whisky.

Pippa stumbled from the car. She stood in a gravel car park before a long, low brick building. An orange neon sign on the roof read *The Welcome Inn* and a smaller sign beneath flashed *Vacancies* in green lights.

Cade guided her to a red door with the number seven painted on it. Inside the hot, stuffy motel room was a double bed, wardrobe and a small fridge beneath a shelf. A toaster and electric kettle sat on top beside a small television. A threadbare rug lay over worn floorboards, and another door led to an ensuite with a shower, toilet and grimy basin.

The air stank of stale cigarettes. Pippa tried to open the front window, but it was firmly stuck with paint. She pointed to the high glass louvres on the back wall. 'Could you open them, honey? I can't reach.'

Cade obliged, then went out to the car and returned with soft drinks and two pizzas. He pulled off his shirt. The dark curly hair on his chest was damp with sweat. Cade poured himself a drink. The whisky bottle stood on the shelf, already half empty.

A big moth flew in through the open window's torn flywire. It fluttered around the bare bulb in the roof. Pippa wanted to catch it and put it outside, but Cade would have scoffed and killed it anyway. Cade held a pizza box out to her. 'Your favourite – pepperoni.'

Pippa forced herself to smile, while above her the pretty moth was bashing itself to death against the light. Her stomach churned at the thought of eating. Cade's face darkened. He didn't like it when she refused what he offered. She was supposed to be grateful.

'I might have a shower first,' she said. 'Wash off the dust.'

Cade's expression grew hungry and his hand brushed her breast. 'Want me to join you?'

'You stay here and relax.' She managed a smile. 'Have that pizza before it gets cold and watch the footy.'

Cade strode over to the screen and tore its plug from the wall. 'The TV stays off.' His eyes travelled round the room and landed on a clock radio beside the bed. 'This too.' He tossed the radio into a drawer. 'I don't want us to be disturbed.'

What? But he loved watching television. The large-screen TV in the lounge room back at Fairview was one of the few things Pippa liked about being married to Cade. Her parents had never owned a television. Dad called it the tool of the devil. When Pippa started watching daytime soaps, she could almost agree with him. All those glamorous, independent women embroiled in scandal after scandal, running their own businesses, having affairs. She was shocked at first, but it didn't stop her watching. In no time the characters became like familiar friends, offering her an escape from loneliness and dull routine.

Cade also loved TV and always had some sports show running in the background when he was home. On top of that, it was footy finals season. His beloved Bulldogs were playing tonight. She couldn't imagine what could stop him from turning on that television.

Pippa escaped to the bathroom and peeled off her filthy clothes. She filled the sink with water, scrubbed them with a small, hard cake of soap, then wrung them out by hand and hung them on the towel rail. They'd dry quickly enough in this heat and, anyway, she had nothing else to wear. She gulped some water from the tap then stepped into the shower. Her eyes closed and she let the rushing water enfold her in a soft, protective curtain, let it lull her into a pleasant trance.

Pippa jumped as the bathroom door opened and Cade pulled back the shower curtain. He stripped off his jeans and stepped into the cubicle. Cade held out his arms and she shrank away. She hadn't meant to. Cade hated rejection, but her response was as instinctive as a rabbit cringing from a fox. It provoked a string of curses from her husband. He withdrew, leaving his jeans in a heap on the floor. She trembled against the slippery wall tiles, wondering whether she'd ever be brave enough to leave the bathroom.

Pippa dressed quickly and sat frozen on the side of the toilet seat. The more time she could give Cade to calm down, the better. But it wasn't long before he called her name. She entered the main room cautiously, feeling the weight of his dark eyes on her. They were red and wild. Cade ran his hands under her damp hair and kissed her neck. Then he backhanded her hard in the face, slamming her against the wall. 'You're my wife. Don't ever say no to me.'

Pippa touched her burning cheek and watched his hands ball into fists. The scene seemed to play out in slow motion as Cade's punch landed in her stomach. She would have screamed if the wind hadn't been knocked out of her. Instead she doubled over in pain and stumbled away. He kicked her in the lower back and legs, adding fresh bruises to the old ones. Seizing her by the hair, he forced her to her knees. 'Will you mind me from now on? Will you?'

Pippa nodded, feeling oddly calm and disconnected as she noted how badly he slurred his words. He was very drunk. And when had he last slept? she wondered.

'Now get up and pour me another drink.' Cade let her go and sat down on the bed.

She gritted her teeth and used the fridge to help her to her feet. Her back ached. Her stomach ached. She could only take shallow breaths, as if she'd been thrown from a horse and winded. Pippa sloshed whisky into Cade's glass until it was full. He emptied it in a succession of small swallows.

'Take off your clothes and lie down with me.'

Pippa pulled back the bedspread, stripped and slipped beneath the top sheet.

He climbed on top of her, his whisky breath making her gag. The mattress squeaked as he heaved and grunted, making a half-hearted attempt at sex, but it was no use. He was far too intoxicated. Cade slid off her body, one heavy leg still holding her down, and started to snore.

Pippa lay paralysed for the longest time, taking stock. Reviewing her life as if watching a movie. She'd married four years ago with such high hopes, eager to leave behind the family farm, Utopia, where she'd grown up. Twenty hadn't seemed too young. Mum was younger when she'd married Dad. At seventeen Pippa had wanted to go to Swan Hill or Mildura to enrol in a course. It would have been nice to live near a river. Her friend, Tracey, from the next-door sheep station had left to study bookkeeping at SuniTAFE, even living on campus. It sounded like a great adventure, but when Pippa suggested the idea, Dad had been horrified, and he was the one who made decisions in their family.

'No daughter of mine will go gallivanting with godless sinners. I know about those places, full of degenerates and atheists. Full of girls dressed like sluts and fornicating in contravention of the scriptures. We didn't spend ten years on your homeschooling so you could run wild as soon as you grew up. You're the oldest, Phillipa. You must set an example for your brothers and sisters.'

So Pippa did just that, working at the little Kilpa general store on

Saturdays and helping teach her siblings at home during the week – feeling like she might wither and die from loneliness and boredom and lost opportunities.

Her mother tried to console her. 'It won't be forever, darling. You'll find a nice young man soon enough, maybe at church. Then you'll have your own family to look after.'

Well yes, maybe. Except that Dad had stopped them from going to church in Kilpa after Father Gerald died and was replaced by a priest born in Mumbai – a priest who'd apparently been a chemist in an earlier life. Her father didn't trust scientists, and he trusted foreigners even less.

'How can a man like that call himself devout?' he'd thundered. 'From now on we will pray within the sanctity of our own blessed land.'

Dad built a little timber chapel beside their house and became a lay preacher. So much for meeting anybody. But in the end, someone had come along – Cade, a man hired to help with the harvest. He was tall, good-looking in a brooding sort of way and was ten years older than Pippa. The age difference didn't bother her. In fact, she'd been flattered to receive the attentions of a mature man and had fallen hard for Cade. He'd seemed romantic and exciting back then, intriguing Pippa with stories of life beyond her narrow world.

He took her on picnics and brought flowers and little gifts. He was kind to her younger siblings. He told Pippa of catching crocodiles up north, mustering buffalo as a chopper pilot and managing a diamond mine in the Kimberley. She'd been gullible enough to believe his tall tales. After an eight-week courtship, her charming suitor not only proposed but had won the approval of her stern father, which was no mean feat. Cade ticked all of Jay's boxes: a Christian conservative farmer with a proud nationalistic bent. He called himself a patriot and flew an Australian flag at his gate. He and Dad had that in common.

After a whirlwind wedding, Pippa escaped the loneliness of her family farm only to swap it for a new kind of loneliness – one far harder to bear. No more singalongs and games with her brothers and sisters. No more afternoons with her mother in the kitchen, bottling quinces, talking and laughing and cracking jokes. No more riding her horse, Pepper, alone in the bush, savouring the delicious freedom of just suiting herself. No more searching for malleefowl mounds and the rare domed nests of emu-wrens. No more harvesting the fruits of wild quandong trees so Mum could make jam. She'd loved the Mallee country back then. But after years of drought and isolation the land had become an enemy.

Pippa's eyes stung with tears and she knuckled them away. No, Cade was not the saviour she'd imagined. Fairview was mortgaged to the hilt, for starters. So much for his promise of a prosperous life. He drank too much, didn't go to church and spent hours each evening on the computer in the spare room with the door closed. What did he do in there? He was moody and jealous and demanding. Pippa had to walk on eggshells around him, and married life soon disintegrated into a procession of dreary days.

After twelve months the violence had begun. At first she could predict the coming storm. Cade's face would grow redder and redder with rage, giving her time to prepare herself. Sometimes she could even calm him down. But after a while he started to snap without warning. She'd endured it for three long years, hoping it might get better, hoping he might change. She'd even got used to it, like someone who'd learnt to live with a savage dog. But Pippa understood now, after that final kick in the back tonight, that she'd been naive and foolish all along. Her thoughts were crystallising as if she was waking up and clearing the fog of sleep. If she stayed with Cade he'd kill her. It was that simple.

So, what was she going to do about it?

CHAPTER 5

Pippa lay in the dark trying to gauge the time. Cade's wrist lay under him so she couldn't see his watch, and the fluorescent wall clock didn't work. After what she guessed was about an hour, she slid carefully out from under her husband, so carefully that the mattress barely moved. She got dressed, ran to the bathroom and shut the door, praying it didn't creak. She turned the light on and searched Cade's jeans. Yes – she had the car keys! Next she went through his wallet: eighty dollars, some change and a bank card belonging to someone called Nathan Jones. There was a driver's licence with the same name and Cade's photo on the front. What on earth? Why did her husband have a fake licence in somebody else's name? There was no time to wonder about it now.

Pippa shoved the wallet and car keys deep into the pocket of her shorts, switched off the light and tiptoed to the front door. This was it. Cade was still snoring steadily. She held her breath and grabbed the handle … It wouldn't turn. Okay, stay calm. Don't be a fumble fingers. She tried again … and again. No use. The door had been locked from the inside with a key.

Moonshine streamed through the small window, faintly lighting the room. She searched the two drawers, atop the wardrobe, in the fridge and under the television. Pippa knew what the key looked like. It was an old-fashioned, heavy-duty metal one, attached to a large plastic tag. She patted down the mattress, careful not to disturb the sleeping man, and then felt around beneath the bed. Nothing.

Cade stirred in his sleep and she backed away, thinking furiously. A small combination safe lay bolted to a shelf in the wardrobe. He must have put the key in there. Pippa sat down on the single cracked linoleum chair and started to shake, dissolving into a puddle of misery. Everything ached: her back, her face, her legs. Pippa rubbed her middle where he'd punched her, wondering if he'd broken a rib. When she'd gone to the toilet, her urine was pink with blood.

A loud scuttling noise on the roof made her look up. The silhouette of a ringtail possum appeared at the high louvre window, then leaped away. Dammit – even mangy possums had more freedom than she did. Gradually, a steely resolve replaced her despair. Cade must believe that she had the courage to leave – the key in the safe proved it. Well, she wouldn't disappoint him. She'd rather die than be in the room when he woke up.

Ever so slowly, Pippa dragged the bar fridge beneath the window. She winced with pain as she climbed onto it. Yes – she could reach the glass louvres. Beginning with the bottom one, she eased the frosted pane from its aluminium tracks, then got down and laid it on the floor. It took less than a minute. Good. Only four to go. But when Pippa reached for the final louvre, she found it was too high. She couldn't lift it out and she'd never fit through the window with it in place.

Pippa climbed down and collected anything that might make her taller. A spare pillow and blanket from the top shelf of the wardrobe. The towels. Even the toaster. And when she piled them all up and balanced the chair on top, she could just reach. She eased the louvre from its tracks, almost falling when the chair slipped. Somehow, she kept her balance and brought the louvre safely down without making much noise.

'Where are you, babe?'

Her heart stalled. She draped the blanket over the pile and raced to get into bed. 'I'm here, honey,' she crooned. 'Just had to use the toilet.'

Cade mumbled something, scratched his crotch and went to the bathroom himself. Please, she thought, please don't turn on the light. In the darkness, her escape pile was a mere shadow against the back wall. But in the light? She refused to think about what would happen if he noticed.

It seemed to take forever for Cade to return. He sat on the side of the bed and buried his head in his hands. 'I'm thirsty,' he said in a voice so hoarse she could barely understand him.

'Lie back.' Pippa wanted to shove him down. Instead she was a pillar of self-control, fluffing his pillow and kissing him softly on the lips. 'I'll get you a glass of cola.' He murmured his thanks and relaxed, closing his eyes.

It took a few interminable moments to unearth the fridge from the pile. With an unsteady hand, she poured him a drink and hurried back with it. Cade drained it in two gulps, then gathered her in his arms. 'You're one in a million, babe, you know that?'

'Go to sleep,' she murmured, stroking his back the way he liked. He soon nodded off.

Pippa waited until he was snoring again, then eased out of bed. She half-filled a glass with cola, topped it up with whisky and sculled. The bracing tonic burnt her throat on the way down. She poured the last of the whisky down the sink, then set to rebuilding her pile. There, that was the best she could do.

She took Cade's phone from the bedside table. It was useless to her – she didn't know the PIN – but it would serve him right to lose it. Pippa dropped it in the toilet, along with his cigarettes. Then she carefully climbed to the top of the pile. It was now or never. She sprang up and dragged herself halfway through the window. Teetering on the sill and biting her lip against the pain, she wriggled forwards. Don't look down, she told herself. What was the point of knowing about the coming fall? Concrete, gravel, blackberries – it made no difference. She was going out that window no matter what.

In the end it wasn't too bad. Pippa landed on a mulched garden bed, only a little the worse for wear. Hardly daring to believe her luck, she ran around to the front of the building. There was the dark blue station wagon, gleaming in the moonlight like a knight in shining armour. Pippa unlocked it, threw open the door and got behind the wheel. She turned the key and the motor roared to life, seeming to make as much noise as a freight train. Any moment, Cade would come pounding out of the room, screaming her name. But who cared, because now she was away, speeding from the car park, wheels spinning on gravel.

She turned onto the main road, heading south, laughing like a maniac as an unfamiliar emotion hit her. Pride. Pride in what she'd accomplished. Pride in overcoming her cowardice. Leaving Cade was a brave thing. Even now, cruising down the highway by herself, she barely believed that she'd done it.

CHAPTER 6

Pippa turned on the radio and tuned in to a local station. It seemed astonishing that the cheerful host didn't know what she'd done. He joked, talked about his dog and behaved like everything was normal, when it wasn't. Pippa was free. That wasn't normal at all.

He introduced a country song – the sassy sound of Taylor Swift singing 'We Are Never Ever Getting Back Together'. Pippa had always liked that song, but now it was imbued with a special significance. She sang along at the top of her voice as she sped through the night, guided by the twin beams of her headlights.

Although Pippa was enjoying the music, what she really wanted to know was the time. The clock on the dash said 12 o'clock, but she soon realised it wasn't working. It could be midnight or near dawn for all she knew. How long would it be before Cade woke up and discovered her escape? She wouldn't want to be a fly on the wall when that startling realisation hit him. Pippa's skin broke out in goosebumps at the thought.

Two more songs and finally a time check – three o'clock in the morning. Pippa heaved a great sigh of relief. After a night of heavy drinking? Without her to wake him up? Cade might not notice her missing for five or six hours.

She was loving driving again and getting to know the car. Her family had once owned a Commodore station wagon and Pippa had fond memories of learning to drive in it. This one slipped out of gear sometimes, but she soon got the hang of it. Going easy on the clutch worked wonders.

She drove on, shifting occasionally in her seat to relieve her aching back, wondering if she was dreaming. It was surreal to be driving down a strange road in the dark without a clue about what to do next. Well no, that wasn't quite true. Next, she'd pick Duke up from the farm. Then she'd have no clue.

The radio hummed away, keeping her company – keeping her connected to the real world. Music. Snappy banter from the host. The weather. Tomorrow would be hot with zero chance of rain. No kidding? The local news was more of the usual: some councillor caught in a corruption scandal, a bushfire up north, a fundraiser for the Wodonga cricket club. Then something more startling came over the airwaves; something that made her skin prickle.

'In breaking news, police are now treating the bombing of the Millburn synagogue two nights ago as an act of home-grown terrorism.'

Terrorism in Millburn? Her father often evangelised about the Jihadist threat, about how all Arabs hated westerners and were waging a war against Christians – and Jews too, apparently, although Jay didn't like Jews either.

The horror of the Bali bombings and the 9/11 attacks on America provoked in him an almost gleeful outrage. Muslims were, without exception, violent and dangerous. And now Islamic terrorism had struck right at the heart of country Victoria.

'One person died in the attack. The victim has been identified as Zadie Mintz, a pregnant thirty-three-year-old mother of two. A spokesman for the local Jewish community said they've been deeply shocked and broken-hearted by this hate crime. If anyone has any information, please call Crime Stoppers.'

Pippa's throat tightened in sympathy. Those poor motherless children. That poor woman. Pippa had been pregnant herself last year – not that she'd told anyone. Cade had beaten her when she was three months gone and she'd lost the baby. She'd hidden in the coolroom, cramping and bleeding among the hanging sheep carcasses while pain swallowed her whole. When it was over all she knew was relief. She couldn't bring a child into her marriage. Not with a snivelling coward for a mother and a monster for a father. But the dead woman's baby would have been planned and wanted, with an adoring family ready to embrace it. The loss of that baby was an utter tragedy.

A favourite song came on the radio, but Pippa wasn't listening any more. Her mind stayed on the newsflash. Pippa knew the historic synagogue in Millburn. She'd admired the building on the few occasions when she'd picked Cade up from the mine. It reminded her of a Roman temple, pale and graceful with twin pillars at the front – looking both exotic and out of place in an Australian country town. A far cry from her own family's crudely built timber chapel. It saddened her to know that a place of such beauty was gone and that a small community had been devastated by the loss of a young mother and her unborn child. The man on the radio had called the bombing a hate crime, and that's exactly what it was.

After two hours of driving, Pippa noticed the fuel gauge dipping low. She stopped at the next service station and turned on the interior light. Time for an audit of what was in the car. It was harder than she expected to exit the driver's seat. Her back twinged with pain whenever she moved, and her legs were stiff and sore. The fresh bruises were turning various shades of red and purple. How embarrassing, having to go in and pay for petrol looking like this.

She examined the contents of the wallet again, marvelling at the fake driver's licence that bore Cade's picture, thinking through the implications of its existence. Dylan had known beforehand that Cade might need a false ID. Why was that? And what in the world had her husband done to make him panic and go on the run? Pippa shook her head, as if to clear such imponderables from her mind. She never intended to set eyes on Cade again, so what did it matter?

Pippa found a torch in the glovebox, then searched the back seat. She found a rag and tied it around her neck – a makeshift scarf to hide the bruises. Nothing else but some tools: spanners, shovels, fencing pliers – and a pile of empty beer cans on the floor. She opened the tailgate, smiling grimly when she discovered Cade's rifle and ammo. He really must have been tired last night to leave his weapon behind. She trembled a little despite the warm night. What a scene there'd be when he discovered it missing, along with the car. Pippa had never known Cade to be without a firearm – it would be like missing a limb.

She explored further, emptying out the rear compartment and lifting up the floor. What on earth? Numberplates – two different sets that looked like they'd been unscrewed from other cars. Pippa slowly straightened her back, feeling more like a fool than ever. She knew Cade for a poor farmer, a cruel husband and a jealous, violent man. She hadn't picked him for a criminal as well. She wondered what form his unlawful behaviour had taken. Robbery, drug-dealing, selling stolen goods? All of the above? Or had he done something even worse? Pippa thought about their broken combine harvester, their rusting house tanks and their box of unpaid bills atop the fridge. The kitchen fan they couldn't afford. If Cade was a thief, he wasn't a very good one.

Pippa had been careful to park in the shadows. Even so, she was drawing unnerving stares from a few drivers who'd pulled in after her. She sat back in the driver's seat, wincing as she moved. Her kidneys were like a pair of burning rocks buried in her back. She went through the wallet again. The bank card was useless without a PIN. Pippa re-counted her money: eighty-three dollars and seventy-five cents should almost fill the tank. No point checking the oil – she had no money to buy more anyway, but she could check the tyres. At least air was free. But when she tried to fit the pressure gauge to the valve, it kept coming off and she couldn't get a reading.

Pippa heard footsteps. She looked up to see a man in a flannel shirt approaching. He stopped a few metres away. 'Having a spot of trouble, love? Want a hand?'

Fear seized her so hard that a trickle of warm wee ran down her leg. The man wasn't Cade, but she still wanted to scream, 'Stay away! Leave me alone!' and flee headlong into the night. Instead she stammered, 'No, I'm fine,' and leaped behind the wheel to rejoin the anonymous stream of passing traffic on the highway.

Pippa turned off the radio, wanting to be alone with her thoughts and feeling so tired that once or twice she thought of pulling over for a nap. But knowing that Cade might steal a car kept her going. He could already be on her trail. She drove until the sun rose and she could no longer ignore the critically low fuel gauge. The thought of stopping again and facing people filled her with dread, but what choice did she have?

The engine had already begun an ominous sputter when she pulled into another service station. This time she headed straight for the pumps, not looking left or right, focused on her task. Pippa filled the tank with two dollars and forty cents left over. She took a long drink from the watering can, then used it to top up the radiator.

Pippa headed for the shop, eyes down, acutely conscious of her visible bruises. Thank goodness the place was largely deserted. She paid for the petrol and the bored middle-aged woman at the counter took little notice. Pippa handed over her last two dollars and forty cents for a twin pack of Mars Bars.

'Ten more cents, hun.'

Pippa almost put the chocolate back, but she was very hungry. Her voice cringed in apology. 'That's all I have.'

The woman took a closer look at her, cocked an eyebrow and gestured to the Mars Bars. 'They're yours.'

This small kindness moved Pippa unexpectedly, and she struggled to keep from crying. 'How far am I from the Victorian border?' She hoped it wasn't too stupid a question. Hoped that she hadn't taken a wrong road in the dark somehow, that she was still travelling south.

'Where are you heading, hun?'

'Kilpa.'

The woman looked blank.

'Near Ouyen.'

'You've got a way to go then. My sister lives there, so I know. It's three hours to Tooleybuc on the border, and another hour to Ouyen.' Her eyes lingered on Pippa's bruises and the oily rag tied around her neck. 'Here.' She handed over two more chocolate bars. 'They're on me.'

Pippa stared at her blankly for a few moments. Then she twisted off her wedding ring and placed it on the counter. 'For you. I don't need it any more.'

Pippa ran back to her car before the astonished woman could react. She gulped some more from the watering can and refilled the empty plastic water bottle in the front seat.

A man a few pumps over wolf-whistled. 'Hey sweetheart. Come over here if you're thirsty.' He held up a six pack of beer cans. 'I've got the good stuff.'

Pippa jumped behind the wheel and sped off. Dawn was breaking – a red glow on the featureless horizon. She opened a Mars bar, biting into the soft, delicious caramel. Food had never tasted so good, and the sugar hit helped to banish her tiredness. Pippa checked the fuel gauge. If the woman in the shop was right, she could be at the farm by lunchtime. God willing, a full tank would get her there to find Duke. She wasn't ready to think about what came next.

CHAPTER 7

It was a strange homecoming. Pippa had left the farm yesterday, yet it seemed a lifetime ago. She turned onto Kilpa Road feeling utterly changed. Could it really only be Sunday?

She drove up Fairview's potholed drive, bursting with conflicted emotions. This was the house where she'd known so much misery, yet it was also where she'd lived for four years. It held her clothes, her personal belongings, the beautiful crockery and cutlery sets that were wedding presents from her parents and aunt. It was a place where she'd first known some autonomy. She knew where everything was. She'd organised the kitchen her way – pretty casserole dishes on show, instead of hidden away in cupboards the way Mum did. Metal hanging racks for shining pots and pans to free up space. Her lovely assortment of pot plants on the windowsill. Despite her fear of Cade, it would be hard leaving it all behind.

Still, she wouldn't be lonely. She'd have her dog, and could she ever use a friend like him right now. Pippa parked at the house, filled with an unfamiliar lightness at the prospect of seeing Duke. But the kelpie didn't bound from the verandah in greeting like she'd expected. She got out and called his name, searched the parched garden and the hay shed. She checked the disused chook house where Duke often hid from Cade's foul moods. Pippa had joined him there more than once. But it was no use. She couldn't find him anywhere.

Damn. Small bush flies clung to her face, savouring the salty moisture of her tears. Damn, damn, damn! Where the hell was Duke? Pippa swayed from side to side as a sudden lethargy overcame her. Adrenaline had been her ally, keeping her alert and running, but now it failed her.

Pippa's eyes grew heavy-lidded and her vision blurred. If she didn't lie down soon, she'd fall down. She tried to think things through. It was dangerous to stay here. For all she knew, Cade had got his hands on a vehicle. He could be right behind her. It would be safer to drive away, hide somewhere and sleep in the car. But what about Duke? Duke was a loyal dog – the most loyal. He was probably out looking for her right now. How would he find her if she deserted him?

Pippa went inside through the unlocked back door. To her eyes the house was already looking abandoned. She gazed about the kitchen as if seeing it for the first time. The dough she'd been kneading lay on the bench, cracked and dry, with flies crawling over it. Pippa resisted the urge to clean. The plants on the sill drooped so she used a jug of water to revive them.

Pippa took one of Cade's beers from the fridge. In four years, she'd never done that. Cade thought beer would make her fat. The liquid slipped down her throat in a blissful icy trail, briefly revitalising her. She sliced a loaf of bread, grabbed some cold cuts and made sandwiches. These she devoured, washed down with another beer. Would it be safer to sleep in the hay shed? No, the car was a dead giveaway. If Cade came, there'd be no hiding from him.

She thought about taking a shower, but her exhausted body complained. Lie down, it screamed. Get some sleep. Pippa called for Duke one last time. When he didn't come, she climbed into bed and closed her eyes – too weary even to be frightened.

Cade woke to a gentle knocking at the door and checked his watch, bleary-eyed. Shit – already after ten o'clock. What the hell was wrong with Pippa? He'd told her to wake him at seven. The knocking came again and he reached under the bed for his rifle. Dammit, he'd neglected to bring it in from the car. His forgetfulness probably had something to do with the hammer in his head, reminding him of how much he'd drunk last night. How stupid could he get? What if the cops were here?

He sat up. Pippa must be in the bathroom. The knocking came again. Stumbling to his feet, he went to the window and tweaked back the curtain. Thank Christ, just the maid. 'Hang on,' he called, then found his jeans on the bathroom floor and pulled them on. He didn't see Pippa. Why was she in the shower when it wasn't turned on? Cursing, Cade unlocked the safe, took the room key and opened the door.

The maid stood there with mop and broom – a forty-something woman with mousy hair, sagging breasts and a soiled apron. She introduced herself as Daphne and popped a piece of chewing gum in her mouth.

'Sorry to bother you, Mr Jones, but I need to clean this suite.' She peered around him into the room. 'Unless you're staying another night?'

He half-closed the door on her. 'No, we're not. Give us a few more minutes, will you?'

The woman stood awhile, silently regarding him, chewing her gum like a cow chewing cud. Cade glanced at her work-roughened hands. She wore a wedding ring. He pitied the poor bastard married to the old bag.

'I'll be back in half an hour,' she said at last.

Cade shut the door and turned to find Pippa. They had to hurry.

It was then he saw it. The little window set high on the back wall – minus its louvres. The makeshift pile of blankets and furniture below. He gaped in disbelief, then rushed to the bathroom and pulled back the shower curtain. The cubicle was empty. Cade screamed in primal fury and ran outside. The car was gone too.

· · ·

Ten minutes later Cade stood in the sweltering reception room talking to the manager. 'My wife had to leave – a family emergency.' The man exchanged a sceptical glance with Daphne, who was hovering in the background. 'Unfortunately, she's also taken my phone and wallet, quite by accident of course.'

'And your car,' added Daphne, with a smirk.

Cade's fist balled up involuntarily. 'So I need the room until my mate picks me up.'

'We'll have to take an imprint of your card again, Mr Jones.'

'I just told you. My wife went off with my wallet.' Daphne giggled. Cade wanted to smash her ugly face. Instead he asked, 'Can I ring from here?'

The manager studied him dubiously, then pushed the landline phone across the counter. 'Dial 1 for an outside line.'

Cade couldn't tell Dylan the whole story – Daphne and the manager were all ears – but he managed to convey the gist of it.

'I bloody told you not to bring her,' Dylan said angrily. 'Hang tight. Someone will pick you up

'Not someone,' said Cade. 'You.'

'Don't be stupid. It's Sunday and I'm working tomorrow. You're six hours away.'

'Take a sickie,' said Cade in a low voice. 'You got me into this and you'll damn well get me out. Otherwise I walk.'

'If you walk, you're nicked.'

'So are you.'

Dylan didn't answer at once. He seemed to be consulting with someone on the side. 'Okay, I'll be there,' he said. 'Stay put.'

'Ha,' said Cade, lost in a red fog of impotent rage. 'Like I have a choice.'

CHAPTER 8

Pippa woke to find a warm form pressed against her. For a horrifying moment she thought it was Cade and was too scared to open her eyes. But the smell of dog and the wet, tickling tongue in her ear left no doubt about the identity of her bedroom companion. Duke.

Pippa laughed aloud, hugging the happy hound and murmuring sweet nothings. 'Well, boy, no time for lying around. We have to get out of here.' She sat up, rubbing her eyes. She was still stiff and sore, but felt more refreshed than she had for days. Was it still Sunday? A glance out the window showed daylight – late afternoon by the look of the sun. Good, she hadn't slept for too long.

Her phone lay on the bedside table. She should ring her mother. For all she knew Ruby had dropped by earlier that morning to pick her up for church. She often did now that Cade had stopped attending. Pippa didn't care about missing her father's sermons – she had a private relationship with God – but she did enjoy being with her family. How long before she'd see them again?

Pippa picked up her phone. She wouldn't know what to say, but it would be good to hear Mum's voice. However, the phone was dead.

She kicked herself for not having put it on to charge before she fell asleep.

She went to the kitchen, ignoring the soreness in her stomach and back, and turned on the radio. She gulped down some Panadol, fed Duke and threw her filthy clothes into the laundry basket. Then she had a shower. The steaming water helped ease her aches. How good it felt to dress in proper clothes again, clothes that covered the tell-tale signs of Cade's violence, making her feel less exposed. In her long-sleeved blue shirt, jeans and western scarf, she could almost believe herself that the bruises had vanished – except for the pain.

Pippa glanced out the window, a fearful urgency building. The drive was deserted now, but Cade could come at any moment. She rushed to pack the car, thinking about all the useful things she'd take if she had more time. Tinned food from the pantry. Everything from the fridge packed in an esky with ice. A bag of onions and another of potatoes. Cade's camping gear.

In the end she took a change of clothes, her sleeping bag, sunglasses, purse, the dead phone and three scarves. Five apples, a quarter loaf of bread and a half-full bag of Duke's dry food went in the back, along with a container of water. As the minutes ticked by, her terror grew. She was so jittery that she almost left before she'd finished packing her few provisions. What Cade would do to her if he arrived now didn't bear thinking about.

Duke sensed her agitation, whining and jumping in and out of the car as if urging her to hurry. Somehow Pippa held her nerve. She found a jerry can of petrol in the shed, poured it into the tank and then ran back inside. As she scanned the kitchen for the final time, her eyes fell on her collection of pot plants. They'd recovered a little since she'd watered them that morning. The violets bravely held their tiny flowers upright, bright bouquets of purple, pink and blue, defying the heat. How many times had they stood between her and her grey world? She imagined them slowly shrivelling to brown nothingness. On an impulse she found a box and packed them in the car, leaving a scribbled note under the little watering can. It read, *Mum. I'm okay. I'll call xo.*

Now, where was her hat, her favourite Akubra? One of the few lovely things that Cade had bought for her. She found it on the back porch.

Lastly, she went to the chook shed and pulled the old cigar tin out from behind two bricks. It contained some sentimental treasures and her meagre savings. Pippa wasn't sure how much money it held, but didn't waste time checking. She threw it on the back seat, whistled for Duke and drove like the devil down the dusty drive without knowing where she was going or looking back.

It was almost five o'clock and Dylan still hadn't arrived at the motel. Cade had spent the waiting hours working himself into a private fury. He couldn't believe that Pippa was gone. Her treachery had left him gobsmacked. Last night when he'd locked the door and stowed the key in the safe, he'd felt a little paranoid. Silly for not trusting his wife. More fool him.

The longer Cade thought about it, the wilder he grew. He'd put a roof over Pippa's head for years, fed and clothed her, provided for her. She didn't have to work like many wives did. Didn't even have any kids to look after, although they'd been trying. What the hell did she have to complain about? True, he had a temper, but what man didn't? He was human after all.

Cade slammed his fist into the bed. He needed a stiff drink and a smoke. But thanks to his darling wife, the whisky bottle was empty and his cigarettes were a soggy mess. Unbelievable.

'Knock, knock.' Dylan stood in the open doorway.

Cade waved him in. 'About time.'

'Steady on, mate. This is your cock up. I said not to bring her. Never trust women, remember? Why the hell didn't you listen?'

'Shut up. Pippa got scared, that's all. We'll check the farm first.'

Dylan shoved Cade hard. 'Are you out of your mind? We're sticking to the plan, driving to the safe house at Dubbo.' He lit a cigarette and offered one to Cade. 'You've got a new identity, for

Christ's sake. The boys have gone to a lot of trouble. There's no going back.'

Cade tried everything: pleading, arguing, threatening – it was no use. How could he explain about Pippa to a man like Dylan? How could he make him understand what she meant? She'd never do anything like this again. He knew how to handle his wife. When he got her back, he'd teach her a lesson she'd never forget.

Dylan was losing patience. 'Forget it, mate. Let her go. She's no threat. You said yourself she doesn't know about the bombing.'

'If we could just drop by the farm—'

Dylan laughed derisively. 'You poor sucker. She's not at the farm. A looker like your Pip? She'll have split with some bloke.'

For whatever reason, the unthinkable hadn't occurred to Cade. Not Pippa, his sweet, church-going girl who was a virgin on their wedding night. Could Dylan be right? Could Pippa have ditched him for another man? This notion rendered him speechless with rage. He could see his naked wife offering her body to a stranger. That gorgeous body that belonged to him.

'Aargh!' Cade hurled the chair at the gaping window high in the back wall.

Dylan grabbed Cade by the arm and marched him outside, almost running into Daphne who was standing by the door. Nosy bitch. Dylan opened the car door. 'I've paid the bill. Now get in.'

Cade did as he was told, gazing silently out the window as they turned onto the highway, heading east. Dylan's words echoed in his brain. *A looker like your Pip? She'll have split with some bloke.* This changed everything. When he found them – and he would find them – he'd kill them both.

CHAPTER 9

Pippa put on sunglasses to hide her face, tucked her hair up under her hat and kept driving. A car came towards her on the Kilpa road, a black Ford ute – Cade. She looked around wildly, but there was nowhere to hide in this dry, flat landscape. Her worst nightmare was coming true. Madness, to think she could escape him.

But in the same moment she understood her mistake. It couldn't be Cade. He'd torched the black ute in Hattah-Kulkyne by the banks of the Murray – she'd seen it happen with her own two eyes. Yet the terror stayed with her, heightened by the realisation that if Cade did come for her, she wouldn't recognise his car.

She turned south at the Calder Highway, desperate to be gone from Kilpa where everyone knew her. She'd stop further down the road, investigate her savings tin and buy fuel. The jerry can of petrol had only quarter-filled the tank. But half an hour later, when passing through Ouyen, she spotted her father's Jeep parked outside the post office. The shock made her swerve, almost hitting a bollard and causing the car behind to honk.

Pippa ducked down a side street and kept driving. Not knowing where you were going was harder than Pippa had imagined. Decisions were called for at every turn, but the decisions didn't matter. So what if she turned this way or that at the coming crossroad? For a while she experimented, alternating between left and right until she was driving through dusty paddocks far from town. She hoped she wasn't lost.

Duke had been dozing on the back seat. Now he woke and joined Pippa in the front, hanging his head out the front passenger window and barking at passing sheep.

'Let's stop, eh boy? Have a drink?' And try to figure out what on earth they were going to do next.

Pippa pulled off a red dirt track and parked in the shade behind a screen of mallee gums. The hot north wind was blowing a gale, and sitting in the car was like being cooked in a fan-forced oven. They drank some water and ate the last of the bread. Then, while Duke went exploring, Pippa found her cigar tin and sat with it under a tree.

She opened the rusty lid, unprepared for the welter of emotions it released. Piece by piece she examined its contents. Sealed in a plastic sandwich bag was a classroom photo of her mother as a grade six girl, with shining chestnut hair and wide, innocent eyes. It had found its way from the mantelpiece into the tin after Cade threatened to burn it during one of his rages. What else? A few special birthday cards. A little diary she'd kept as a child. A green satin hair band – the goodbye gift from her friend Tracey when she'd left to study in Swan Hill.

The money lay under a square of purple taffeta – an off-cut from the party dress Mum made for her when she was ten. Pippa carefully counted out the five-dollar notes she'd managed to squirrel away by withholding change from Cade after their fortnightly shop. One hundred and thirty dollars. She could add to that the five dollars in her purse.

Pippa put the notes back in the tin with a rock on top to prevent them blowing away. She was pleased at first. It seemed like quite a lot of money. But when she thought about how long it had to last, she started to sob. Cade's money was all gone. A tank of petrol and some change – that's what her paltry savings would buy her. Whatever would she do then?

Duke arrived back, whining and licking away her salty tears. Then he laid his head on her lap and promptly fell asleep. She hugged him tight, taking comfort in his unconditional love. Duke didn't care about money or marriages or where they'd sleep that night. He didn't care that Cade might be hunting them down. All he cared about was being with her. When they were together, Duke was happy – it was as simple as that. There was a time when Pippa had believed her husband would feel the same way.

How had she been so naive? It wasn't like her own parents were happily married. Dad was a complete dictator, so why had she thought her marriage would be different? No, that wasn't fair. Dad had never been violent like Cade, and he loved his family. But he was unbearably bombastic and controlling. Pippa didn't know how her mother put up with it.

Sometimes, when her father stayed overnight with the Ouyen church deacon, Mum would drink sherry late at night – lots of sherry. On these rare occasions she'd talk of her long-since-dead dream of becoming a nurse. She'd talk about wanting to travel and see the world. She'd confess all sorts of regrets and dashed hopes. As a teenager Pippa would stay up with her during these drinking sessions, partly to help her to bed before she passed out, and partly to listen to stories of her life before Dad.

Pippa found it hard to reconcile Drunk Mum with Normal Mum. Normal Mum rose at dawn to bake bread and make jam. She read the Bible and led Sunday school and taught four children at home. Drunk Mum talked of hitchhiking to see country bands and dying her hair pink. Of stealing beer from eskys at grown-up parties and having a crush on Dave, the coach of the local football team. After five or six large sherries Mum would start rambling, talking nonsense, but Pippa always remained with her until the end. She owed her mother that. Mum loved her more than anybody else in the world – apart from Duke, of course.

Pippa closed her eyes. Such maudlin thoughts would get her nowhere. What she needed was a plan, and driving around aimlessly until her petrol ran out was hardly that. She picked up the green hair band. Perhaps she could go to Swan Hill and find Tracey? But that bookkeeping course would have ended years ago, and Tracey hadn't kept in touch. She could be anywhere now.

Something sharp lodged in Pippa's throat. For the umpteenth time she wished that Tracey hadn't left. What a relief it would be to talk things through with her old friend – with any friend for that matter. How was it possible that she'd become so isolated?

Mum had mentioned a cousin in Stanthorpe, but that was in Queensland. Pippa made a quick calculation. She could probably only drive for six or seven hours on a new tank of petrol. Queensland wasn't an option.

Pippa took her money out again to re-count it. A flutter of white in the bottom of the tin caught her eye. As she reached for it, the wind whipped it away. Pippa gave chase, but lost sight of it. Duke leaped to the rescue, extracting his prize from beneath a honey-myrtle bush and depositing it into her hand, before laying down to nap again.

She turned the old paper napkin over. Two words were scribbled on the other side. *Andrew* and *Currajong*. Pippa instantly recalled when she'd written them. She'd been about sixteen and Mum had been particularly drunk that night. The bottle of McWilliams sherry was nearly empty when her mother came out with an extraordinary story. She said that she'd had more than a crush on Dave, the footy coach – she'd been madly in love with him. They'd slept together after he promised to marry her, but he was twenty and she was fifteen and her parents found out. The family moved away from the district, and when they discovered Mum was pregnant, they put her baby boy up for adoption.

Ridiculous. Just another of Mum's drunken fantasies. But Pippa had been intrigued enough to ask questions. The baby was called Andrew, apparently. He'd grown up in the upper Murray town of Currajong, in Victoria's high country. He worked with horses. That's all Mum said before she slumped over and Pippa helped her to bed. In the morning, Mum had no recollection of the previous night – that was the way of these things. But Pippa remembered. She'd written down the boy's name, along with the name of the town.

'*Andrew. Currajong.*' Pippa spoke the words out loud to make them sound more real. The story must be nonsense. Mum was a devout Christian. Not exactly the sort of person to have a fling and a baby out of wedlock. That was the sort of thing that happened in Pippa's daytime soaps.

Still … she stared at the scribbled names. If by some miracle the story was true, it meant she had a half-brother somewhere. And if it wasn't true, Currajong was as good a destination as the next. Early that morning she'd crossed the Murray at Tooleybuc, which wasn't much more than an hour from Ouyen. The upper reaches of the river couldn't be too far away. At a pinch she could just follow it upstream.

Duke yawned, then stood and barked at her. She kissed his soft nose, thankful that he'd retrieved the napkin. Grateful for the sense of purpose the old scrap of paper had given her, however misguided that purpose might be.

Duke barked again. 'You're right. Time to go.' Pip gathered her treasures. 'We're heading for the high country.'

After several wrong turns, Pippa found her way back to the Calder Highway. Solitary gum trees cast long shadows across flat paddocks of sheep and wheat as she headed east, stopping at the first service station she passed to fill up and buy a map of Victoria. How she wished for a smart phone with Google maps. But even if her basic phone had been charged, it could only text and make calls.

The sun hung low in the sky, sinking in a blaze of fire, casting the high, rainless clouds in brilliant shades of crimson and gold. But Pippa barely spared the sky a glance. She'd long since grown immune to the glory of Mallee sunsets. All they meant was more days of drought. Her stomach rumbled as she pulled away from the pumps, but she didn't want to waste money on food. An apple would do. After buying petrol she only had thirty-five dollars left. Who knew how long that would have to last?

A relentless north wind blew a gale as Pippa parked at an empty truck stop to find her bearings and let Duke have a run. She wiped dust from her stinging eyes and spread the map out awkwardly on her knee. Now to find Currajong. Her finger traced the blue squiggly line of the Murray River back towards its headwaters, where she lost it in a green sea of national parks and state forests. So many romantic, tongue-twisting names: Tallangatta, Tintaldra, Khancoban and Kosciuszko. Then she spotted it – Currajong – six-hundred-and-fifty kilometres east of her current location. Roughly a seven-hour drive. The last radio time check had said six-thirty. Excellent. She'd had a sleep at the farm, and with a bit of luck the little town was within reach of the station wagon's fuel tank.

Dusk couldn't fall fast enough for Pippa as she followed the road east again, praying for the shield of night. Cade couldn't see her in the dark. She almost missed the Chinkapook turnoff. What a relief to finally be away from the main highway. Pippa stroked Duke's soft head where he dozed beside her. 'Don't worry about a thing, mate,' she whispered, 'We'll drive all night and be in Currajong by morning.'

CHAPTER 10

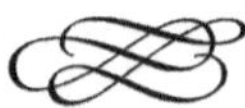

Pippa couldn't drive all night after all. By midnight she was almost asleep at the wheel. After skirting the large town of Wodonga she turned onto the Murray Valley Highway and looked for a secluded place to sleep. Pippa parked behind a stand of tall gum trees, got out of the car and explored the area with her torch to make sure she was alone.

Despite the darkness, Pippa sensed that she'd left the Mallee country behind. The air here was cool, and fragrant with wild mint and eucalyptus. A chorus of frog calls throbbed through the night. The dirt beneath her feet was black, not red. She picked some up and squeezed. It formed a loose, moist ball in her hand instead of running straight through her fingers. And the size of the trees! They towered so high above the car that her torch beam couldn't find the top branches.

Pippa climbed into her sleeping bag and stretched out as well as she could on the back seat. Duke scoffed a cup of dry food and curled up on the floor beside her, licking his lips. Pippa tried to ignore the empty, gnawing feeling in her belly; she was so hungry that she almost nibbled on Duke's kibble. Instead, she started her third apple and was asleep before she'd finished it.

. . .

Pippa woke to the carolling of magpies instead of the desolate cawing of crows. She sat up, stiff, sore and shivering, to find herself in a picture-postcard world. Dewdrops sparkled on leaves. Rolling, green paddocks lay beyond the trees. Fat cows and calves grazed knee-deep in lush pasture, their sleek grey coats shining in the early morning light. A range of distant peaks loomed beyond the rising sun – misty blue and mysterious. She exhaled, forgetting her aches and pains, even enjoying the novelty of being cold. Perhaps her brother lived in those far-flung mountains. Perhaps not. But she knew one thing for certain. Currajong lay somewhere up there, less than two hour's drive away. And her future also lay there – brother or no.

She drove east into the foothills of the Great Dividing Range. The road revealed myriad marvels and Pippa's spirits soared. Sweeping landscapes appeared around every turn. Forested hills and valleys. Wide rivers spanned by historic trestle bridges. Misty floodplains alive with waterbirds that she'd only seen in books. Duke cocked an ear each time she oohed and aahed.

At six-thirty Pippa stopped at a roadhouse cafe in Tallangatta, a small town on the shores of a lake so vast that she couldn't see the end of it. Currajong was only an hour away and Pippa was no longer frightened. This was a different world – Cade couldn't find her here. Pippa combed her hair with her fingers. She'd celebrate with break-fast and hang the expense.

Pippa's mouth watered as she ordered the Truckies Bargain Break-fast: eggs, bacon and toast for fifteen dollars along with bottomless cups of coffee. Half-a-dozen diners sat scattered about the cafe. She chose an isolated corner table and watched the wall-mounted TV while she waited. A morning news show was on, and she wanted to see the weather.

Suddenly Pippa froze. Right there on the television was their black Ford ute – the one Cade had torched two days ago. She couldn't see the number plate, but recognised it by the dented front panel and taped up headlight. A creeping horror gripped her as a reporter said the car had been captured on CCTV leaving the scene of the synagogue bombing at Millburn last Friday night.

Shocking footage of the smouldering ruins followed.

'The police are searching for three suspects, including Dylan Dean Moore, a known member of an extremist militia group known as the Renegades.' A photo of Dylan appeared on the screen. 'A quick-thinking staff member at Cobar's Welcome Inn motel overheard two men discussing the bombing at the weekend and alerted police. Moore's fingerprints were found in a guest room.

'The search is on for the second man and a female accomplice who stayed at the motel last Saturday night. The man is described as in his early thirties, dark-haired, with a heavy build and going by the name of Nathan Jones. He and Moore were last seen driving east in a white Hilux ute.

'The woman is described as in her twenties, of slim build with fair hair and driving a dark blue, early model Commodore station wagon with New South Wales plates, registration number VEE 957. If you have any information please call Crime Stoppers.'

Pippa's appetite fled. Her dark blue Commodore station wagon with the numberplate VEE 957 was parked, nose in, right by the large cafe window in plain sight of everyone inside. It may as well have had a neon sign over it. Her heart raced as a flight reflex flooded every cell. Pippa ran from the cafe, jumped into the car and took off, turning down the first side road she came to and parking behind a bank of pine trees. Taking great, heaving breaths, Pippa tried to process the implications of what she'd seen and heard.

She turned on the radio to catch the seven o'clock morning news. The hunt for the bombing suspects led the bulletin. Shit! She wasn't dreaming. So much for Arab extremists. The shame of blaming some nameless Muslims flooded in, making her empty stomach lurch. She'd pictured the terrorists as bloodthirsty, half-civilised outsiders wearing turbans and exotic robes. Instead, they were white Australian men who wouldn't rate a glance if you passed them in the street. They wore their hate on the inside. Damn that Dylan, spreading ugliness wherever he went, recruiting her husband to his despicable cause.

Duke cocked his head, his liquid amber eyes wide pools of concern. Pippa's hand trembled where she stroked him. And as the horror sank in, things began to make terrible sense.

Cade had bombed the synagogue and killed that young mother. That's why he hadn't come home last Friday night. That's why he'd as good as kidnapped her and gone on the run and torched the car. The police were hunting him, and hunting her as well. What in the world was she going to do?

She should turn herself in and tell the truth. Identify her husband for the police and plead innocence. It was the right thing to do, but in the same instant she knew she didn't have the courage. What if they didn't believe her? Cade would be out for revenge. He'd implicate her if he could, and so would Dylan. And if they let Cade go for some reason? He'd track her down and kill her, nothing surer. Like he'd killed that poor woman in Millburn. No, thought Pippa, not like that. Cade would have something slower and even more terrifying in mind for her.

She took a swig from her water bottle. Her fingers shook so much that she couldn't hold it still. The liquid spilled down her shirt, soaking through to her skin, giving her a chill. The small pride she'd felt at her escape from Cade ebbed away. Now fear wholly ruled her. She wasn't just hiding from her husband – she was hiding from the whole world.

It took a long time for Pippa to stop shaking. She felt paralysed, frozen, tempted to fade into blissful oblivion and give up on the cruel world. But that wasn't an option. She had Duke to consider. So she settled on a plan, cowardly as that plan was.

Thank God for Cade's tools. Pippa used the spanner to remove the station wagon's numberplates. Then she pried up the floor of the rear compartment, chose a Victorian pair from the spares and fitted them to the car. What to do with the old ones? Take them with her and find a more remote place to hide them or dump them here? In the end she couldn't bear to put the incriminating plates back in the car, so she used the shovel to dig a shallow hole. As an afterthought she tossed her phone in after the plates and buried the lot. She wasn't sure how, but had heard that people could be traced via their mobiles.

Pippa may have lost her appetite, but her body was growing faint from hunger, so she forced herself to eat an apple. It tasted sour and floury with a rotten middle, but she forced most of it down. It was her second-last apple and she couldn't afford to waste food. She thought wryly of the big breakfast she'd abandoned at the cafe; the fifteen dollars spent for nothing.

Just twenty-three dollars left, and now she'd be spending that on a home hair colour. Pippa had helped Mum cover up her grey for years – secretly, of course. Dad would never approve of that small vanity. So Pippa knew what to do: she'd buy a colouring kit from the super-market in Tallangatta, then find somewhere with a tap and a basin. A park rest room might work. She could hide in the cubicle while the colour developed. Then she'd head for Currajong to look for her brother. How she hoped that Mum had told her the truth.

CHAPTER 11

The brumby stallion snorted and reared, his silver mane shining like the glittering crest of a wave. Levi stood back and admired his prize. Damn, that horse was beautiful, even lovelier than their current palomino sire, Phoenix.

Levi had named the horse Thowra, after the mysterious stallion in Elyne Mitchell's famous *Silver Brumby* books. He and his boss, Drew, had been trying to capture him for months, and yet last night Thowra had simply appeared in the small dam paddock, doubtless meaning to entice the brood mares away under cover of darkness.

However much the heavily in-foal mares might have been tempted by his beauty and charisma, a steep bank made jumping out of the paddock more difficult than jumping in. Thowra could have made the treacherous leap back to the bush, but they couldn't, and the brumby stallion had been loath to leave them behind. So when Levi went out that morning, Thowra was standing there like an early Christmas present.

Levi snapped some photos on his phone. He wished he could show off Thowra in person and share this moment of triumph, but he was quite alone. Drew and Samantha, the owners of Brumby's Run, were away on their honeymoon. Levi thought back to the grand celebrations held next door at Kilmarnock Station last Saturday – twin sisters and a double wedding. Even the gilded invitation he'd received had been grand; handpainted with wattle and waratahs on fine satin-bound linen paper:

The party had been the biggest bash the district had seen for years – two hundred guests and the celebration lasting through till Sunday. But now the party was over, and Levi had been left to care for Brumby's Run solo for two weeks until the honeymooners returned.

Brumby's Run was an Australian stockhorse stud and wild horse sanctuary, offering refuge to brumbies captured in the high country – animals that were otherwise at risk of going to slaughter. Two registered brumby stallions, Jarrang and Phoenix, stood at stud there, alongside Australian stockhorse stallion, Phantom. A herd of older brumbies roamed free in the upper pastures, offering visitors a chance to see these iconic heritage horses in their natural state. Promising youngsters were broken in and offered for sale.

It was a big job for one person, managing a thousand acres and almost fifty horses, even without running treks high into Balleroo National Park. Notoriously changeable alpine weather meant that trail rides wouldn't recommence until summer. Five brood mares were due to foal soon. There were visiting mares for the stallions to serve, and half-a-dozen youngsters undergoing education.

Levi wasn't meant to be doing the job singlehanded – he was meant to have someone helping him. But their last station hand had resigned shortly before the wedding and Drew hadn't had much luck replacing him. Plenty of people had shown interest, but few were suitable. Some applicants who were sufficiently experienced with horses had been offered trial jobs, but none had actually turned up.

Drew and Sam were still hopeful. Sam had hugged Levi just before leaving for her honeymoon on Saturday night, giddy with excitement and optimism. 'Don't worry. With any luck the perfect person will just turn up out of the blue.'

Levi wasn't holding his breath, so he'd sent a shout out to his friend, Nullah Nelson, who travelled the rodeo circuit.

'Sure, I'll come up and give you a hand,' he'd said. 'My shoulder's buggered anyway from holding onto them bulls. It could use a rest.' That was good news, but Nullah wouldn't arrive for another few days. Until then Levi was on his own.

Thowra reared again, golden forelegs punching the air. He was growing more and more agitated, trotting around the little paddock, kicking at the fence to test its strength. Time to move him into a secure stockyard with higher rails. Levi couldn't risk losing Thowra now, not with talk in town of an upcoming brumby cull. Liberty might mean death for the palomino stallion.

Levi took down the sliprails to the reinforced stockyards and stepped back, hoping Thowra would be tempted by an open gate. The stallion stared at the opening, then shook his head as if declining Levi's invitation. His muscles bunched, standing out like ropes beneath his gleaming skin. From a standing start and with one astonishing bound, he cleared the fence and tore down the track past the house.

What a horse! Levi whistled in admiration. Thank goodness he'd shut the front gate – five-barred and almost two metres high. Even Thowra would struggle to jump that. Levi hurried down the drive after the escapee, planning to get behind him and herd him back up to the mares. He pulled down the brim of his hat, squinting into the sun. Wait, the gate wasn't shut after all. It stood swung wide with an old station wagon parked beyond. Levi watched in dismay as Thowra thundered towards it, silver tail streaming behind like a pennant in the wind.

At the last moment, a dishevelled, dark-haired girl jumped from the car and ran to the open gateway, waving her hat and shouting. But Thowra was almost upon her and could taste freedom. He charged past, making her leap aside. Now a dog jumped from the car. To add insult to injury, it chased Thowra down the road, causing him to gallop even faster away from Brumby's Run. The dog returned to the car when the stallion was almost out of sight. Levi swore and slapped his thigh with his hat. Of all the damn fool things to happen.

He strode down the drive to confront the culprit, brimming with disappointment and frustration. 'What the hell did you think you were doing, opening that gate?'

The young woman stood, hat in hand, staring down at her feet as if ashamed to meet his eyes. She was pretty, early twenties, with short blue-black hair that didn't seem to match her fair skin. It also looked like it had been hacked short with blunt scissors, but what did he know about women's hairstyles? That rough cut could be the latest fashion. As if sensing criticism, she jammed the hat back on her head. The dog ran up to him, a fine red kelpie, wagging his tail and panting from the chase.

'That's Duke,' she said.

Levi stroked his head and murmured hello. He took an instant liking to the animal. Losing Thowra wasn't the dog's fault, after all, and it didn't hurt that Duke looked a bit like Levi's own dog who'd died last month at the ripe old age of sixteen.

The girl raised her dusty face to his, her big eyes a startling blue and filled with remorse. 'I didn't see your horse until it was too late.'

Levi's frustration waned and curiosity took over. Who was she?

'I was wondering …' Her quiet voice trailed off. She pointed to the large sign above the gate. 'I was wondering – is this the Brumby's Run where Andrew Chandler lives?'

Then it dawned on him. She was one of the station hands who'd applied for a job and been offered a trial. Levi sized her up – tall, with slim hips tapering to long, straight legs. She looked like a stiff breeze might blow her over. Still, Drew wouldn't hire someone who wasn't capable of the job. 'You took your sweet time coming, but I could sure use some help around here.'

A smile lit her face, turning mere prettiness into a certain ethereal beauty. Levi was captivated.

'So you're Andrew Chandler,' she said. 'I'm very pleased to meet you.'

'Me? No, Andrew's away for a couple of weeks.' He offered his hand. 'Levi Goldstein, at your service.'

The girl didn't shake his hand. Instead she shrank back, and her faint smile fled. Well, stuff that. She'd just lost him a horse he'd been chasing for months. Surely he was the one with a right to be unfriendly, not the other way round.

'My apologies for not being Drew.' His sarcasm seemed lost on her. 'And who, may I ask, are you? If I'm giving you a job I'd best have a name.'

'A job?'

'You're here to try out for the position of station hand, right?'

She stared at him with the strangest expression, as if she believed him mad. But just when Levi thought he'd made a mistake, she said, 'I'm Poppy. Poppy Forrester and yes, I want a job.'

'Even if I'm not Drew Chandler?'

Here came that disappointed look again. 'When will Andrew be back?'

'No one around here calls him Andrew.'

'When will Drew be back, then?'

'Never mind. You'll be working for me and I'm right here.' The kelpie bounded up and pushed his nose into Levi's hand. 'So this feller's part of the package?' He stroked the dog's ears. 'If he chases our horses again you'll be out on your ear.'

Poppy nodded.

Not much of a talker, this one. 'You'll get bed and board, plus award wages paid cash in hand while you're on trial. If you work out, there's a raise and a permanent position in it for you. Okay?'

Poppy shuffled her feet and nodded again.

'Right, now drive up and stow your gear in the bungalow behind the house. It's used for guest accommodation during the trekking season. Have your pick of the bedrooms. No one else is here. Take the morning to settle in while I head into town for supplies. I'll be over after lunch to stock up the kitchen and fill you in about the working week ahead.'

Without a word Poppy whistled for the dog, got back in the car and drove up the track towards the house.

'I'll shut the gate then, shall I?' he said to himself, shaking his head and looking after the car in bemusement. He was a good judge of character. He prided himself on being able to read people, but this time his instincts failed him. Levi had absolutely no idea what to make of Miss Poppy Forrester.

CHAPTER 12

Pippa parked at the timber bungalow that stood about fifty metres behind the main house. The building nestled into the base of a steep bank that was swathed with flowering wonga wonga vines. However, Pippa couldn't admire the pretty purple blossoms, teetering as she was on the brink of emotional and mental overload. She crossed her arms on the steering wheel, closed her eyes and let her head sink down.

Pippa's thoughts swam in a thick soup of confusion. Duke pawed at her knee and whined with concern. She shook her head to clear it and sat up. 'You're right,' she murmured. 'Let's go inside.'

The modest building consisted of four bunk rooms off a central hallway, a bathroom with a washing machine, and a small kitchen diner. Where was the back door? She found it at the end of the hallway, completely blocked by a heavy wardrobe. Pippa piled her few belongings in the farthest bedroom, pulled up the blind and frowned at the window. The flywire screen and wind-out mechanism offered no path for a quick escape.

Pippa glanced in a little mirror atop a chest of drawers and froze. For a moment she thought someone else was in the room. A hollow-faced girl stared back, a girl with dark eye circles and wild black hair sticking out in all directions. A hairdresser Pippa was not, but what could she expect when her only tool had been a blunt penknife? She'd keep her hat on until she could fix her hair somehow. The good news was that with the cut and change of colour, she looked quite different from the Pippa who'd woken up that morning. So different that she barely recognised herself.

Duke licked her hand and jumped onto a bottom bunk with an approving bark.

'Don't get too comfortable.' She felt restless and trapped by the four walls. 'We won't be staying long.' Well, what was the point? Andrew wouldn't be back for weeks. But the truth was they had nowhere else to go.

It had been easier than she thought to discover where her brother lived – if that's who Andrew Chandler really was, and if Mum's drunken confession could be believed. She had to admit that was a lot of ifs. After discreetly asking around town, she'd quickly narrowed her search. It seemed there was only one Andrew who worked with horses in Currajong, although the name caused some confusion. Levi was right, everyone knew him as Drew. She'd arrived at Brumby's Run that morning, sick with nerves, yet also excited and hopeful that she might soon meet her long-lost brother.

What a disaster. She'd opened the gate just in time to let the most beautiful stallion she'd ever seen escape down the road. Duke had taken it upon himself to pursue the escapee until it was out of sight, making completely certain that she couldn't remedy her error by catching the horse. Then a man had come tearing down the track, gesturing and shouting, understandably angry. She'd have been angry too were the shoe on the other foot. Not an auspicious way to meet her brother.

But it wasn't Andrew. The angry man's name was Levi Goldstein. Was he Jewish? If so, that presented Pippa with a few headaches. One, she was currently racked with guilt because her husband had bombed a synagogue and killed a young Jewish mother. Two, Pippa was wanted as an accessory for the same terrible crime. Surely just by looking at her, Levi would be able to see her vicarious shame. And three, well … She'd grown up listening to Dad preach so much negative stuff about Jewish people, about how morally bankrupt they were. As kids, he wouldn't even let them wear jeans because they'd been invented by Levi Strauss. It seemed silly to her now, but after a lifetime of internalised mistrust, she couldn't shake her disquiet about Levi.

A shadow darted by the window, startling her. Just a passing bird, but in that same instant Cade's face had flashed across her mind's eye, making her shudder and cry out. Duke whined in sympathy. Maybe her misgivings about Levi were simply because he was a man.

But whatever her reservations, she certainly owed Levi: for a job, a place to stay, and for the loss of one gorgeous golden horse. Pippa could still picture the stallion racing towards her, still feel the thrill of his presence.

Pippa's stomach clenched and a wave of dizziness swamped her. She wouldn't be able to think if she didn't eat something soon. As if reading her mind, Duke barked and led the way to the kitchen. She opened the fridge, expecting it to be empty – Levi had said that he'd gone into town for supplies – but the little freezer at the top contained half a loaf of bread and a packet of bacon.

'We've hit the jackpot,' she said. Duke grinned back at her and licked his lips.

Pippa put bread into the four-slice toaster and dumped the lump of frozen bacon into a pan. Soon, cooking smells were making her mouth water. Her empty belly gurgled loudly enough for Duke to cock his head at the sound.

She found tea bags, sugar and long-life milk in the pantry, along with Vegemite and jam. There was even a block of chocolate. Twenty minutes later Pippa was sitting down to the most delicious breakfast she'd ever eaten. Duke, who was polishing off his own plate on the floor beside her, wagged his tail in agreement. It was amazing the clarity of mind that a full belly gave. The little bungalow felt more like a haven now than a trap.

Pippa's optimism grew. Why had she been so disheartened? If all went well, in two short weeks she'd meet her brother. She'd found a job, albeit accidentally, and somewhere to live. According to the news broadcast, Cade had last been sighted hundreds of kilometres away and there was little to connect Pippa Black to Poppy Forrester.

She'd chosen Forrester because that was the surname of the main family in *The Bold and the Beautiful*, and Poppy because it was close enough to Pippa. She should at least react to it when someone called her new name. Pippa made a mental note to think of herself as Poppy from now on, even if nobody else was around. She found a rubber band in a kitchen drawer and wound it around her thumb, tight enough to be uncomfortable. It would be her new name reminder and she would only take it off at night. She couldn't afford any slip-ups.

After four rounds of bacon on toast Poppy was finally full. She sipped on her second mug of tea – hot, sweet and reviving. Duke yawned, stretched out on the mat and went to sleep. Poppy yawned in unity. How she'd love to walk down the hall to her room, climb into the bunk bed and close her eyes. But it wouldn't be safe. Levi would be here soon and she had to remain on guard.

Her gaze fell on the sunny kitchen windowsill. Poppy fetched her plants from the car and began arranging the pots on the sill, watering them and nipping out browning leaves. Time slipped away. Last of all came the African violets, adding a welcome splash of colour to the monochrome kitchen.

A knock at the door made her jump and provoked Duke into a flurry of barking. Poppy peered out the corner of the window. Levi stood there, carrying a box of groceries. She'd been so overwrought upon their first meeting that she'd barely noticed his physical appearance. Now she had a chance to watch him unawares.

Tall, broad-shouldered and lean-hipped, Levi was every inch the cowboy, from the top of his bushman's hat to the tip of his leather boots. Close to her own age, she guessed, or a little older. Hair the colour of ripe wheat. And was that a dimple in his chin? Poppy studied the chiselled angles of his face. She was reluctant to admit it, but he was exactly the sort of man she'd dreamed of as a girl.

Levi glanced sideways at the window and she ducked away, hoping he hadn't spotted her. The knock came again and Poppy opened the door. Levi tipped his hat in an old-fashioned way and glanced at the pots on the windowsill. 'You didn't waste any time making yourself at home.'

'Is that a problem?' she asked, instantly on the defensive. 'I can take them down.'

He gave her a curious look and deposited his offerings on the kitchen bench. A cornucopia of fresh produce: spinach, tomatoes, carrots, kiwi fruit, bananas, apples and oranges. Olives and a round of cheese. More bacon, along with sausages and eggs. Poppy stared, astonished, automatically adding up the extravagant cost of the groceries. This couldn't all be for her.

She eyed Levi suspiciously. 'Do I have to cook for you, then?'

His brows rose in surprise. 'You're joking, right?' Poppy flushed at her mistake. 'Actually, it's the other way round,' he said. 'I'm throwing some steaks on the barbie tonight, out on the deck behind the house. I do it most nights. Too lazy to clean the kitchen, I guess. You're welcome to come by.' Duke put his paws on the bench and sniffed the sausages. Levi laughed and put them in the fridge. 'You're invited too, mate.'

Poppy backed up and shook her head. Bad enough that she had to spend the next couple of weeks here alone with Levi. She wouldn't be socialising with him as well.

Levi shrugged. 'Suit yourself. I'll meet you at the top hay shed in half an hour.'

'About that horse,' she said. 'The one that got away.'

'His name's Thowra.'

'Thowra. Has he run off into the bush?'

'He has.' Levi tossed a rosy, red apple into the air.

'I feel terrible.' And she did. Poppy couldn't shake the idea of the beautiful stallion. The thought of him made the hairs on her arms stand on end.

'Don't feel terrible.' Levi caught the fruit and took a bite. 'Because you're going to help me get him back.'

CHAPTER 13

Poppy drew the blinds after Levi left, locked the door again and put away the groceries. In spite of her full stomach, she salivated over the treats in store for her: fresh strawberries, avocados and plump red grapes. She'd never been able to afford such things back home and Cade wouldn't have eaten them anyway. He was a meat and three veg type of man who almost never ate fruit. She snacked on some grapes and then had a shower, relishing the feel of clean clothes against clean skin. Time to meet Levi up at the hay shed.

Poppy stepped onto the porch and stopped short. Something was wrong. Well, maybe not wrong, but different. An unfamiliar quality to the air, heavy and hushed, smelling of earth and eucalyptus. A loud, mournful call sounded from the sky and dark shadows rippled along the ground. Six huge black birds soared overhead, so low that she instinctively ducked. She'd never seen anything like them. Golden cheek patches and bright yellow tails contrasted with glossy black feathers. Their broad wings flapped deep and slow in an oddly fluid motion that gave their flight a dream-like quality. They sailed away, making strange wailing *whee-la* calls.

Poppy watched them leave with a feeling of reverence. And then she saw another unusual sight – a dark shelf of clouds boiling up from behind the mountains and closing in from the west. Mallee storms didn't look like that, but she knew what the clouds meant.

Poppy wasn't back home on the farm. She wasn't praying for rain to deliver Kilpa from the despair of drought. But that didn't diminish her joy at the coming storm. For a born-and-bred Mallee girl, rain would always mean hope. Poppy pulled her hat down hard on her head, whistled up Duke and headed for the hay shed with a spring in her step.

The hay shed was flanked by a row of stables on one side and a long row of yards on the other. A herd of horses grazed high on the hillside, tossing their heads in the wind as clouds ate up the blue sky. Three of the yards contained stallions: a chestnut, a palomino and a shining black. They arched their necks and pranced alongside the rails. Poppy had never seen so many beautiful horses.

Levi was driving a tractor, moving a big round hay bale into a paddock containing five plump mares. The plumpest of them, a fine-boned bay with a zig-zag blaze, ignored the hay. She pawed the earth and looked around anxiously at her sides. Levi secured the bale in the metal hay feeder and gestured for Poppy to come into the paddock. 'First, tie up your dog,' he said.

Poppy found a length of baling twine and attached Duke to a ring on the side of the shed. 'Stay,' she said without much confidence. The dog was an escape artist, able to miraculously free himself from the most secure tether. She never could work out how he managed it.

Duke commenced a mournful howling. Pippa sighed. He was also the most vocal dog in the world, a canine chatterbox. 'Stop that.' He lay down on the hay, whining occasionally, never taking his eyes off Poppy until she disappeared around the corner of the shed.

'This is Comet.' Levi slipped a halter on the bay mare and scratched behind her ears. 'I think it's her time, don't you?'

'Her time?'

'To foal. According to her service certificate she's not due until next week. But she's showing all the signs. Check out her udder.'

Poppy dutifully knelt down, not knowing what she was looking for. The mare's udder was full and shiny, with what looked like tiny icicles dripping from the teats.

'What do you reckon? Will she drop today?'

Poppy looked up at his expectant face. She'd never even seen a mare's udder before, but she had to say something. 'Yes, I think so.'

Levi nodded approvingly and handed her the leading rein. 'Put Comet in the big loose box at the end, and give her lucerne hay and water.' Fat plops of rain bounced off the rim of his hat. 'Then I'll show you the youngsters that we're breaking in, six in all. You can pick two of them to work with yourself. By the time Drew gets back we want them trotting and cantering on both reins, backing up, picking up feet and loading into floats.'

Poppy swallowed hard. She'd read every horsey book in the library, but the only horse that she'd actually ridden was Pepper, the roan gelding her father had acquired on her tenth birthday. She'd been begging for a horse ever since she could talk, and Mum had finally persuaded Dad to find her one. Pepper was advertised as free to a good home in the local paper. She soon discovered why. He was cold-backed and rebellious. He bolted and bucked and shied so violently at kangaroos that it was all Poppy could do to hang on. She often didn't, but she loved him nonetheless, and at least he'd taught her horsemanship.

As a girl she'd loved to gallop off into the scrub, sometimes disappearing for hours. Those were some of the few times that her life had seemed her own. But Pepper was an old plodder now, quiet and lazy, hard to rouse past a shambling trot. Riding him was a far cry from breaking in youngsters.

She'd often tried to persuade Cade to buy a horse. 'It can help us muster the sheep,' she'd said, but he wasn't convinced. For some reason he didn't like horses and she didn't know why.

Poppy led Comet to the stable and settled her in the roomy stall at the end. She laid a hand on the mare's shining flank, now dark with sweat. Kicks and thrusts of the unborn foal rippled under her fingers.

Comet snorted and pawed at the straw. Poppy stroked the mare's nose and murmured soft, sympathetic words.

Poppy hated births. They might be about new life, but they were also about suffering. She'd seen ewes struggle to deliver babies that were too big or presented the wrong way. And she'd seen them die in agony while Cade refused to call the vet. On top of that, she'd been assistant midwife at the homebirth of her own twin brother and sister. She remembered Mum screaming, racked with pain and exhaustion, while Dad paced the hall quoting Genesis.

'To the woman He said,

I will greatly multiply your pain in childbirth,

In pain you will bring forth children;

Yet your desire will still be for your husband,

And he will rule over you.'

Poppy had despised her father in those times. Mum endured all the hurt while he took all the credit, boasting at church the following Sunday that God had given him more children. Poppy had listened, silently fuming. God hadn't given him more children – Ruby had. And she deserved better than a return to household duties within days of giving birth.

Comet rolled her eyes. 'You poor darling.' Poppy had her own Bible quote for Comet, from the New Testament, of course, and slightly edited to suit the occasion. 'When a mare is giving birth, she has sorrow because her hour has come, but when she has delivered the foal, she no longer remembers the anguish, for joy that a horse has been born into the world.'

Amazingly, Comet seemed calmer, nibbling at some sweet hay and taking a deep draught of water from the offered bucket. Poppy kissed the mare's nose. 'I'll be back soon,' she said, and slipped out of the stall.

Duke had somehow freed himself and was gambling around Levi like a pup.

'Next time, tie him up like you mean it,' he said, clipping a leading rein to the dog's collar. 'Duke can come with us as long as he stays on the leash. You need to train him not to chase the horses.'

He sounded stern, but Poppy couldn't help noticing that Levi seemed delighted to be leading Duke. The two of them had certainly hit it off.

Levi glanced up at the darkening sky. 'Do you want to get a coat?'

'No,' said Poppy, who didn't have a coat. 'I'll be fine.'

They walked down a laneway past the stallion yards to one of the small paddocks beyond. Six horses cavorted within, rearing and bucking and chasing each other. They looked as wild as the surrounding forest. Surely these weren't the horses Levi expected her to ride?

'These are the three-year-olds,' he said, proudly. 'Aren't they something?'

That was an understatement. A big black gelding spotted Levi, trumpeted a greeting and careened towards them. The others followed, manes and tails streaming in the wind.

'This black one's mine, aren't you, Zorro?' Levi rubbed the animal's arched neck over the fence. 'But you can pick out two of the others. The buckskin's a handy mare, if a bit pushy. And that bright bay at the back? He's smart as a button. Still got some buck in him though.'

Poppy shut her mouth, which she realised had been hanging open. 'What am I supposed to do with them?'

He gave her a quizzical look.

'I mean … where are they up to with their training?'

'They've all been backed and mouthed. It's just a matter of consolidating what they've learnt and working on their paces. Smoothing their transitions and so on. You know what I mean.'

She didn't. She had no idea.

'So which two do you want?' he asked.

Poppy studied the three-year-olds who were crowding together, turning their tails to the wind. Who to choose? The big black gelding taken, thank God. The bay who still had some buck in him was out of the question, as was the pushy buckskin. That left a pretty paint colt, a liver chestnut gelding with a heart-shaped star, and a dapple-grey filly who seemed to be on the outer. She stood to one side, head held high, looking longingly over at the others. The paint colt suddenly lunged at her, ears flattened and teeth bared. He aimed a vicious bite at her rump.

Poppy shouted and leaped the fence, running to the filly and shooing away her attacker. The filly bent her head, allowing Poppy to smooth her mane and whisper some comforting words. 'I'll take this one,' she called to Levi, finding it hard to make herself heard above the rising wind. 'And the chestnut gelding.'

'Righto. I'll run those two into a yard for you in the morning. You'll be totally responsible for them – feeding, riding, the works. How does that sound?'

In spite of her doubts, that sounded like heaven. It had always been her dream to work with horses.

Now the storm struck in earnest. It roared over the ranges, tossing the treetops with a savage fury. Rain beat down while lightning split the sky, chased by loud rolls of thunder. This was the kind of storm that Kilpa residents could only dream of.

'Let's get out of this rain.' Levi opened the gate for her, and they ran back to the hay shed, holding onto their hats as the storm redoubled its efforts.

'What made you pick Mist?' asked Levi, once they were under cover. 'She'll be a challenge. That filly has some trust issues.'

'Mist looked like she needed a friend, and I don't like bullies.'

Levi's gaze caught hers. He didn't seem so bad after all. And was that approval in his warm brown eyes? Before she knew it, they'd shared a smile. Poppy quickly composed her features into their usual expression of opaque neutrality. She hadn't meant to smile. It had felt strange to curl up the corners of her mouth and crease her face in pleasure. She'd almost forgotten how.

CHAPTER 14

Levi spent the rest of that rainy afternoon completing Poppy's tour of Brumby's Run and showing her the ropes. He introduced her to their stallions standing at stud and showed her the visiting mares, sent there by their owners to go in foal to one of the stallions. He took her into the foothills to visit the seventeen trail horses, currently turned out to await the start of the summer trekking season.

Poppy, although shy as ever, displayed a keen interest in everything he showed her. Her passion for horses was genuine, and he loved seeing it break through her reserve, but some things troubled him. Her refusal to discuss the pros and cons of western versus stock saddles and bits, for example. Her blank look when he talked about lunging and desensitisation training. Her seeming ignorance about breeding mares and stallion management. She didn't even know who Abbey was.

'Abbey?' he asked, incredulous. 'He's an Aussie legend. There's even a song written about him. Jet black – no white at all – and referred to as a freak by those who saw him perform. From the age of eighteen months that horse won every campdraft competition he entered. Then when he was in his prime, tragedy struck. Abbey's owner, Harry

Ball, was killed in a car crash when the pair were driving home from the Warwick rodeo. Harry's broken-hearted widow swore that Abbey would never be ridden again. So she sent him to stand at stud with Theo Hill at Quirindi. From the moment Abbey's first foals hit the ground people realised they were super special horses. He went on to become the greatest stockhorse sire of all time.'

Poppy listened with rapt attention as Phantom paced his yard, giving the occasional imperious neigh. Yet she didn't say a word. What was it with this girl? So sincerely interested in all aspects of the job, but still so closed off. He'd never met someone who was such a contradiction.

'Well, what do you think?' he prompted. 'It's getting mighty lonely over here, talking to myself.'

'So this black stallion, Phantom, is related to Abbey?' she asked, hesitantly.

'Related?' said Levi. 'He's a direct throwback, with a double cross in his pedigree. Have you any idea how special that is?'

Clearly she didn't. Poppy turned away and lowered her eyes in that unnerving way she had. Levi immediately regretted the tone of his last remark. He hadn't meant to sound disparaging or judgemental. But he'd helped Drew draft the 'help wanted' ad, and a knowledge of horse breeding and blood lines had been a key component of the job description. He couldn't imagine Drew giving a trial to someone who was ignorant of those things. Unless, of course, Poppy had lied on her application. It was an unsettling thought.

'Where did you work last?' he asked.

Poppy stepped back, staring at him warily. A sudden gust whipped off her hat and he caught it. She looked wildly beautiful standing there. Astonishing blue eyes. Raven hair, dark as Phantom himself, tossing crazily every which way. Scarf whipping in the wind. Poised like a cornered brumby, ready to flee.

Duke moved to Poppy's side. She clutched the kelpie around his handsome red neck, as if he might ward off some unseen threat. Levi hadn't meant to scare her. It seemed like a reasonable enough question, but it had clearly knocked her for six. Poppy sure was a strange one. Sometimes she didn't even seem to know her own name. He'd call it, and she'd look surprised that he meant her, even though they were alone at Brumby's Run.

The silence hung between them, magnifying the sounds of the abating storm: the pitter patter of raindrops falling from the gum tree canopy to the leaf litter below, the wail of the waning wind. His suspicion was growing that she'd lied to get the job.

'I asked where you worked last.'

'On a farm in the Mallee,' she said in a halting voice.

There was so much more that Levi wanted to know – was entitled to know. How long had she worked at this Mallee farm? Was it a stud farm or a training facility, or both? What were her main duties? Had she ever taught students to ride, or coached people on their own horses? Did she finish off youngsters for sale, or did she start them as well? A desire to know all about Poppy gripped him, and it went beyond professional curiosity. He wanted, no, needed, to know more about his enigmatic new stablehand – a whole lot more. But there was something so fragile, so vulnerable about her, as if she'd regard the most standard of questions as a hostile interrogation.

Damn it, he hated being put in this position. Levi took one final glance at her anxious face and wide eyes before deciding to let the matter drop. He could always contact Drew and Sam to ask them about her, but they'd warned him not to interrupt their honeymoon unless it was an emergency. This was hardly an emergency. So what if Poppy wasn't as knowledgeable about bloodlines as she'd made out? That was no crime, and it wasn't like anyone else was knocking at the door for the job. She was keen enough and seemed like a fast learner. So long as she could handle horses and ride a green youngster, she'd do.

Levi handed Poppy back her hat. 'I've shown you enough for today,' he said. 'Could you go and check on Comet for me? I'll be there shortly to fit her with a foaling alarm.' Levi took out his phone. 'If she foals tonight I might need your help. What's your number so that I can text you?'

Poppy sighed in a defeated way. 'I don't have a phone.'

What? Levi looked at her askance. Who didn't have a phone?

'I lost it,' she added.

'Where?' he asked. 'If it's an iPhone you can sign in with mine and find its last location.'

'It wasn't an iPhone.' An element of frustration was creeping into her voice, making her pale cheeks flame red. 'It wasn't even a smart-phone, okay? It was one of those crappy flip phones with no apps or internet.'

Levi hadn't even realised you could still buy dumb phones. 'Okay, but we'll need some way to communicate until you can replace it. I'll organise a two-way radio for you in the meantime.'

Poppy nodded and for once met his gaze openly. Her eyes bore the haunted look of a hunted deer. 'I was wondering …' she said. 'Could I please use your phone to ring my mum?'

'Of course,' he said. 'Go down to the house. There's a landline in the kitchen. You'll get better reception with that.'

Levi watched, intrigued, as Poppy set off down the track to the main house with Duke trotting at her heels. He was convinced that she was hiding something. When he had time, he'd look through the responses to the Brumby's Run online job ad and try to find Poppy's resume. That might provide him with some answers.

Duke sat on the lino at Poppy's feet, gazing up at her. 'Wish me luck, boy.' She shouldn't have brought him inside without asking, but she needed her dog for moral support.

Poppy dialled the number with trembling fingers, then lost her nerve. She took the rubber band off her thumb, where it was cutting off the circulation. It hadn't worked anyway. She'd grown used to the pain.

Mum had no mobile phone. Dad didn't think she needed one. He said it would be a waste of money, even though he had the latest Samsung Galaxy and spent half his life on it. So in order to call her mother, she'd have to ring the old rotary dial phone that sat on the hall table. Poppy took some deep, steadying breaths. A clock on the wall said four o'clock. For a moment Poppy couldn't remember what day of the week it was. Only Monday, as hard as that was to believe. It seemed like she'd been on the run for months, not days.

Poppy tried to imagine the scene at Utopia. It might be a good time to ring. Twenty-year-old Ron, the next oldest, wouldn't be there. He'd found work at a garage in Swan Hill and never seemed to go home any more. Fred and Ian would probably be out in the paddocks, and they rarely answered the house phone anyway. Dad was a risk, of course. He could be anywhere.

Mum would be in the back room, finishing up the day's home-schooling lessons for the ten-year-old twins. Poppy imagined the scene. Luke and Janie, eager to go outside and play. Mum urging them to pack away their books and Bibles. Her soft chestnut hair caught up in a neat bun. Her kind blue eyes, their corners wrinkled from smiling. Warm spicy smells coming from the kitchen: cinnamon, ginger and the scent of freshly baked bread. The mouth-watering aroma of slow-cooked lamb stew simmering on the range. Ruby was the cornerstone that made Utopia a happy home, in spite of Jay and his overbearing ways. Poppy's throat grew tight. When would she see Mum again? The sense of loss overwhelmed her.

The empty feeling wasn't only for her. It was for her mother too. Did Ruby know that her oldest daughter was wanted in relation to a terrible crime? Or did she think that Poppy had vanished for some other reason, perhaps the victim of foul play? For the umpteenth time, Poppy prayed that Mum had found the hastily scribbled note that she'd left under the little watering can in the kitchen at Fairview. What had it said? *Mum, I'm okay* or something like that. Not very reassuring, but better than nothing.

Poppy tried dialling the number again. If Mum didn't answer she'd have to hang up. Nobody else could know that she'd called. She held the receiver to her ear, heart thumping against her ribs. There was the ring tone, and then a voice.

'Pastor Jay Sullivan speaking.'

Poppy slammed the phone down and burst into tears.

CHAPTER 15

Levi was searching for the foaling alarm on the rear porch when he heard crying coming from the house. He went in through the laundry, careful not to let the screen door bang behind him, and walked quietly along the hall to the kitchen. Poppy sat slumped on a chair, sobbing with great shuddering sighs, oblivious to his presence. Duke was sitting on her feet, looking up at his mistress with worried brown eyes. With her shiny nose, tear-streaked face and dark hair sticking out at all angles, Poppy looked about fifteen years old. Her distress and the sheer vulnerability in her eyes provoked in him a fiercely protective feeling.

'Poppy?' he asked, wanting to give her a hug. 'What's wrong?'

She leaped up and whirled to face him, scrubbing her palms over her eyes.

'Is it your mother? Is she ill?'

'No, nothing like that.' She was struggling to compose herself. 'I don't want to talk about it.'

'Fair enough.' Levi moved to put the kettle on. 'Sit there and I'll make us a cup of tea. Then I'll show you how to fit the alarm on Comet. Unless you've used one before?'

Poppy shook her head. With a few final sniffs she sat back down, eyes downcast.

Levi was more convinced than ever that she wasn't a seasoned stud hand. Anyone experienced with brood mares would know how to fit a simple foaling alarm.

He busied himself while the kettle boiled, dropping tea bags into mugs, putting the sugar bowl on the table and taking milk from the fridge. He tried not to crowd her. Somehow he knew that she'd leave if he put her under any pressure. On an impulse he found a pretty blue-and-white jug for the milk. Now where was that packet of Tim Tams? And why was he behaving like this was some sort of tea party?

At last Levi sat down at the table with a plate of biscuits and two mugs of tea. 'Milk?' She nodded and he tilted the little jug. 'Say when. Now how about sugar? And would you care for a biscuit?

Duke barked assent, jumped up at the table and took a Tim Tam.

'I didn't mean you,' laughed Levi.

Poppy took a sip of her tea and looked at him over the rim of her cup. Was that a smile? Yes. Poppy's face lit up with amusement as the dog escaped out the kitchen door with his prize. Levi grinned, feeling like he'd won the lottery. What the heck was wrong with him?

Poppy walked up to the stables with Levi feeling much calmer. So she hadn't been able to talk to her mother. That wasn't the end of the world. There was always tomorrow.

If she was honest with herself, Levi had a lot to do with her improved mood. She'd been humiliated when he found her crying in the kitchen. Cade always mocked her when she cried, but Levi's response had been so gentle, so charming – so unexpected. Making tea like that and not pushing her to disclose what was wrong. Letting Duke steal the biscuit. It made her smile again just to think of it.

The afternoon had gone pretty well, considering. If not for the cloud hanging over her, she would have even enjoyed it. Brumby's Run was a far cry from the depressing dust bowl of Cade's farm back at Kilpa. (She always thought of Fairview as Cade's farm – not hers.)

Poppy hadn't known that such natural beauty could exist outside the pages of travel magazines. The fragrant air and paddocks thick with grass and wildflowers. The well-maintained fences of neat hardwood post and rail. The bevy of beautiful birds, including colourful parrots that flashed through the treetops like living jewels. And best of all, dozens of the loveliest horses imaginable.

Here, nestled in the protective ring of the mountains and living under an assumed name, Poppy was starting to feel safe. Her thoughts turned to Levi. He was a bit bossy, but since he actually was her boss, she supposed that was all right. He certainly hadn't tried to harm her. And in spite of Poppy's fear of men, she couldn't help noticing how attractive he was. Heaven only knew why. After the way Cade had treated her? It was a miracle that she could look at any man without throwing up.

But Levi was dodging her defences, flying under her radar. She liked watching him. His back, tall and straight as a pine tree. His strong jaw and Roman nose. That dimple. And it wasn't just his looks that impressed her. It was the sweet way he talked to Duke. The easy way he swung into a saddle. Their shared passion for horses.

Levi gestured for Poppy to follow him into the loose box. Comet was restless, spinning in circles and pawing at the straw. Poppy soothed her, refilled her water bucket and used a rake to clean her stall, while Levi fitted the mare with a leather headstall. Then he took a slim leather pouch from his bag and called Poppy over.

'This is the transmitter pouch,' he said. 'We use Velcro to attach it to the bottom of her headstall like this. Then we slip the monitor in, making sure that it faces down.'

Comet shook her head a few times, and then permitted Levi to fit the monitor.

'How does it work?'

'The transmitter activates ten seconds after the mare lies down flat. It sends a signal to the receiver that I keep with me. So, for example, If I'm in bed at night, and that's when mares generally foal, it will beep loudly to alert me. It saves a lot of sleepless nights, I can tell you.'

'What if Comet just lies down for a rest?'

He gave her a quizzical look. What had she said wrong?

'Mares in late pregnancy avoid lying flat on their sides until they're in labour. If it was a false alarm the transmitter would tell me, but that's never happened.'

Oh. She supposed she should have known that. Despite her eagerness to learn, Poppy's enthusiasm was flagging. The truth was she was dog-tired. Poppy unsuccessfully tried to stifle a yawn.

Levi was studying her with more interest than seemed called for. 'That's enough for today.' He gave Comet's rump an affectionate slap and pinned Poppy with curious eyes. 'Have you come far? Where's home?'

The question made Poppy squirm, chasing all her carefully prepared lies from her head. If she didn't have a good answer, it was best to say nothing at all. She set her mouth in a stubborn line and knelt down to look at Comet's udder, pretending not to hear him. The waxy icicles had fallen from the mare's dark teats, which were now dripping fluid.

'Take a look,' she said.

As Levi knelt down, his thigh pressed against hers. Poppy sprang away, frightening Comet into a rear and tipping over the water bucket.

'Whoa,' soothed Levi, taking hold of the mare's headstall. He glared at Pippa, who was standing uneasily in the corner. 'What the hell were you thinking? You're supposed to be keeping her calm, not scaring her to death.'

'Sorry.' Her voice was barely a whisper. She hated having frightened Comet, but Levi had frightened her first, and now she felt trapped with him in the enclosed loose box. He'd touched her thigh. By accident or on purpose? It shocked her to think how swiftly her previous fears and suspicions had returned.

Levi knelt back down, shaking his head, and checked the mare's udder. 'You're right, she's leaking milk.' Comet turned her head to snuffle his back and he felt her flank. 'She's in early labour.'

Poppy edged along the wall and let herself out of the box with a sense of relief. Levi seemed nice, but so what? Cade had seemed nice too at the start. She was acutely aware of the remoteness of Brumby's Run and that, apart from Levi, nobody knew she was here. At least she hoped they didn't. She pictured Cade's furious face and shuddered.

Levi looked over to where she was peering over the stable door. 'Looks like I won't get much sleep tonight, with or without the foaling alarm.'

Despite her fright, the idea of a new foal coming was exciting. 'Who's the father?'

'Our own Phantom. Comet has Wardance in her pedigree, so this foal will be Australian stockhorse royalty.'

Levi stood up slowly, holding out an upraised palm towards Poppy as if she was the skittish horse instead of Comet. 'I might need some help when the foal comes.'

Poppy was thinking hard, weighing up the pros and cons. She wanted to be there when the foal was born, but she didn't want to be cooped up with Levi in the stable again. But she did want to keep this job.

'Come down to the house for a two-way radio,' he said. 'I'll call you when it happens.'

Comet nuzzled Levi's cheek, then snorted in his face, making him laugh. Poppy smiled too. If she was going to spend the next two weeks here, she supposed that she'd have to trust him. Duke seemed to, and so did Comet. Her mother always said that animals were a good judge of character.

'Of course,' she said at last. 'I'd love to help.'

Her answer provoked in him a broad grin that seemed rather out of proportion to the reasonableness of his request. After all, helping mares with foaling was probably part of her job.

Poppy followed him back to the house. Tree trunks cast long shadows over the path, while late afternoon sunshine gilded their leafy canopies in green and gold. She thought she might never grow accustomed to the beauty of these mountains.

'Could I ring my mother?' she asked. 'I couldn't reach her last time.'

. . .

Poppy picked up the phone while Levi went to fetch the two-way radio. She could feel the blood pounding in her ears. She didn't have time to wait – Levi would be back any minute. Damn it, just make the call!

It rang three times before her mother answered. 'Hello?'

Yes! 'Mum, I can't talk for long, but I want you to know that Duke and I are okay.'

An audible gasp, then her mother's dear voice. 'Thank God. Pippa. Where are you?'

'I can't say, and you can't tell anyone that I rang, not even Dad … and especially not Cade.'

Footsteps sounded from the hall. 'I have to go, Mum. Love you.' Poppy put down the phone, feeling the sting of approaching tears. She knuckled them away as Levi came into the kitchen.

He looked at her curiously. 'Does talking to your mother always make you cry?'

His gentle teasing tone was just what she needed. Poppy felt the tension drain out of her. 'I'm just happy, that's all.'

'Glad to hear it.' He offered her the radio. 'Remember to keep it with you.' She took the receiver, and he showed her which channel to use. 'The Currajong post office sells phones, by the way.'

She flushed a little. That was no use to her. How was she supposed to buy a phone without ID?

'Feel free to use the house phone in the meantime.' Levi seemed reluctant to let her go. The dinner invitation still stands,' he said. 'Steaks on the barbie at seven o'clock.' He tousled Duke's ruff. 'You too, mate.'

'I'm pretty tired,' said Poppy. 'Some other time.'

She turned her back on him and stepped off the verandah. Pleading tiredness may have been an excuse, but it wasn't a lie. She was suddenly bone-weary, struggling to keep her eyes open. Rounding the corner of the house, she spotted an open toolbox. She lifted three screwdrivers, a hammer and some fencing staples before heading for the bungalow. All she wanted to do was sleep, but there was something she needed to do first.

Once inside, she locked the door, pulled down the blind and gave Duke a cup of kibble, slipping a few more pieces into her pocket. She snacked on some fruit, way too tired to cook or even take a shower. The blocked back door bothered her. It turned the bungalow into a trap. Pippa tried hard to shift the wardrobe, but it wouldn't budge. Maybe tomorrow when she had more energy.

Instead she went into her bedroom, studied the casement window and pulled off the insect screen. How to remove the winder? The screws must be under the bottom sill. She fetched a large knife from the kitchen and pried the hollow piece of timber free. Then she chose a screwdriver. Yes, a perfect fit. Now that she had access, it was easy to unscrew the mechanism. She hid the winder beneath the bed and pushed the pane of glass. It swung freely from the top hinge.

Duke whined as Poppy climbed out the window onto a narrow path. Good, she could exit in either direction. She climbed back inside, and Duke greeted her as if she'd been away for hours, gambolling around her feet and licking her fingers.

'Okay,' she said. 'Your turn.'

Poppy climbed out again, held the window open and called for Duke to follow. Encouraged by a piece of kibble, Duke scaled the sill and joined her outside. After a few more practices, Poppy was satisfied that both of them could swiftly escape out the window if necessary. She hammered a stout fencing staple into the timber window frame, hoping it wouldn't split. Fortunately, the frame survived. She took a piece of baling twine from her pocket, threaded it through the staple and tied it to the bunk with a quick release knot.

Now the window couldn't be pried open from the outside. A pointless precaution, perhaps. Cade could just smash the glass, but Poppy felt better knowing that he couldn't get in without making a noise. Not that Cade would get that close without Duke warning her. She fed the kelpie the last bits of kibble from her pocket.

The sun was dipping low when Poppy pulled down the blind. She lay on the bunk and pulled the doona up to her chin, trembling – whether from cold or nerves she didn't know. Despite her weariness, Poppy's brain fought slumber. Was it safe to sleep here in the bungalow? The locked door wouldn't keep Levi out if he had a mind to come in. He'd have a key. She was acutely conscious of being all alone at Brumby's Run with a stranger. She shivered more violently, and Duke laid his warm body against her.

Poppy hugged him tight. Duke liked Levi, liked him a lot. That was reassuring. Then a sudden fear hit her. Did Duke like Levi too much? Would he bark to warn her if Levi let himself in, or would he merely wag his tail? Poppy felt around on the floor beside her bed, found the hammer and slipped it under the covers. Only then, with her fingers curled around its smooth handle, did she allow sleep to claim her.

Cade slammed down his phone and lit a cigarette. He wasn't supposed to contact anyone from his old life, but this was the second time he'd called Pippa's mother. Ruby had sounded worried, saying that she hadn't seen or heard from her daughter. Cade didn't believe her. She was a lying bitch. How he wished he could talk to Ruby face to face – then he'd get the truth.

He stared out the window of an old farmhouse on the outskirts of Dubbo. It was prime land hereabouts. Fat cattle, lush grass and shady paddock trees glowed in the light of the setting sun. A far cry from drought-stricken Fairview. He took a deep drag of his fag, feeling a gnawing resentment towards the farmer who owned the place. It was all right for some.

He and Dylan had spent the last two nights stuck in limbo at the farmhouse, waiting for Renegades HQ to finalise their futures. Dylan had been told not to return home or to work. He was known to the police, and they'd apparently been sniffing around his place asking questions. Having Dylan there with him was the only thing stopping Cade from stealing a car and hightailing it back to Kilpa.

He'd spent the last few days swearing, chain-smoking and muttering to himself. Drinking whisky until his head felt like an over-ripe watermelon. Seeing Pippa out of the corner of his eye. Smelling her shampoo. Reaching for her in bed. Sometimes he thought he was going mad.

Cade licked his fingers and scrubbed at a dirty patch on the windowpane. A young woman had come into view on a quad bike, checking the cows and calves. Not bad – slim with fair, flowing hair. She looked like Pippa. He went outside, discarded his cigarette on the concrete path and headed for the paddock.

'Oi!' Dylan sang out to him from the back door. He hurried from the house, hopping on one leg while pulling on his second boot.

Cade stopped and scratched his chin.

'Where the hell do you think you're going?' Dylan caught up with him and glanced at the woman in the paddock, nonplussed. 'You mad bugger. That's not Pippa. You do know that, don't you?'

Cade glared at him. Of course he damn well knew it. Pippa was off somewhere with another man, making a fool of him every minute of every day. He marched to where the cars were parked and tried the driver's side door of Dylan's vehicle. It was locked. He tried the next.

Dylan swung Cade round hard by his shoulder. 'Your missus won't be at the farm.'

'Maybe not, but I have to know.' He could hear the desperation in his voice. Pathetic, what she'd reduced him to.

'Tell you what,' said Dylan, in a tone he might use to a stubborn child. 'I'll send one of the boys around to check.'

'No,' said Cade. 'It has to be me.'

'Well, it can't be you,' yelled Dylan, losing his temper. He took some steadying breaths. 'We're in this together. If the pigs catch you, they catch me.' He dragged his palms over his face. 'Come back inside, mate. Dazza can go get pizza and beer while we talk.'

Cade, in a daze, allowed himself to be guided back to the house. Dylan was the best friend he'd ever had and he needed him. But Dylan was wrong about one thing. Cade had lost his wife, his job, his home – even his name. He felt like a ghost. And how could the police catch a ghost?

CHAPTER 16

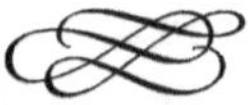

Poppy slept for twelve wonderful, restorative hours. She would have slept for longer, but as morning crept in the window, a flurry of barking from the hallway startled her awake. She grabbed the hammer and sprang from bed. Fear gripped her groggy brain. She tugged at the knot in the baling twine, releasing the window. Instinct screamed at her to flee, but what about Duke? He'd stopped barking – why? She struggled for breath, imagining Cade kicking in the dog's skull, leaving him a silent, quivering heap in the corner. And then she heard it – a knocking at the front door. Poppy exhaled, her panic abating. Cade wouldn't knock. She had to pull herself together.

She crept into the kitchen. Duke was wagging his tail and scratching at the door. 'It's me, Levi,' called a familiar voice.

Poppy unlocked the door. Levi stepped inside, eyeing the hammer in her hand. She quickly put it down. Dark patches stained his jeans, and straw suck out from under his hat. For some unaccountable reason she had a sudden urge to comb the stalks from his sandy-coloured hair with her fingers.

Levi picked up the two-way radio receiver lying on the table. 'You need to turn it on.'

Oh. 'Have you been trying to reach me?'

'Comet's had her colt and I could use a hand.' He looked her over. 'When you're ready.'

Poppy could feel the heat rise in her cheeks. She must have looked more of a mess than Levi did. Slept-in clothes. Bleary eyes. Tangled hair. 'Are Comet and the foal okay?'

'It was a difficult birth. The colt's weak and hasn't fed from mum yet. He needs to have that first drink of colostrum.' Levi turned on the two-way. 'If he's not on his feet in an hour we'll have to milk the mare and bottle feed him.' He handed her the radio. 'I have to get back. Leave Duke in the bungalow.'

She watched him stride up the path to the stable at a half-run. He really cared about the horses. Poppy hadn't met that sort of softness in a man before. Of course, caring for the horses was his job and the new colt was valuable, but it was more than that. Poppy had the feeling that Levi would be equally concerned for the welfare of any animal, whether it was valuable or not.

And Levi was right to be concerned about Comet's foal. Poppy understood the importance of colostrum, a magic elixir of protein, fat, vitamins and, most importantly, antibodies that helped newborns ward off deadly infections. The lambs at Fairview needed it too and without it they usually died.

Dad had taught all his kids how to milk ewes who'd lost their lambs, and he kept the bags of frozen colostrum in the back freezer to feed to orphans. Poppy had tried to convince Cade to do the same thing, but he couldn't be bothered. 'If they die, they die,' he'd said. It was hard not to contrast Cade's callousness with Levi's natural compassion.

Keen as she was to see the foal, her rumbling stomach demanded breakfast. After all, she had a fridge stacked with goodies and it was time to enjoy them. She threw eggs, bacon, spinach, thick tomato slices and fresh basil from her windowsill garden into a pan. Then she toasted some bread and slathered it with fresh farmhouse butter. Soon she and Duke were enjoying a hearty cooked breakfast. One burp and two mugs of tea later, and she was ready to greet the latest arrival at Brumby's Run.

. . .

Poppy knelt beside the small bundle nestled in the straw, all tangled legs and soft grey fur.

'You're the most precious thing I've ever seen,' she whispered, stroking his velvet nose while Comet kept a watchful eye.

Poppy looked up to see Levi leaning against the stable door, smiling. Her delight upon meeting the foal caused her to lower her guard and she returned the smile. He really was very good-looking, with his generous mouth, and dimpled chin, though the set of his jaw did suggest a stubborn streak. But it was his intelligent brown eyes that she liked the most – warm and kind with a hint of humour.

'The image of his father,' whispered Levi, proudly watching the foal.

'But he's grey,' said Pippa.

'Not for long. Black horses are born the colour of smoke. He'll shed out to pure ebony. Now fetch me that stainless steel bucket over there,' he said, 'and hold Comet. I hate this bit. Never was much good at this milking malarkey. I'm all thumbs.'

'Let me do it,' said Poppy.

He seemed surprised. 'You've milked mares?'

'No,' she admitted. 'But I've milked plenty of sheep. I'm an expert.'

'Sheep?' he said, in an amused voice. 'Tell me, that farm in the Mallee where you worked … Did it run sheep or horses?'

Poppy hesitated, but decided to tell the truth, hoping that she wasn't thereby shooting herself in the foot. Something told her Levi was onto her anyway. In any case she liked Levi and didn't want to lie to him. 'The farm ran sheep and grew wheat. But there were horses too. Or at least one horse.' She made the correction in keeping with her new spirit of honesty. 'A stockhorse called Pepper. I rode him all the time.'

'Aah … and have you ridden any other horses?' She shook her head. 'Righto … and what age was this stockhorse?'

She had to think about how to answer that one. Pepper was the same age as she was, twenty-four years old and he could still bring the sheep in for shearing. But Poppy had started riding Pepper when they were both ten, so it seemed fair enough to give that age. It would also sound better than twenty-four.

Levi looked at her with a thoughtful expression on his face, like he was trying to make his mind up about something. 'You do realise that mustering sheep on a trained ten-year-old stockhorse is a far cry from breaking in youngsters?'

Poppy stood up and pressed her lips together. She wanted to add that when Pepper first arrived at the farm he wasn't a trained stock-horse at all. He was a rogue, barely rideable. But she was afraid that it would sound self-serving.

'Do you want me to milk Comet or not?' she said, a little cross. 'If foals are anything like lambs, their digestive tracts can only absorb colostrum for the first twelve to twenty-four hours. Every second counts, so we shouldn't be standing around chatting—'

Poppy stopped talking abruptly, nervously shifting her feet and retreating from Levi. Had she really said those words? If she'd dared speak to Cade like that, he would have smacked her in the mouth.

Yet far from being angry, Levi apparently agreed with her. 'You're right. Go get the bucket and I'll hold Comet.'

The colt whinnied, high and shrill, causing his mother to nuzzle him, trying to nose him to his feet. He made a half-hearted attempt to stand and collapsed back into the straw.

'When was he born?' she asked.

'Almost three hours ago.'

Poppy bent down to look at the mare's bag. It was shiny, tight and sore looking. When Comet moved her leg the teats squirted milk, or more accurately, colostrum. If, like sheep, mares produced the high-est-quality colostrum only for the first twelve hours after foaling, Poppy couldn't afford to let another drop go to waste.

She knelt down on one knee and positioned the bucket on the other. 'Is this Comet's first foal?'

'It is.' Levi soothed the anxious mare, who cow-kicked when Poppy attempted to press her bag. 'But I've handled her teats daily to get her used to them being touched. She's still ticklish though.'

Ticklish? Quite an understatement, thought Poppy. She touched Comet's bag again. A violent kick tipped the bucket over. Her bag was painful and tender, not ticklish.

'Careful,' said Levi. 'Do you want me to do it?'

'Patience,' murmured Poppy.

She kept her head in Comet's flank and her shoulder against her stifle so she could feel the first sign of a kick. When the mare bunched up her muscles, Poppy tapped her leg. 'Stop that!' she said, firmly. Comet put her ears back, but stood still. Poppy used the leaking milk to moisten and lubricate her fingers. When Poppy then gently pulled a teat, Comet merely flinched.

Using her left hand to hold the bucket, she used her right hand to massage first one teat, then the other. Comet relaxed as pressure released from her overfull bag, stimulating her to let down her milk. Soon two steady streams drummed loudly into the tin bucket. It was like milking a giant sheep, really. Poppy hummed to herself, enjoying the familiar task.

Levi was peering around Comet's neck, trying to see what was happening. Poppy ignored him, concentrating on the job, rhythmic hand movements lulling her into a state of meditation. After ten minutes she was done. Poppy stood up and showed Levi the bucket. It contained more than a litre of creamy yellow colostrum.

'Yes!' cried Levi, spooking both Comet and Poppy. 'That's fantastic. Last time I milked a mare I was lucky to get quarter of that amount.'

Poppy watched his animated face, sharing in his excitement, alarmed by his passion. For an awful moment she thought he was going to kiss her. For an awful moment she wished that he would.

Instead, Levi simply took the bucket from her. 'Can you get me the funnel and the feeding bottle?'

Poppy took the required items from an insulated bag in the corner of the stable.

'Now use the funnel to fill the bottle while the milk's still warm.'

Poppy did so, wondering at how small the bottle was, not much bigger than a human baby's.

Levi must have noticed her surprise. 'Newborn foals only drink a little at a time. I'll be happy to get two hundred and fifty mils into him.' He handed her the bottle. 'Be my guest.'

Poppy gave a happy sigh and settled down in the straw beside the foal. He didn't need any encouragement, sucking strongly as soon as the rubber teat touched his lips. Within a minute he'd drunk the lot.

She looked enquiringly up at Levi, who grinned and held out his hand for the bottle. He refilled it and she offered it to the foal again. He drained that one as well, then lay flat on the straw and went to sleep.

'You've done a top job, Poppy. You really have.' Levi's voice brimmed with admiration.

A warm feeling of relief and accomplishment suffused her whole being. 'We can't keep calling him the foal,' she said. 'Can we name him?'

'Drew's already picked out a name – Night King for a colt.'

'Night King?' Feeling playful, she lay down in the hay and cuddled the dozing foal, tugging at his ears. 'He's too little to be a king,' she laughed. 'Can we call him Prince for now?'

'Sure.' Levi repacked the insulated bag. 'I'd better get this extra colostrum to the fridge. Might catch an hour's sleep as well. I've been up all night.'

As he turned to go, Comet gave her sleeping colt a mighty shove with her nose. Prince snorted with indignation and scrambled to his feet. Poppy and Levi cheered in unison. Prince shook his head and, with shaky first steps, nuzzled his way along his mother's flank. When he found her udder, he latched on and nursed noisily, little tail wagging.

'Make that two hours sleep,' he said with a grin. 'And thank God we won't be bottle-feeding Prince ten times a day. That's your job now, mum.' Levi threw his arms around Comet's neck and kissed her. The mare nickered in protest at this familiarity.

Poppy blinked at them. She'd never seen a man hug an animal – not even a dog – let alone kiss one.

Levi offered his hand and she took it without thinking. He helped her to her feet. She brushed straw from her clothes as he gave Comet one last affectionate slap on the neck. 'Look after these two for me, won't you Poppy? They're special.'

'Aye aye, captain.' She stood tall and saluted, proud to know that Levi trusted her with such precious charges, heart bursting with happiness. She was going to like this job.

CHAPTER 17

Levi didn't sleep for two hours after all – it was more like four. When he woke he lay in bed for a long while, thinking about Comet and her colt. Thinking about Poppy. So he'd been right about her not having worked with horses. Well, he'd forgive her for that and give her a chance. She was a quick learner. She'd been honest with him and Levi valued honesty. Heaven knows how she'd wangled a trial, but Levi no longer believed that she'd lied on her online application. It seemed that she'd never submitted one, or if she had, he couldn't find it. Yet despite Poppy's lack of experience, she'd really come through for him this morning. She understood animals and had a tender way with them.

Levi thought back to yesterday. She'd seemed so reserved – scared, even – barely able to meet his eye. That hadn't boded well for the job. Horses, especially young, green ones, didn't respond well to timid people. It took a confident trainer to inspire confidence in a nervous colt or filly. Yet she'd shown courage in protecting Mist from the aggressive paint colt. She hadn't taken any nonsense from Comet, making the skittish mare stand up and accept being milked. And what had she said to him? *We shouldn't be standing around chatting.* She'd been right, but it took some guts to tell your boss off, however mildly, on the first day of a job.

Levi imagined that her initial shyness had a lot to do with the unfortunate circumstances of their first meeting. She'd lost him Thowra. At the time he'd thought her a negligent fool, who didn't seem to care that she'd lost his horse. But now that he knew her better, he realised he'd been wrong. Her seeming indifference was due to shame and embarrassment. Poppy would have cared very much about the mistake she'd made. She loved horses as much as he did, that was clear.

Levi stretched and got up. Perhaps he'd make coffee to help him wake up. No, he was in too much of a hurry, too eager to see Comet and her colt. He pulled on his boots, slapped on his hat and checked himself in the mirror, wishing he'd shaved. Who was he kidding? He was just as eager to see Poppy. The girl had him thoroughly intrigued. Her charming combination of shyness and boldness. Her slim, graceful body that looked like it could do with a good feed. Her beautiful face, brilliant blue eyes and funny haircut.

Finding her crying in his kitchen yesterday had triggered some powerful protective emotions. If Poppy was in some kind of trouble, he wanted to help. Nullah often teased him, saying he had a hero complex and was always trying to save someone or other. Maybe it was true. Levi's early experiences of being tormented in the schoolyard had given him a keen sense of justice. Back then he'd been his sisters' champion, even when he copped abuse for it. He'd lost friends by calling out racism or ill treatment. He'd been fired from one job because he stood up to the boss who'd been hitting on a young jillaroo. He simply couldn't stand bullies or bigots.

Levi opened the fridge, gulped some milk from the carton and fixed a quick sandwich for a lunch on the go. He planned to work with the youngsters that afternoon and he couldn't wait to find out how good a horsewoman Poppy really was. He imagined riding with her up into Balleroo National Park, showing her the waterfall, the platypus in Snake Creek, the cypress pine forests of Maroong Mountain. Levi whistled a tune as he headed for the stable. The future suddenly seemed very bright.

Poppy finished brushing Mist and took the plaits out of her mane. The filly pawed and whinnied impatiently. Poppy stood back to admire her. What a beauty! Mist looked just like the picture Poppy had on her bedroom wall as a child. How often had she dreamed about that dark dapple-grey with the arched neck and proud eyes? She'd cut it from a calendar and made a wish every night that the image would come to life. And now, miracle of miracles, that horse stood before her in the flesh, even lovelier than the picture.

They were readying the youngsters for a training session. When Levi yarded her two – grey Mist and the chestnut gelding named Copper – Poppy had been shaking in her boots. The pair had charged around the yard, snorting and trying the gate. They'd looked far too wild for her.

Levi had gone to fetch his favourite three-year-old, Zorro, leaving Poppy to get Mist ready. She doubted that she could manage the fractious filly, who didn't seem to have a walking speed, but instead pranced wherever she went. Yet once she'd fed Mist and brushed her and put soft waves in her dove-grey mane, Poppy changed her mind. How would it feel to ride such a vision? Like dancing on air, she decided. Now where was Levi? It was time to get this show on the road.

At that moment Levi appeared around the corner of the stable leading a plump palomino mare. 'Meet Goldilocks,' he said. 'One of our trail horses.' Mist neighed an excited greeting, but Goldilocks ignored her, resting a back foot and appearing to doze off.

'She's sweet,' said Poppy, untangling a knot from the mare's creamy mane. 'Why did you bring her in? Is she hurt?'

'She's for you,' he said. 'So I can see how well you ride.'

'But I'm riding Mist,' said Poppy, heart sinking. 'You said so.'

'That was before I knew the full extent of your riding experience was on an aged stockhorse called Pepper.' Levi's coppery brown eyes twinkled with amusement. 'Put Mist in the box next to Zorro and I'll show you the tack room.'

'But …'

'No buts. You ride Goldilocks or you don't ride at all.' His expression brooked no argument.

'Can I ride Mist if I pass the test?'

'We'll see.'

After saddling and bridling Goldilocks, Poppy mounted her in the rectangular sand arena, keenly aware of Levi's scrutiny. It felt marvellous to be on a horse again, seeing the world between her neat, golden ears. The mare stood perfectly still, seeming half-asleep. 'What should I do now?'

'Start on your right rein,' he said. 'First at a walk, then at a trot.'

'Right rein?'

'Clockwise,' he said. 'Go clockwise.'

She tapped her mount with her heels. Goldilocks went straight into a canter, carting her rider to the gate and skidding to a halt. It took Poppy a moment to recover her balance.

'Try again,' he called.

Poppy tugged on the right rein and kicked. Goldilocks swished her tail, pinned back her ears and didn't move.

Levi smothered a smile. 'Don't kick. Use your lower legs and seat. Show her who's boss.'

Don't kick – how was that supposed to work? 'You're making a fool of me, Miss Goldilocks. I really need this job, so *move*,' Poppy muttered under her breath, all grit and determination. She sat deep in the saddle and squeezed with her lower legs as Levi had suggested. To her surprise the mare moved off smoothly, walking counterclockwise around the arena.

'Right rein,' he called. 'Go right.'

She tugged on the right rein. The mare tensed her neck, jaw gaping wide in protest.

'Gently,' he called. 'And use your left leg behind the girth. Outside leg to inside rein.'

This time, instead of pulling, Poppy's fingers loosened the left rein and lightly squeezed the right. At the same time, she moved her left calf back a fraction and pressed it against her horse's side. Goldilocks promptly changed direction. Poppy laughed and glanced over to Levi, who gave her the thumbs up.

After walking a lap around the arena, she asked for a trot. Goldilocks obliged, her gait surprisingly fast. Poppy was enjoying herself. When Goldilocks shied at a low-flying bird and broke into a canter, Poppy let her have her head. And when she headed for a low jump in the centre of the arena, Poppy urged her on. They cleared the obstacle in fine style and trotted back to meet Levi in the centre of the arena.

'Not bad.' He looked pleased. 'But I never said to take that jump. You're a bit of a rebel, Miss Poppy. You need to learn to do as you're told.'

The irony of this comment was not lost on Poppy. All her life she'd done as she was told. She'd been a brow-beaten, docile, obedient slave. She loved that Levi didn't know that. She loved that in the space of two short days he was calling her a rebel. Her – Miss timid-as-a-mouse Pippa Black. She'd never been prouder.

Poppy beamed down at Levi, wondering at the vast contrast between him and Cade, thinking how different her life would have been had she married such a man.

Levi spent the next half an hour putting Poppy through her paces. She had a lot to learn, but Levi was a good teacher, if a tad demanding.

'Your hands are too high. Keep them on her wither.'

'Stretch your heels down and balance the ball of your foot on the stirrup.'

'Look up. Focus on where you're going.'

'Those reins are too tight. Imagine there's a baby bird in each hand. You don't want to squash it, but you don't want to drop it either. That's the pressure you need on her mouth.'

And, 'Don't hold your breath. Hum a tune or something.'

How the hell did he know she'd been holding her breath? It always happened when she concentrated hard and it made her tense up.

Finally, he called her into the centre of the sand arena. 'Not bad.

You may be self-taught, but you have plenty of natural ability, a deep seat and a good connection with your horse.'

Poppy basked in the unfamiliar glow of praise. 'So, can I ride Mist now?'

'Watch me do a session with Zorro first. If you still want to ride Mist after that, go for it.'

Poppy watched with rapt admiration as Levi worked Zorro. What a horseman! He managed the fiery three-year-old with patience, skill and an instinctive understanding of his mount. Poppy was close to having a fangirl moment.

The pair practised transitions between walk, trot and canter. They practised circles, rein backs, changing direction and trotting over poles. At the end of the session Poppy could see how much progress they'd made. Zorro was calmer, he'd lowered his head and seemed more balanced in his movements.

'Your turn,' said Levi when he'd finished.

Poppy mounted Mist in the round yard under Levi's watchful eye. The filly felt like a coiled spring beneath her, all bunched muscles and flared nostrils. But instead of being frightened, Poppy was eager to rise to the challenge.

In contrast to Zorro's bold paces, Mist seemed hesitant and unsure. 'You're a nervous Nellie,' whispered Poppy. 'Just like me.'

'Reassure her,' he called. 'Talk to her, stroke her neck.'

With Levi's able assistance, Poppy soon had Mist moving forward freely. As the filly gained confidence, her prancing gait returned. Poppy had been right. Riding Mist was like dancing on air, and she was in heaven.

After half an hour Levi called time. 'I was wrong,' he said, stroking Mist's dappled neck. 'You're a good match for that filly. She needs a soft touch.'

Just as Poppy was about to dismount, Duke bounded into the yard. Mist snorted and reared. Poppy barely kept her seat.

'I told you to tie him up when we're riding the youngsters,' said Levi, grabbing the dog's collar.

'I did,' called Pippa, but the damage was done. Thoroughly

spooked, Mist charged off and gave a tremendous buck. Poppy flew from the saddle, hitting the top rail as she fell, tearing her shirt open on a sharp splinter. Levi rushed to where she lay face down on the sand. 'You're bleeding,' he said, kneeling. 'Let me see.' He lifted her torn shirt away from the wound.

'No!' She scrambled away from him. 'It's just a scratch. Don't touch me.'

'Okay.' He backed off, showing her his open hands. 'I'm sorry.'

Poppy climbed unsteadily to her feet, clutching the rail. Duke pressed himself against her, whining in sympathy. He seemed to know he'd done something wrong. She stroked his ears. 'It's okay,' she whispered. 'You didn't mean it.'

Levi was staring at her, his expression grim. Poppy tried to hold the torn flap of her shirt shut. Had he seen the bruises on her back? They must still be there. It had only been a few days since she'd left Cade.

She burnt with embarrassment as reality crashed in. Between the excitement of Prince's birth, the thrill of riding Mist and her newfound admiration for Levi, she'd almost forgotten the deadly predicament she was in. She couldn't let it happen again.

'I'm fine,' Poppy said as firmly as she could, feeling blood trickle down her back. 'But I need to get changed. Can we call it a day?'

'I'll put Mist away.' He took the mare's reins and gave her a searching look. 'If there's something I can do …'

'No, nothing.'

Levi led Mist to the gate, then turned. 'You did a great job, Poppy. You really did.'

Poppy didn't reply. She stood shaken and rigid by the rail, feeling numb, willing him to leave.

CHAPTER 18

For the next few days Levi trod very carefully around Poppy. Since the fall she'd retreated into her shell. He could barely get a word out of her. But Levi was a patient man. He didn't expect her to open up to him, not yet. She'd need time to conquer her embarrassment. He hoped that, in the end, she might confide in him.

Levi couldn't put the sight of Poppy's horribly bruised back from his mind. Her skin had been an assortment of colours – not the result of a single accident. Blue, purple and black. Yellow, green and pale brown. Someone had inflicted the injuries over an extended period of time. It made his blood boil. A boyfriend or husband? Poppy was such a mystery, so tight-lipped about her history. If she was on the run from her past, now he understood why.

Keeping the knowledge to himself was emotionally draining. He found it hard to concentrate and was forgetting things. He forgot to order the new delivery of lupins and oats. He forgot to pay the electricity bill. He constantly second-guessed himself. Did he ignore what he'd seen, or confront Poppy and offer to help? Did he allow his feelings for Poppy to grow, or close them down?

Because there *were* feelings. Poppy was his last thought before going to sleep and his first thought in the morning. He pictured her slender neck, determined chin and enigmatic blue eyes. Levi dreamed of Poppy's shy smile, a smile he'd seen so rarely.

He looked for her each morning. She started work early and could be found dishing out feeds or mucking out stables. For although she was distant with him, Poppy remained tireless in her duties, devoting herself to the horses with a true passion. Levi was sometimes a little jealous of all the hugs and kisses she dispensed to them each day.

Simply put, without saying a word, Poppy was driving him crazy. Levi wished his friend Nullah would come. He could use somebody to talk to. He wouldn't betray Poppy's privacy by disclosing what he'd seen, but surely he could discuss his dilemma in general terms. After all, Nullah was his oldest friend.

Four o'clock on Friday and Levi had never seen a more glorious afternoon. The cloudless, silver-blue sky rang with the cry of curra-wongs. Sunshine played on gum leaves. The scent of wattle wafted from the forest. Poppy was feeding out hay in the yards, dawdling at Comet's gate to watch the foal play. Had that girl only been at Brumby's Run since Monday morning? It seemed like she'd been inhabiting his thoughts forever.

They'd achieved a significant milestone today – riding Mist and Zorro out of the arena. Levi had led them up the broad track past the stables and broodmare yards. Past the dam and turnout paddocks. Into the wild uplands that served as a sanctuary for a herd of twenty brumbies. Then through the gate leading to Balleroo National Park and into the forest beyond.

They cantered for a while, giving the horses their heads, letting them expend their youthful pent-up energy. Then they settled into a long, swinging walk through the candlebarks, catching views of the shining valley below through occasional breaks in the trees. Each glimpse provoked cries of delight from Poppy. The majesty of the mountains was breaking down her barriers.

The horses had mainly behaved themselves, apart from the odd high-spirited pigroot from Mist. Poppy had sat out the small bucks easily. Levi watched her admiringly, impressed by both her horsemanship and the way her neat bottom fitted in the saddle. Her baggy check shirt could not entirely conceal the swell of her breasts. He was enjoying himself.

Upon reaching the old stock route, they pulled up their horses.

'Years ago, men used that track to drive cattle into the high country for summer,' he said. 'It starts down on the road at the corner of our southern boundary and leads up to Dead Man's Hut.'

'I know the legend of that hut,' she said. 'The old man that lived there was obsessed with capturing a herd of enchanted brumbies. He swore they could fly and become invisible.'

'That's right,' said Levi. 'A cattle duffer, by all accounts. Earned his living stealing cleanskin calves and branding them himself. Nobody knew his real name, but everyone called him Brumby Jack. Staying alone in the bush for years on end can send someone a bit mad. He spent more and more of his time chasing this imaginary herd led, he said, by a magical white stallion.

'One day Brumby Jack's horse turned up in Currajong with an empty saddle and caked in sweat. Riders went to check on him. They found Jack lying in the yard with a catching rope clutched in his dead hands. It was snubbed to a post, but the noose was empty, and the gate was still shut. Jack's skull had been kicked in. People still talk of ghost horses roaming these mountains.'

'Is the hut haunted?'

'I sure hope not,' laughed Levi. 'We take the more experienced riders up there in the trekking season. The accommodation is pretty primitive, but there's a rainwater tank and a fireplace. Yards for the horses. The gear goes up the day before in the Jeep. When the visitors arrive after a long day's ride we meet them with cold drinks, a campfire-cooked meal and an authentic high-country experience.'

'I'd love to go there one day,' said Poppy, as Mist grazed on some sweet snowgrass.

'You will,' grinned Levi. 'That's where we'll catch Thowra and his brumby friends, just as soon as Drew and the others get back. Or have you forgotten about my wayward golden stallion?'

Poppy had the grace to flash him a charming mea culpa smile. 'Catch Thowra? Exactly how do you propose to do that?'

'I'll tell you later – on one condition,' he said.

'What's that?

'Join me for a barbeque tonight. It's my birthday and I don't want to eat alone.'

Poppy laughed aloud, a joyful, musical sound. 'You win. I'd love to.'

Levi fussed about the kitchen, adding more parmesan cheese to the salad and buttering extra slices of bread. The steaks were marinating in mustard, vinegar and Worcestershire sauce, the drinks were chilled, and he had sausages on hand for Duke.

A knock came at the back door. Levi looked up as Poppy and Duke entered the kitchen. She looked freshly showered and very young, with pink, scrubbed cheeks and damp hair slicked back. It wasn't the first time he'd been struck by her startling combination of blue eyes, fair skin and jet hair.

Poppy wore her signature scarf, a tan shirt and patched blue jeans that had been heavily soiled the day before. She must have washed them overnight. Poppy seemed to only have three shirts and two pairs of pants – the blue jeans and a worn pair of moleskins. Levi sighed and shook his head, annoyed that he actually knew how many sets of clothes she had. What was wrong with him? He covered the salad bowl with a tea towel.

'Can I help?' she asked.

'Yes, keep your hound away from the meat tray. And see that yellow envelope on the shelf? That's your first week's pay.'

Poppy opened it and counted out the notes, whistling in approval. The sound caused Levi to tingle all over. Damn that girl, she was getting a hold on him without even trying.

They sat on canvas chairs around an outdoor table, waiting for their food to cook. Steaks sizzled on the wood-fired, homemade brick barbecue standing in a patch of grass near the back door. Drinks sat in a galvanised feed bucket filled with ice. Levi grabbed himself a beer and poured Poppy a glass of riesling.

'I've never drunk wine before.' She tasted her drink. 'It's delicious.' By the time he got up to turn the meat, she was on to her second glass. 'Is it your fair dinkum birthday today?'

'It is. I'm twenty-seven years old.'

'I don't have a gift for you,' she said.

'Your company is gift enough.' Levi winced. Had he really said that?

They chatted about horses, the weather, the bad load of hay full of dock seed. When the meal was ready they ate heartily, appetites whetted by a hard day of physical work. Duke, full of sausages, dozed beneath the table as twilight turned into evening.

Poppy pushed aside her empty plate with a sigh of satisfaction.

'Tell me about Thowra.'

'He wasn't born a brumby,' said Levi. 'He was a six-month-old foal at foot, ready to be weaned, when a wild stallion stole his dam from Stan Grant out at Dandalong Station. They recovered her, but not the colt.'

'He's so beautiful, he doesn't seem real. How can you be sure that Thowra is Stan Grant's colt?'

'He has the Dandalong Station brand,' said Levi. 'An S inside a D. Last Monday was the first time I was close enough to see it for myself. Thowra's a direct descendant of Champagne Charlie, a foundation stockhorse, but also one of the most influential palomino sires in Australia. He was an attention grabber wherever he went, with a superb front, lovely length of rein and a classic refined head. But it was his colour that really set him apart. Coat like a newly minted gold coin, and a mane and tail of pure silver. I'll find some photos for you tomorrow. Charlie's the spitting image of our Thowra.'

Poppy was clearly intrigued and Levi couldn't be happier.

'Stan offered a huge reward for the colt's return. Dozens tried, but Thowra outsmarted them all. So for the last five years he's been roaming free, causing havoc by stealing station mares. Seems that none of them can resist him.'

'I can understand why,' said Poppy, listening to his story with rapt attention.

'Last autumn Stan gave up the search in disgust. He withdrew the reward, saying the horse was more trouble than he was worth. "Anyone who catches that bugger can keep him," he said.'

'And you did catch him,' said Poppy. 'And then I let him go.'

'We'll get him back. I have a plan.'

'You promised to tell me,' she said.

'Well …' He tossed a twig into the coals, causing a little flare. 'Problem is that my plan keeps changing.'

Poppy giggled. 'You lured me here under false pretences,' she said with mock outrage.

Though the meal was finished, neither of them seemed inclined to call it a night. As the wine loosened Poppy's tongue, their topics of conversation grew more personal.

'Have you ever been married?' She poured herself another drink, emptying the bottle.

'No.' Somewhere in the dark an owl hooted. 'What about you?'

'I was once,' she said. 'A long time ago. It didn't work out.'

'Oh?' He sensed that she wanted to talk and it was best if he just listened.

'He was an awful man, my husband.'

Ah, did that explain the bruises? And if it did, that *a long time ago* reference was probably untrue.

'Do Jews marry in a synagogue, the same way Christians marry in a church?

Her question took him aback. Levi hadn't realised that she knew or cared about his background. He never liked it when people mentioned his Jewish heritage out of the blue. It meant they'd been dwelling on it.

'Sometimes,' he answered. 'And sometimes they marry at home, or at a reception venue, or in a park, just like anyone else.'

'Christians must marry in church,' she said. 'The union must be consecrated in the eyes of God, otherwise it's not a real marriage. My father says that a couple married outside of church are sinners, and will be condemned to misery on earth and hell in the hereafter.'

Poppy had delivered her rather bleak remarks as if learnt by rote. Their chat was taking a strange turn, one Levi didn't much like. 'Were you married in a church?' he asked.

She nodded.

'And yet you say you were miserable. Maybe a good marriage depends less on where it takes place, and more on the love between the two people.'

This seemed a radical concept for Poppy. 'Is that what Jews believe? That love is more important than God?'

'No, it's what I believe.' He could feel his frustration growing. He didn't have to justify anything to her. 'Why are we even talking about this?'

'I was curious.'

Levi opened another stubby of beer. 'Well be curious about something else.' He stood and poked the dying fire beneath the grate, smothering it with ash.

'Do you know anything more about when Drew will be back?'

His irritation rose another notch. She asked him this every single day. 'Who's Drew to you anyway?' he said. 'Why the fascination?'

Poppy called Duke over, as if the dog might protect her from the question.

'Did you know that Drew was married last Saturday up on Maroong Mountain?' he said. 'I guess that makes him and his new wife sinners.'

Poppy sculled the last of the wine. 'You're cross with me.' Her eyes shone wide in the pale glow from the house.

Levi slapped at a mosquito on his thigh and sat down, wondering how to explain his discomfort to someone who seemed to have no idea. 'What's me being Jewish have to do with anything? It's an aspect of my heritage, that's all. Like having parents born in Greece, or being Indigenous.'

'I didn't mean anything by it.'

How often had Levi heard that same line? 'Maybe not, but plenty of people do.' He felt his face crease in anger and was glad it was dark. 'I'm the great-grandson of a Holocaust survivor. Last weekend a woman died when some bastards bombed a synagogue in Millburn. My mother knows the family. Someone blew Zadie Mintz up because she was Jewish. Can you blame me for being defensive?'

Poppy dropped her wine glass. It shattered on the mossy stone pavers at her feet. Next moment she was gone, vanished into the gloom beyond the porch light.

CHAPTER 19

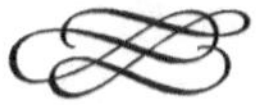

Poppy lay curled on her bed in a fetal position, hugging Duke tight to her clenched belly. Her head spun from the wine, clouding her thinking. Not that any amount of thinking would help. Levi's words echoed through her brain. *My mother knows the family.* It brought Cade's crime way too close to home. He'd killed that young mother and now Poppy felt dead too. There was no escaping her husband. Cade might not know where she was, but he was still managing to torture her.

Duke whined and licked her face. His coat was wet with tears, although she hadn't realised she was crying. The fear was back; the fear that she'd been starting to conquer during this last magic week. It crawled over Poppy like a great black spider. Familiar sights and sounds terrified her. Grevillia bushes rustling against the wall, shadows playing at the window, possums growling on the roof – these things suddenly seemed filled with sinister intent.

A knock came at the kitchen door and Duke bounded off in a flurry of barking. Poppy froze. He no longer barked at Levi, so who was there? She took fast, rasping breaths, struggling to drag air into her lungs. She wrenched herself upright and forced her paralysed limbs to move.

'Duke,' she called softly. 'Come here.'

Within seconds the dog was at her side. Poppy found her car keys, undid the baling twine window tie and scrambled out the window. Duke followed with a practised leap. 'Shh,' she whispered, holding onto his collar and creeping down the side of the bungalow.

She dared to peer around the corner. The shadowy figure of a man wearing a cowboy hat stood at the door. It wasn't Cade. Well, of course it wasn't. With Cade, the first thing she'd know would be his hands around her throat.

The stranger dumped a swag on the bungalow porch and peered in the window. He knocked one last time, then walked over to Poppy's car. Out in the open, bright moonshine showed him clearly – an Aboriginal man dressed like a stockman.

The stranger leaned against her station wagon and lazily rolled a cigarette. Dammit, he was going to steal her car. Poppy didn't have the courage to confront him, but if she went round the back of the bungalow the other way and slid down the bank, she could get to the house without him seeing her. Thank God for the moonlight. Reluctant as she was to face Levi, it was better than facing the stranger alone.

Levi hadn't gone inside. She found him sitting with a beer at the outdoor table, listening to music on a small transistor radio. He bent to pat Duke.

'There's a man,' said Poppy, breathless and urgent. 'He's trying to steal my car.' Levi looked up at her in confusion. Poppy grabbed his arm and pulled him from his chair. 'Come on, get your torch. We have to hurry.'

Levi followed her, and she followed Duke, who bounded ahead of them, barking. The stranger was still lounging on her car, bold as brass. 'There,' she said, pointing.

The man looked around and waved.

'That's Nullah,' said Levi.

'You know him?'

'Sure.'

'So he's not trying to steal my car?'

Levi chuckled. 'No offence, but that old bomb isn't worth stealing. I told Nullah to stash his swag in the bungalow.'

Poppy was staring, open-mouthed, her mind still woozy with drink.

'Sorry, did he wake you?' said Levi. 'It's only eight-thirty. I thought you'd still be up.'

Nullah strolled over to them. He was shorter than Levi, but not by much – lean as a bullwhip, with a three-day stubble and a huge silver belt buckle that gleamed in the moonshine.

'G'day.' Nullah offered his hand.

Poppy backed off, feeling vulnerable despite Levi's presence. 'Why's he here?'

'I told you about Nullah,' said Levi. There was an edge to his voice. 'The friend who'll help us catch Thowra?'

The thought of this stranger sharing her quarters made Poppy desperate. 'No.' She shook her head. 'Can't he stay in the house with you?'

'What's wrong with me sleeping in the bungalow?' asked Nullah.

It was more of a challenge than a question. Poppy was too upset to notice, and the wine had washed away her customary filter of civility.

'You're—' she hesitated, seeing Levi's furious face.

'I'm what?' said Nullah. 'Go on, girl. Spit it out.'

Duke whined and went to sit by Nullah's feet. For a long time no-one spoke.

'Grab your gear, mate,' said Levi at last in a low voice. 'And stow it in the room next to mine. I'll meet you back at the house in a few minutes. We've a lot of catching up to do.'

'Righto.' Nullah retreated into the darkness.

She exhaled. Thank goodness Levi understood.

'And in the morning, Miss Poppy Forrester, you can pack your bags. Nobody insults a friend of mine that way.'

Poppy didn't immediately grasp his meaning. 'Pack my bags? So you want me to move into the house instead of Nullah?'

'No, I want you to leave. You're fired.'

'I'm sorry. I didn't mean …'

'Yeah, yeah. I know. You didn't mean anything by it. Too bad.'

His words hit Poppy like missiles. She was too stunned to speak.

Levi chucked Duke under the chin. 'Goodbye, boy. It's been nice knowing you.' And with that he followed Nullah into the night.

Poppy sat in the bungalow kitchen, feeling numb. The shock of being fired had sobered her up. Pity it hadn't happened before she was so rude to Levi's friend. Even now she found it hard to believe that the two of them were mates. In her experience, blacks and whites did not form friendships.

In her experience. Poppy was starting to realise that her experience may be steering her wrong in some very fundamental ways. Her short time at Brumby's Run was opening her eyes to a different way of being. She'd never gone to school, never had peers, apart from Tracey, and Tracey's parents attended Dad's church too. Her school friends were her siblings. Her understanding of the world had been framed by her parents – mainly her stern father – and to a lesser extent by Cade. What if that understanding was all skewed?

Dad's face swam before her, thundering from the pulpit. As a girl, Poppy had often been frightened of the larger-than-life figure who ruled his wife and children as a dictator, answerable to no-one but God. To hear him tell it, almost everyone was going to hell.

Then she'd married Cade. Mum said that daughters married men similar to their fathers, and in some ways Poppy had. Both Dad and Cade were Mallee farmers. They were also controlling, critical and intimidating, although Cade had taken intimidating to a whole new level.

After marrying Cade, her father's charismatic hold on her had weakened. She began to explore the scriptures herself, and not just the passages Dad prescribed. She found that the Bible held many inconsistencies, and that the Old and New Testaments were like two different books. Dad picked chapters and verses to support his agenda, while selectively ignoring ones that contradicted it. She suspected that he even made up some verses. Maybe 'Wives, praise and obey your husbands as you praise and obey the Lord' was somewhere in the Bible, but if it was, Poppy couldn't find it.

Cade was a man far more full of hate and intolerance than her father. She'd quickly discovered what kind of a person he was, yet she'd meekly believed him when he ranted about Australia being swamped by Asians and Muslims. About Aboriginals being thieves. About single mothers being sluts and whores. An overwhelming wave of disappointment left Poppy weak – a wave of disappointment in herself. What was wrong with her? Had she ever had one independent thought in her life?

Levi was Jewish. According to her father and husband that automatically made him an awful person. Yet Levi was the sweetest, kindest man she'd ever met. And what about Nullah? Levi called him his oldest friend. Duke had gone to stand beside him. The only awful person had been her. She'd bought tonight's disaster down entirely upon herself.

What should she do now? A wave of humiliation swamped her, combined with a rising desperation to put things right. She couldn't leave without at least trying to make amends. She'd go back to the house this very minute and apologise to Nullah, then hope that he and Levi would forgive her.

A knock came. Levi half-opened the door, and she beckoned him in. Had he changed his mind? Hope surged through her and she came to a surprising decision. If Levi let her stay, she'd tell him the truth about who she was. No more lies and obfuscation. No more fear about being found out. She felt lighter just thinking about it.

'About your friend,' she said, not waiting for him to speak. 'I was rude and I'm sorry.'

'Too late.' Levi slapped a yellow envelope on the table. 'Your severance pay. Thought I'd save you the trouble of coming by the house tomorrow.'

Poppy swallowed hard. The lightness was leaving her. 'I said I was sorry.'

His gaze was flinty and hard – no forgiveness there. He pulled out a chair and gestured for her to sit opposite him. 'Let me tell you a story. Nullah and I grew up in a town where anyone different was fair game. I was bullied at school for being Jewish. So were my sisters. But that was nothing compared to what Nullah and his mates went through. First there were the names. I can't tell you how hurtful they were. I won't even repeat them now.'

Poppy listened with growing horror.

'Slugs in lunch boxes. Dead rats in desks. Crude comments and vicious gossip. It was relentless. I copped it too, of course, because Nullah and I stood up for each other no matter what. Teachers shrugged and did nothing. Then there were the bashings. In year nine Nullah was beaten so badly by a pack of boys that he wound up in hospital. He was smart – smarter than me. Nullah always got good grades, but he left school after that to go jackarooing. I felt like I'd let him down.' Levi pushed the envelope across the table to her. 'I vowed that I'd never let him down again.'

Levi stood up. 'Just so you know where I'm coming from.'

Poppy watched him leave, soaked through with shame and shock. How little she knew of the real world. And what a very fine man was Levi Goldstein.

CHAPTER 20

Poppy spent a sleepless night. By the time first light tiptoed through the trees, she'd come to some painful conclusions about who she was and the beliefs she'd accepted without question all her life.

Now that she'd made her decision, Poppy was in a hurry to get it over with. She'd packed her things the night before, murmuring apologies to the absent Nullah for raiding the kitchen cupboards: some food, a knife, fork and spoon, a small saucepan. It was safer to stock up at Brumby's Run rather than risk being seen shopping in town. She tried not to think of it as stealing – more like borrowing. Finally, she borrowed the little transistor radio on the bench, collected her pot plants from the sill and took a final look around. There, all done.

Poppy drove into Currajong, nerves ajangle, marvelling at what she was about to do. Fighting to maintain her resolve. She shouldn't second-guess herself. Making this call was the right thing. According to Levi, the police hadn't apprehended the bombers. She had to share what she knew about Dylan and Cade. She owed it to Levi and to the woman who'd died. She owed it to a grieving husband and two little girls, to a whole community reeling from Cade's cruelty. She owed it to herself.

The main street of Currajong was deserted in the grey dawn. She parked opposite the post office and crossed the road to the public telephone outside. Dammit, no phone book. Poppy ran back to the car for pen and paper, then rang 000.

'What is your emergency?' came a reassuring female voice.

'I need the number for Crime Stoppers.'

'One moment, please.'

Poppy wrote down the number with fumbling fingers, took a long, steadying breath and made the call.

Ten minutes later Poppy returned to the car, shaken by the enormity of what she'd done and ashamed that she hadn't done it earlier. Cade had committed that brutal crime, she was sure of it, so she'd identified him as the bomber. Anonymously, of course, but by doing so she'd also identified herself. She was Cade's wife. It wouldn't take long for the law to realise that Phillipa Black was the mystery woman in the dark blue station wagon. Not today, perhaps, or tomorrow, but soon. No matter. The sacrifice was worth it if it helped bring Cade to justice. Poppy had given up trying to predict what would come next in the chaos that had become her life. The police would find her, or they wouldn't. She'd take one day at a time.

The threat seemed less real because, in some important ways, Pippa Black no longer existed. So how could they find her? This time last Saturday she'd been Cade's dutiful wife, a cowed woman who didn't dare defy him, didn't dare to question him or hold opinions of her own. That person was no more. By contrast, Poppy Forrester had found the courage to leave Cade, forswear his bigoted beliefs and report his crimes to the authorities. Poppy had even developed feelings for another man. What a difference seven days had made. It reminded her of something she'd read in an old book of quotes, though she couldn't remember who'd said it: *There are decades where nothing happens; and there are weeks where decades happen.'* Last week was one of those weeks.

Poppy let Duke out. He explored the broad stretch of grass beside the road, christening the bushes that he came across. A sudden crawling sensation made her shiver as a bank of clouds scudded across the sun. *Someone is walking over your grave,* Mum would have said. Poppy had a different explanation, an irrational feeling that Cade knew what she'd done, as if some message had been arrowed straight to him through the ether. She squinted her eyes tight, scared to open them for fear of seeing Cade's furious face staring back at her through the windscreen. How would he feel if he knew? If he knew that not only had she abandoned him, but that she'd betrayed him to the police as well? She shuddered. His rage would be truly terrible.

Poppy checked the clock on the outside of the post office building – six-thirty. She wanted to phone her mother, but it was too early. Dad was bound to answer if she rang at this time. Early calls were generally from a member of his congregation seeking emergency spiritual guidance. Dad enjoyed those calls. He loved nothing better than to dole out his heaven-sent wisdom.

Poppy waited for the service station to open. She filled up with petrol, wearing sunglasses and her hat pulled down tight. It was all she could do to avoid running from the shop. Was it her imagination or could she feel the attendant's eyes studying her? How ironic. She had a pocket full of cash, hundreds of dollars, more money than she'd ever had for herself before. And yet here she was, too scared to spend it.

At eight o'clock she returned to the post office, called her mother and got straight through. 'Mum, it's me.'

'Pippa – thank the Lord. Are you all right, darling?'

'I'm fine, Mum. I left you a note at the farm, saying that I was okay. Did you find it?'

'I found nothing at the farm, not even Duke. Is he with you?

'Yes, he's safe.'

Mum must have been alone and able to talk freely. She launched into an interrogation. Poppy could have hardly got a word in, even if she'd wanted to.

'Stop talking, Mum, and listen. You … you might hear some bad things about me on the news.'

Her mother erupted in a flurry of frantic questions.

'Cade has committed a terrible crime, but I had nothing to do with it. You have to believe me.'

Her mother fell briefly silent, processing what she'd heard. 'My darling child, from the day of your birth you've been the dearest, kindest girl a parent could ask for. Nobody could convince me otherwise, not if they had all the proof in the world. Cade, on the other hand …'

The equivocation in Mum's voice surprised her. 'I thought you liked Cade?'

'You and your Dad did, so I went along. Truth was, there was always a darkness about him. It made me frightened for you.'

'You never said.'

'No.' Was that a sob? 'I held my peace. I've done that far too many times. It was wrong and I'm sorry.'

Poppy was stunned. It seemed she wasn't the only one who'd been doing some soul-searching. Time to take advantage of her mother's sudden attack of honesty.

'Tell me, do I have a half-brother named Andrew? He calls himself Drew, right?'

Mum stuttered, struggling to get her words out. 'You know?'

'So it's true,' Poppy whispered, as much to herself as to her mother.

The sobs came louder now. 'I always meant to tell you …'

'Never mind. Just know that I'm fine, and that I love you. Look, I have to go. Talk soon.' She hung up the phone while her mother was mid-sentence.

Poppy drove back along the road towards Brumby's Run. More clouds were rolling in, obscuring the mountains in a dark pall of grey. A week ago, the sight would have filled her with joy. Not today. Her battered station wagon was no four-wheel drive. Rain could make the old stock route impassable.

She drove slowly, looking for the gate marking the boundary between Brumby's Run and neighbouring Kilmarnock, a cattle station and quarter horse stud. According to Levi, Drew's adoptive father owned it and Drew had grown up there. Poppy passed the entrance gate with its impressive bluestone pillars and grand sign, *Kilmarnock*, etched in black granite. It seemed her brother's childhood had been one of wealth and privilege. She felt a surge of envy. What if she'd been the one adopted out, spending her childhood in the shadow of beautiful Maroong Mountain, instead of in the heat and dust of the Mallee? How different might her life have been?

She went back to scanning the road ahead. There on her left – a wide farm gate set between two stout boundary fences and flanked by timber yards and a cattle ramp. She vaguely remembered having passed it when she first drove to Brumby's Run. A sign said *Road Closed. No Public Access*. The gate led to a broad, gravel track running uphill, wide enough for two cars to pass. That must be the old stock route, the one leading to Dead Man's Hut.

An ancient shearer had once told Poppy of mustering cattle from the mountains back in the day, and of staying in the historic high-country huts. 'I camped at a fair few in my time, my word I did,' he'd said, enjoying nothing more than to share his recollections. 'Each hut had its own history, its own stories. Some huts dated back to the 1860s and were built by pioneers. They gave shelter to stockmen, foresters, gold miners and even bushrangers.'

Her favourite yarn was the one about Dead Man's Hut, but she also liked the story of Mad Lucy's Hut. 'It was the last building standing of a ghost town in the Mount Delusion State Forest west of Swift's Creek,' the shearer said. 'Lucy Strobridge lived and died there; a woman known as the mysterious Maid of the Mountains. She turned her back on the world and became a recluse, with secret caves and tracks all over the forest. It's said she haunts the place, and visitors to the hut can still smell the smoke from her cigars.'

'What's your pick of the huts?' she'd asked.

'Well, that's easy. I proposed to my wife in the hut at Mount Terrible.' Poppy loved all the dangerous-sounding names. 'My missus jokes she only said yes because she was crazy with cabin fever. We were snowed in for a week.' He'd chuckled at the memory.

Poppy had always been intrigued by these tales of romance and adventure high in the remote mountains. Now it was her turn to add her own chapter. She would hide out at Dead Man's Hut. Levi said that nobody went there until summer, and that was months away. Maybe she'd become a modern-day Maid of the Mountains, build her own shack in the wild back-country ranges and live as a hermit. Cade would never find her there. Poppy dragged open the rusty gate, and its hinges promptly fell off the decaying post. She leant it up against the fence and set off up the track.

Five minutes later the weather closed in. Rain fell softly at first, but increased in intensity until it was lashing the ground in an unbroken curtain. Poppy could barely see two metres in front of her, but still she climbed, stopping occasionally to get out and assess the lay of the land. She lost her way a few times and had to scout ahead. As long as Poppy could find the track she felt confident to continue, albeit at a crawling pace.

After two hours, though, she began to doubt her navigational skills. A fog had descended, so the car was travelling within the rain cloud, rather than beneath it. With no radio reception she didn't know the time. With no sun she couldn't judge direction. They seemed to be skidding sideways as often as they went uphill, and bone-jarring corrugations jolted the car like giant speed bumps. Only when she came to a dilapidated sign did she realise she was still on track. *Balleroo National Park*. She let out a loud whoop, startling Duke.

Poppy's joy was short-lived. The terrain quickly grew rougher, and the rain was relentless. The track narrowed and narrowed again, as ruts deepened and turned into rivulets. If there'd ever been gravel, it had long since washed away. The sky turned from grey to black, changing day to night. Rain turned into hail, pinging off the windscreen and piling in shallow drifts. Sheet lightning flashed across the ranges and dammit … there, right in front of her, lay a fork in the road.

'Which way?' she asked Duke. 'Bark once for left and twice for right.'

The dog cocked his head and barked three times. 'Hmm, I'll take that as twice,' she said, 'and assume that you just can't count.'

Poppy turned right. Hail turned to rain and the fog cleared a little, giving her a better view of the way ahead. The going here was fair, the track rocky instead of muddy, and not too steep. After more hours of precarious driving, of second-guessing herself and almost getting bogged, Poppy came to another sign: *Hut 8 km* → She hugged Duke. 'You clever, clever boy!'

A bolt of dazzling light split the heavens, followed by a dull boom of thunder. Duke leaped into the back seat, lying flat on the floor and whimpering. Poor thing. Poppy stopped the car. She didn't blame Duke for being scared. She was scared herself, as lightning sizzled through the clouds, taking snapshots of the ridges and valleys, burning a fleeting image onto her retina. Thunder roared, the ground shook – and ever so slowly the car began to lean.

What was happening? Poppy opened her door. It was hard to see clearly in the gloom, but the saturated soil at the edge of the track seemed to be subsiding, forming a treacherous landslip. Even as she watched, more earth crumbled away, plunging down a precipitous slope to the valley below. She turned on the engine, hoping to drive her way to safety, but it was too late. The car was tilting fast.

Poppy slid across to the passenger side and called to Duke who was still huddled in the back. 'We have to get out.' A deafening clap of thunder made the dog crouch lower. The car lurched sideways with a sickening, grinding sound. It lay at an angle, half-hanging from the track. Any moment now it could slide over the brink.

Poppy climbed out and pulled off her belt. With shivering fingers, she yanked open the back door, looped the belt through Duke's collar and dragged him from the car. The rain hit them with force, drenching them through. Twin waterfalls swelled and cascaded down the opposite bank. Runnels rushed across the road, further washing it away. Her teeth began to chatter. She was only wearing a thin shirt and jeans which were thoroughly soaked. Poppy hadn't brought a coat when she left Fairview. She hadn't imagined that she'd need one.

In no time she was drenched to the bone. The rain was like icy needles piercing her skin. Poppy weighed up her options. Should she try to recover her belongings? It would be risky. The tailgate was stiff and the force needed to open it might be enough to unbalance the car. But everything she owned was in there, including the food they'd need to survive.

She had to try. Poppy buckled Duke to a tree using her belt and approached the car. It was now or never. She wrenched open the tailgate. The car shuddered alarmingly, but stayed put. Poppy yanked the bags from the back and stowed them within a shallow hollow she found in the opposite bank, along with the box of pots. Her plants would appreciate a good soaking. At least someone would enjoy the rain.

Next she grabbed the rifle, heaved out the ammo boxes and stashed them with her other gear, screening the lot under a pile of leafy twigs. Good, that was most of it. As she returned for the bags on the back seat, a creaking sound made her look up. Poppy briefly glimpsed the falling branch before all went black.

When she woke, blinking up at the grey sky, she found Duke's warm form pressed against her. He'd somehow worked his way free. That dog was a canine Houdini, and just as well. His body heat might well have saved her from hypothermia. Poppy didn't know how long she'd been lying there. The rain had slowed to a drizzle, and the sun was attempting to break through the clouds. She was grateful for its wan warmth. Poppy's head throbbed and her left knee hurt. Her frozen fingers explored her scalp and found a giant bump. She was unaccountably comforted by the knowledge that one of Cade's beatings would have left her in far worse shape.

Poppy looked around and sighed with relief. The car was still there, balanced on the brink, although at a more extreme angle than before. She gazed at it longingly. Dare she risk retrieving the rest of her stuff? The car lurched alarmingly. There was her answer.

Poppy stretched her legs and winced. Her knee pained her, but not too seriously. With any luck it was bruised, not sprained. The splintered branch beside her hardly looked big enough to have caused so much damage. It must have cracked her square on the head to knock her out.

Duke stretched too, then whined at her to get up. The task seemed impossible, but what choice did she have? Who would help her if she didn't help herself? Nobody knew where she was. Bloody hell, she didn't even know where she was – not precisely.

Poppy stared ruefully up at Duke, who looked very much like a large, drowned rat. 'Come here.' The dog obligingly moved closer. She reached out a stiff hand, grabbed onto his collar, and with the assistance of a stout stick, managed to stand. Her feet were numb, like two dead lumps of wood, and she very nearly crashed back to the mud. But as she hobbled about, feeling returned to her toes.

'That's better,' she said. Duke wagged his tail. Poppy rummaged around in the bags she'd managed to save. Finding a piece of baling twine in her pocket, she used it to tie a small bag of kibble to the dog's collar. She hung a bag with biscuits and bread around her own neck. Then she nudged the rest of the provisions further into the hollow with her good leg and replaced the leafy twigs on top. Poppy gazed up the track to where it vanished into the forest. 'So,' she said. 'I guess we take Shank's pony.' Duke looked puzzled and cocked his head. She stroked his wet ears. 'It means we walk.'

Poppy reluctantly waved goodbye to the blue station wagon. It had been her means to escape Cade, and a reliable getaway car and ally. She wished it luck as it teetered on the edge of the track.

Poppy set off, limping through the drizzle and leaning heavily on her stick. Water dripped off her nose, ran into her eyes and trickled down her neck. She envied Duke his warm coat of fur.

According to the sign, the hut was eight kilometres away. She didn't know what time it was, though the lengthening shadows told her it was getting late. She didn't even know if they were on the right path. What if the sign had been switched around somehow? What if it was a cruel prank? Poppy trudged on through the mud for what seemed like hours.

Occasionally the cloud cleared. She was too cold and tired to notice the views down the mountain to the misty-blue valley beyond. Poppy thought of nothing but planting one foot in front of the other.

And then, there it was. Through a screen of gum leaves, the shape of a timber slab hut emerged. Poppy hobbled faster. Water dripped from its rusty tin roof into a corrugated iron water tank. It had a rickety chimney at one end, and a porch at the front, supported by rough-hewn poles. Stockyards flanked the hut, and a stream in full spate sprang from a nearby granite bank. It rushed past the ramshackle building, plunging through a thicket of tree ferns to a chain of rocky pools below. An iconic, picture-postcard scene.

Poppy forgot about her headache and her growling stomach. She forgot about her frozen feet and aching knee. The hut was a perfect antidote to misery, more rustic and romantic than she could have imagined.

She unlatched the door and pushed inside. How good it felt to be out of the rain. Her eyes were drawn to the stone fireplace, complete with dry kindling, split firewood and a box of matches. She whispered a silent thank you to the thoughtful person who'd provisioned the hut so well. How lovely it would be to dry out before the flames. But she couldn't muster the energy to light a fire.

Poppy untied the bag from Duke's neck with fumbling fingers and poured some kibble on the floor. Duke scoffed it and wagged his tail hopefully. She gave him a little more. 'Not all, mind. It has to last.' She looked for the bread in her own bag, groaning as she pulled out a sodden loaf. Maybe she could dry it out later. The packet of Salada biscuits had fared better. She tore open the plastic and took a bite, but she had no saliva, and the dry, salty cracker made her gag.

It didn't matter. She had no appetite anyway. Shivering violently, Poppy stumbled to the bunks and was pulling off her wet clothes when she spotted a bottle of brandy on the timber mantle above the hearth. She fetched it, then wrapped herself in two coarse woollen blankets and sat on a bunk. The mattress was surprisingly comfort-able – either that or she was exceptionally tired. Duke settled content-edly beside her with a yawn. She gulped the brandy. It sent a delicious rush of warmth through her body and the pain in her knee receded. Poppy swigged more and more until the rough timber walls swam before her eyes. She lay down and was asleep by the time her head hit the hessian pillow.

CHAPTER 21

Levi finished feeding out hay under the dull grey sky. He was in a very bad mood. What a bugger of a day. Torrential rain had prevented him from working with the youngsters. The feed room roof was leaking. A visiting mare that he'd believed safely in foal had come back into season. And worst of all, he missed Poppy. She'd been on his mind ever since he woke, distracting him from his daily tasks. Whether it was dealing with the farrier in the morning, managing the brood mares at lunchtime or working with the stud stallions that afternoon, only half his mind had been on the job.

Levi had swung by the bungalow first thing, hoping to say goodbye, but she'd already gone. Well, what did he expect? He'd fired her after refusing to accept her apology. If he missed her, it was entirely his own fault. He jumped on the four-wheeler and, after first unbogging the bike's trailer, headed back to the stables. Levi automatically looked around for Duke, who loved following the bike, almost whistling for him until he remembered. Dammit, he even missed Poppy's dog.

Levi parked at the hay shed but stayed sitting on the bike, thinking. It wasn't just that he missed Poppy. He was worried about her too. The sight of her bruised back haunted him. Had he sent her away into danger? She was free from whoever had hurt her, but did she have somewhere safe to go once she left Brumby's Run? Not to her family, it seemed. He recalled Poppy crying in his kitchen after the phone call to her mother, and the strong feelings it had stirred in him. But he had to protect Nullah. He could not excuse the sort of prejudice that she'd showed towards his friend.

Bigotry revolted him. Levi knew from personal experience the hurt and damage it caused. From an early age, Levi's parents had taught him that some people, a small minority, would dislike him simply for being Jewish. They'd been right. The attack on the synagogue had resurrected memories of the bullying he'd endured as a schoolchild. His father had told him not to take it seriously, saying that kids would be kids and it was harmless enough. 'Sticks and stones can break your bones, but names can never hurt you, eh? How many times do I have to say it? Your family faced far worse during the war.'

So Levi had learnt not to bring his pain and humiliation home, even when the persecution went beyond name-calling. Even when a group of laughing girls pulled his pants down in the middle of the playground to see if he was circumcised. Even when boys beat him up behind the shelter shed, tormenting him with Hitler salutes. Dad had been wrong. The antisemitism Levi had experienced as a boy wasn't harmless. There was a vicious under-current of real hatred behind it. The synagogue bombing was proof of that.

The sun made an appearance through the clouds. Nullah came around the corner carrying a bundle of letters. He'd gone into Currajong for supplies and to check the mail.

Levi climbed off the bike. 'You took your time,' he said with a scowl.

Nullah grinned. 'Don't take it out on me. You're the one who sent her packing.'

'What are you on about?'

'That girl, Poppy. You've been like a bear with a sore head all day, mooning over her.'

Levi shot him a baleful look and snatched the mail. 'I fired her because of you.' He glanced at a brochure about farm bikes. The kelpie in the photo looked like Duke.

Nullah shrugged. 'I don't remember asking you to fight my battles.'

Levi looked up and his taut expression softened. 'You don't have to ask,' he said, gruffly. 'It's my job.'

Nullah hooked him fondly around the neck and delivered a mock punch. 'If you're that keen, you should have cut the girl some slack. She'd have come round. To know me is to love me, after all.'

'Who said I'm keen on her? And anyway, it's too late now,' he said in a gloomy voice.

'Call her. Tell her to come back.'

'She doesn't have a phone.'

Nullah laughed. 'Mate, is that what she told you? By the way, someone's been up the old stock route. The gate's come off.'

'That doesn't mean a thing. The post was rotten.'

'Yeah, but the gate didn't lean itself back up against the fence, did it? Hope it's not bloody brumby hunters. I heard they shot twenty horses out Bogong way – mares, foals and all.'

Brumby hunters? A chill ran through him as he thought of Thowra. 'Hold the fort,' he said. 'I want to take a run up to the hut.'

'What, tonight? There's only two hours of light left.' Nullah shook his head. 'Can't it wait until morning?

'No, it can't.' If brumby hunters, or any hunters for that matter, planned to set up base at Dead Man's Hut, Levi had to act quickly. He'd been salting the yards up there for months. Native alpine pasture, such as snowgrass, was low in sodium, and brumbies were irresistibly drawn to mineral licks and buckets of salt. For the last two months there'd been signs that horses were regularly coming in for his offerings, and as far as Levi knew, the only brumbies living on Maroong Mountain were Thowra's mob. If hunters managed to trap them in the yards, they'd be sitting ducks.

'With all this rain the track could be impassable,' said Nullah.

Levi gave him a grim smile. 'Well, I'm about to find out, aren't I? Will you take care of things until I get back?'

Nullah clapped him on the shoulder. 'Go on then. It might make you forget about that sheila.'

Not bloody likely, thought Levi. Miss Poppy Forrester seemed to have taken up permanent residence in his head.

It was five-thirty before Levi was ready to go, packed with a few nights' provisions just in case. He said goodbye and headed for the start of the stock route. The gate was leaning up against the fence, just as Nullah said. It hadn't been like that yesterday. Levi always glanced at it when he drove by.

He scouted around on the wet earth, but all trace of footprints or tyre marks had been obliterated by the storm. He glanced at the sun. Having seen off the clouds, it was sinking in a rosy glow, promising a fine day tomorrow. That was a bonus. He didn't fancy tracking poachers in the rain.

The hut lay only forty kilometres north of the road, but it would still take hours to get there. The going was rough along the stock route at the best of times, and after a day of torrential rain, who knew what state it might be in?

The first part wasn't too steep and Levi made good time. He knew the route well. Thanks to a good coverage of gravel and well-defined runoff channels, it had weathered the storm without much damage. But after twenty kilometres or so it became a different story. The gradient increased sharply, and each time the track levelled out, axle-deep water lay over the road.

It was slow and slippery going – no faster than a walking pace. Levi had to use low gear and concentrate hard to pick the right line of direction. At one point a rock slid down the left bank and bounced off the Jeep's bonnet, leaving a deep dent. Encroaching twilight played tricks with his depth perception, making it hard to judge distance. Maybe Nullah had been right about waiting until morning.

Levi fared better when night fell properly. The Jeep's headlights cut brilliant swathes through the dark, highlighting potholes and branches across the road. He kept close to the crown of the track to avoid the soft edges, and kept his nose pointing uphill. He never crossed sideways. That's how rollovers happen.

By eight o'clock Levi was but a few kilometres from the hut. On rounding a steep spur, he slammed on the brakes as a huge stag bounded in front of the Jeep and vanished into the night. He took a steadying breath. That was close. The headlights showed a splintered branch across the road, so he took his torch and got out to move it. The wind was picking up, moaning eerily through the treetops, causing his skin to goosebump. Then he saw it – a massive landslip had opened a chasm in the road ahead, taking out the right-hand half of the track. Dammit. It was either get past or be stranded there all night. He couldn't turn around, and reversing down the treacherous path in the dark would be suicidal. Perhaps if stayed hard against the bank …

Levi tripped over something. He shone his torch to the ground, and his heart stopped. Next to the loose rock that he'd kicked was a sodden red and yellow checked piece of fabric – Poppy's scarf. He looked over to the landslip, then approached it, step by terrified step, and peered over the precipice. Poppy's blue station wagon lay ten metres down the cliff, trapped mid-fall by trees. Its headlights still shone, and the passenger side door gaped open.

'Poppy,' he screamed. 'Are you there? Can you hear me?'

Nothing. Levi ran back and tried to raise help on the radio. No reception. He was on his own. Levi manoeuvred the Jeep as close as he dared to the edge. He attached his tow rope to the winch, letting it down the cliff until it reached the car. Strapping his gloves on tight, he prepared for the descent.

Levi wasn't a fan of hanging off ropes. Nullah had once talked him into abseiling down a rock face. Levi had slipped from an overhang and his carabiner had jammed. He'd hung there, suspended in space, certain that any moment he'd plunge into the abyss. He didn't – Nullah had him expertly belayed by a top rope. But those few minutes of spinning wildly in the void had haunted his nightmares. Levi ignored his lurching stomach. This was no time for misgivings. He hooked the torch to his belt, looped the rope around his waist and lowered himself over the edge.

It was pitch black. The wind whipped through the trees as Levi blindly climbed hand over fist down the cliff. He'd hoped that the station wagon's headlights might illuminate the scene, but their light shone into thin air and was swallowed by the night. No matter, he had his torch. Levi gripped the rope tighter, fearful of what he might find.

When he reached the station wagon, Levi propped his heels against the roots of a spindly snow gum clinging to a crack in the rocks. So far, so good. Checking the interior required him taking one hand from the rope. Slowly, carefully, he let go with his left hand and used it to free the torch from his belt. He could feel the burn in his shoulder and side. This was crunch time. He shone the beam into the car, frightened to look, bracing for what he might find.

It was empty. Levi's knees buckled with relief, and it was all he could do to maintain his one-handed grip on the rope. He checked again, just to be sure, and a sudden terror gripped him. If she'd fallen from the open door ... He steeled himself against the possibility. No, Poppy must have escaped in time. She was somewhere up there on the track, he had to believe it.

Levi began his perilous ascent. Hope was a prime moving force. He virtually sprang back up the cliff, desperate to find Poppy. She might have crawled off, injured, into the bush. He hauled himself back over the edge and tried the radio again. Still dead. Levi stared into the black forest, grateful for the light of a half-moon rising over the mountains.

He walked along the steep left-hand bank looking for a place where Poppy might have moved off the road. Something glinted in the light of his torch. In a shallow hollow, behind a screen of leaves, he found a treasure trove: plastic shopping bags filled with soup cans, packs of noodles, dog food and more. A collection of pot plants. A saucepan that he recognised as one from the bungalow at Brumby's Run, and the transistor radio as well.

Levi felt like cheering. If Poppy had time to retrieve her belongings from the car, it was unlikely she'd gone over the edge with it. He examined the items again, surprised by the rifle – an old Remington – and the ammo boxes stacked against the bank.

Why had Poppy taken this remote route in the rain and with such an unsuitable vehicle? And why had she gone so well armed? Levi scrubbed his palms across his face, trying to make sense of it. She was heading for the hut; there was no other explanation. A deep flush of guilt crept through him, making his chest tight and sore. He'd wondered if Poppy had somewhere safe to go after he fired her. Now he had his answer. She was desperate and out of options.

Levi stowed the tow rope away. Then he packed Poppy's sodden things in the Jeep, carefully wedging her precious pots into a space where they wouldn't be upturned. Now he just had to get past the landslip. He took some time examining the track, measuring the width of the safe section, and then measuring the width of his vehicle. As long as he hugged the bank he should be fine.

With gritted teeth, Levi reversed a few metres and went up a gear. He took off fast, hoping momentum would see him safely past the washaway. The track stayed firm. In half an hour he'd be at Dead Man's Hut. Please God, let Poppy be there too.

CHAPTER 22

Poppy lay in fitful sleep, plagued by terrifying dreams. Dreams of stumbling, heavy-limbed and naked, through a nightmare forest of mud and trees and rocks and rain. Pursued by ravenous wild animals: bears and wolves and lions – animals who invariably turned into Cade when they finally seized her.

Duke jumped from the bed. She stirred, missing the comfort of his warm form pressed against her. The hut was freezing. The blanket slipped off her shoulder, exposing a breast to the chilly night air.

'Poppy?'

She gathered the blanket around her, staring in horror at a figure looming in the doorway. It shone a torch in her direction. She should have known Cade would find her. Poppy found the brandy bottle under her pillow and gripped it by the neck. She was no longer the helpless coward that Cade used to know. He wouldn't kill her without a fight.

'Poppy, it's me – Levi.'

Levi? Yes, it must be. Her husband didn't know her new name, and Duke was wagging his tail. Adrenaline drained from her stiff body, and she sagged with relief, half-expecting for a contingent of police to march in behind him.

'What are you doing here?' he asked, moving closer.

Poppy was suddenly aware that she wore no scarf. She pulled the blanket up to her chin, but it was too late. Levi's sharp intake of breath told her that.

He came to kneel by the bunk. Ever so slowly, he reached out a hand and folded the blanket away from her neck, exposing the bruises. 'Who did this to you?'

Poppy started to sob. Levi sat beside her on the bunk and gradually pulled her close, gently and quietly, the way he'd handle a frightened filly. Bundling the blankets around her, he cradled her in his strong protective arms in a way she'd never been held before. The way she'd always wished to be held. And suddenly the floodgates opened. She poured out her story, leaving nothing out. Not her fundamentalist father, or Cade's beatings, or the torched ute. Not her hope that Drew might be her long-lost brother. Not the bombing, or Cade's guilt or how she'd been wrongly implicated in the crime.

'And then the car slipped and a falling branch knocked me out.' She showed him the bump on her head. 'I'm here because I'm on the run,' she said. 'From Cade and from the police. Poppy Forrester isn't even my real name.'

'Tell me,' he coaxed, his low voice brimming with tenderness. 'Tell me your name.'

She'd rarely heard that sort of kindness in a man's voice.

'Phillipa Black,' she said. 'Pippa for short, but I never want to be her again. Pippa is weak and afraid and completely unlovable. I'm staying with Poppy.'

A cold gust of wind blew in the doorway, making the old tin roof creak. 'Let's warm this hut up and get some light.' Levi bent to kiss her forehead and she didn't move away. His lips briefly touched her skin in an electric moment that she wished would last longer. Levi closed the door and knelt to build a fire.

Poppy noticed her clothes lying in a wet heap on the floor. How could she be so relaxed, knowing that she was naked under the blanket? Maybe it was all the brandy. She found the bottle and took another warming swig. Her thoughts turned to why Levi had come to the hut.

'Did you see my car on the way up here?'

Levi took his time answering, waiting until flames crackled in the hearth before turning around. 'I did.'

'Thank goodness. I thought it might have slipped off the road. Did you see how close it was to the edge?'

Levi poked the fire and added a small log.

'Can you take me to it?' she said. 'Maybe you could winch it back to the centre of the track.'

'I don't think so.' Levi gave the fire a final poke and came to sit beside her. 'That's some story you just told me.'

Poppy took another swig of brandy and handed him the bottle. Levi set it back on the mantle, then went outside and returned weighed down with bags and boxes. He lit a kerosene lamp and hung it from a beam, banishing the darkness. He picked up her wet clothes and draped them on a wooden chair by the fire. Then, he opened a rucksack and threw her one of his T-shirts, a jumper and a pair of trackpants. 'Get dressed. Don't worry, I'll turn around.' He made himself busy, tipping tins of tomato soup into a saucepan and resting it on a rusty grate above the hearth.

Poppy put the clothes on, relishing Levi's scent. It was in the weave. She limped over to stand beside him. 'Can I help?' She found a ladle and stirred the soup. 'I had a loaf of bread, but it's soggy.'

Levi took the spoon from her. 'Let me make dinner,' he said, laying his hands on her shoulders. 'You go rest that knee.'

As he turned to guide Poppy back to bed, she kissed him. It seemed the most natural thing in the world. Levi's lips met hers, tentative at first, then more firmly. His mouth was warm and sweet and tender in a way that she'd never known. She kissed him harder, feeling the unfamiliar heat of arousal.

The kiss seemed to last forever. 'You're so beautiful,' he whispered, holding her tighter. His lips found the soft hollow of her throat as if he meant to kiss away her bruises. The act astonished her. All her married life she'd been disgusted by the marks Cade left on her skin.

They were hideous and shameful, a sign of worthlessness and weakness, something to be hidden and denied. And yet here she was, her ugliness exposed, and Levi called her beautiful. It was a revelation.

Poppy wrapped her arms around Levi's neck, closed her eyes and melted into him. He picked her up, carried her to the bunk and laid her down. She shivered in anticipation, not believing it was possible to want a man so badly. So it was a letdown when Levi gently extricated himself from her embrace.

'Don't go,' she murmured. 'Stay with me.'

'You're exhausted – and full of brandy to boot.' He spread the blanket over her. 'Get some sleep.'

He called Duke up beside her and the dog snuggled in. She could feel Levi tucking more blankets around her before she drifted off.

Levi watched as Poppy fell asleep, fighting an urge to take her in his arms again. Their kiss had sent his spirits soaring. He recalled her small, snow-white breast peeking from under the covers when he'd first arrived. Charming. Heck, that girl would look good wearing a chaff bag. With a jolt he understood that he was falling for her, and hard. That hadn't happened for a very long time.

Levi took the soup off the fire. Poppy needed rest more than food, and he needed to think. Where to start? He'd barely processed a fraction of what she'd told him. Her violent husband had bombed the synagogue, killed Zadie and now Poppy was a suspect in that terrible crime. Levi desperately didn't want to believe that she was involved. He felt like he'd known her forever, but in truth it wasn't much more than a week. How could he be sure? He couldn't, but he could take a leap of faith. He could trust in his ability to judge character and decide to believe in her innocence.

Then there was Cade, her monster of a husband. Levi's teeth clenched to think of the man who'd murdered a pregnant mother and tortured Poppy. Even now he could see the choke marks on her exposed neck. Levi could hardly conceive of the hell she'd lived through for the past four years. She'd escaped from Cade and reported him to the police. That had taken courage, and he prayed that the bastard would be swiftly apprehended. But until then Cade remained a threat. The best thing Poppy could do would be to turn herself in and clear her name. In the morning he'd try to convince her of that, but it had to be her decision. He wouldn't make it for her.

And what about Poppy's belief that she was Drew's half-sister? It was possible. Drew had been adopted. What a buzz that would be, calling for the next big Currajong celebration. But once again, Poppy had to approach Drew and ask the question herself. From the sound of it, Poppy had never had much control over what she thought or did, not until this last week. Her opinions had been shaped by bullies and bigots. Her power had been usurped by the men in her life. Levi didn't plan to continue that tradition.

Poppy woke the next morning to find sunshine streaming in the windows. She glanced around, panicked that Levi might have up and left during the night. No, there he was, slicing thick slabs of bread on the rough timber table. She yawned and stretched, thinking back to her monumental confession of the night before – and thinking back to the kiss. Levi knew who she was, and what she'd done, yet he was still here. It seemed inconceivable.

'Hungry?' he asked, noticing that she was awake. 'There'll be tea, buttered toast, and Vegemite if you want it.'

Her stomach rumbled so loudly she was sure he would hear.

'No milk though,' he said. 'We'll have to take our tea black.'

Poppy got up and went to sit by the hearth. Her knee barely hurt. A steaming red kettle sat on the hob. The fire must have burnt all night because the hut was wonderfully warm. 'Drive me back to the car,' she said. 'There's powdered milk in a bag on the back seat.'

Levi pulled up a chair and sat beside her. 'Can I kiss you good morning? I've been waiting for you to wake up.'

The request took her by surprise. It seemed she wasn't the only one thinking about the night before. 'Yes,' she said, feeling pleased and rather important. 'You may kiss me.'

His finger traced the curve of her cheek and lifted her chin. Then his mouth found hers and the world went away. They could have been the last two people on earth. Yet when Levi let her go, his expression turned serious. 'Now that I've officially kissed you good morning, there's something I have to tell you. Do you want the good news first, or the bad news?'

Poppy sprang up and looked nervously around the hut. 'It's Cade, isn't it. He's come to Currajong.'

'No, nothing like that,' said Levi, quickly. 'But you won't like it just the same. Come and sit down with me.'

Poppy listened in despair as Levi explained that her trusty station wagon was lodged ten metres down the cliff. 'Can't you winch it back up?'

'Nope, not with my Jeep anyway.'

'But what will I do without my car?' Poppy thought better of this small lie. She'd made up her mind never to lie to Levi. 'Well, technically it's not my car. I stole it from Cade and fitted fake plates. But I'm still terribly fond of it. It saved me, you know.'

Levi's eyebrows flew upwards. 'Fake plates? You sure are full of surprises.'

'What about my stuff?'

'You can forget about anything left in the car. But that gear you stashed by the roadside is safely in the back of my Jeep.' He sent her a searching look. 'Including the rifle. You're packing a lot of ammo. What were you planning – World War Three?'

'The rifle and ammo belong to Cade.'

'You know how to use it?'

'Grew up shooting rabbits for the pot. I'm a better shot than my brothers. If Cade comes, I'll be ready.'

'About that.' Levi shifted his long legs. 'You can't stay here.'

'Why?'

'It's not safe. Turn yourself in, and tell the truth. We'll go to the Currajong Police Station together.'

Poppy stared at him in disbelief. 'They won't believe me.'

'If you had nothing to do with the bombing, they can't prove that you did.'

'If?'

'I meant ...' He dragged a hand through his hair. 'They'd need evidence.'

She looked at him askance. 'Are you kidding me? They have evidence. I went on the run with Cade. People saw me with him and Dylan at the motel. I dodged the cops, changed my name and hid out at Brumby's Run.'

'All circumstantial,' he pointed out.

'And if they catch Cade?'

'When,' corrected Levi.

'He'll be out for revenge,' she said. 'Cade will do everything possible to implicate me.'

Levi frowned. 'It's your call.' He stood and gathered her stiff body into his arms. 'But you can't run forever. That's no way to live.'

He stroked her tangled hair and Poppy slumped against him, swallowing the sobs rising in her throat. 'Did you mean it when you said it's my call? You won't give me away?'

'You have my word.' He raised her chin, staring at her with a disconcerting intensity. 'But I ask one thing in return.'

'Yes?' she whispered, becoming lost in the pools of his eyes.

'Take back your name. No more Poppy Forrester.'

'You don't understand,' she stammered. 'Poppy Forrester she's ... she's amazing. She's brave and clever and great with horses. And she's funny sometimes, though she doesn't always mean to be. And best of all, Levi Goldstein likes her.'

He smiled at that. 'I like Pippa Black more.'

'No, you don't!' she shouted, pulling away from him. 'Black is Cade's last name. I never want to hear it again.'

'Fair enough. Who were you before you married that jerk? What's your maiden name?'

'Sullivan.'

'Pippa Sullivan.' He spoke the name slowly, rolling the Ls around on his tongue. 'I like it.' The red kettle whistled. Levi got up, poured boiling water into two mugs, and started jiggling teabags. 'So we have a deal then?'

'How do you mean?'

'I don't tell anyone that you're here, and you take back your name. The way I see it, Pippa Sullivan was always brave and clever. Oh, and good with horses. A natural, I'd say. Only she was never free to show it until now.'

Levi threw the teabags into the fire where they landed with a soft hiss. 'Your tea, Miss Pippa Sullivan.' He bowed and handed her the mug, before toasting slices of bread on a green stick in front of the fire.

A shiver ran through her to hear those words spoken aloud. Pippa Sullivan – the name she'd been born with. It took her back to a time of innocence, to a time of hope for the future. Levi was right. She didn't have to be a made-up soap opera character to find her courage. Like the Cowardly Lion in *The Wizard of Oz*, she'd had it all along. Pippa watched Levi, crouching with his broad back to her and felt a surge of love. He'd helped her reclaim her name, her identity, her sense of who she was. Was there any greater gift?

CHAPTER 23

They spent the rest of the morning getting to know each other better, in the light of their new romantic understanding. They stowed away the provisions that Levi had brought with him, along with Pippa's meagre offerings.

'I don't believe it!' she said when Levi came in the door with her pot plant collection. Pippa spent a happy half hour arranging the pots on one windowsill, then switching them to the other. In the end she moved most of them back to the original sill and placed the blooming violets on the porch flanking the front door. Flowers made the hut instantly feel like home.

Levi sometimes touched her as they worked: a light clasp of her shoulder, a stroke of her cheek, a gallant kiss of her hand. Pippa looked forward to these small gestures of affection. Each touch made her as giddy as a girl, although she was too shy to reciprocate.

Levi produced a joint of corned beef from his esky, along with potatoes and carrots. Pippa put the meat into a cast iron pot of water and seasoned it with salt and fresh leaves of mountain pepper berry that Levi had picked.

'Come on,' he said when the hut was more or less shipshape and their lunch was bubbling on the fire. Levi took her hand and led her outside. A pale sun was starting to warm the earth. They were greeted by a chorus of birdsong and a forest sparkling under the rain-washed sky. Once again Pippa marvelled at the beauty of these mountains.

At the rear of the hut was an open-sided shed. Levi pointed to the hay bales and bags of salt within. 'Remember how I said you were going to help me get Thowra back? Well here's your chance. I've been coming up here once a fortnight to salt the yards and feed out hay, but it's not enough.'

'Do you reckon Thowra's mob's been here?'

'I do, and with you able to feed out daily, we'll have a much better chance of catching them.'

She beamed at the news. Guilt over losing the stallion had hit her hard, especially with an aerial-shooting brumby cull coming. She'd like nothing better than to restore Thowra safely to Levi's care.

Pippa explored the stockyards. Levi showed her how to set the trap mechanism that would close the gate behind the horses, and they spread out bales of hay and tubs of salt. They fetched buckets of water from the creek to fill the troughs, and Pippa stopped to watch a host of darting tadpoles.

'It's like Disneyland here,' she said. 'Where I come from, the creeks dried up years ago. Even the Murray is a muddy ditch.' She leaned closer to the water. 'Look, there are little minnows.'

Levi laughed. 'Don't let Charlie hear you call them minnows. They're mountain galaxias. The only minnows around here are plague minnows, an introduced species that preys on our native fish.'

'Who's Charlie?'

'Drew's sister-in-law. She married a Balleroo park ranger. They're both environmentalists with a special interest in the bogs and water-ways of the park.'

'So it was Charlie who taught you about the fish?'

'Not just about the fish. She's an encyclopedia when it comes to wildlife, especially amphibians.' He pointed to a fern-fringed pool. 'See those pretty gold tadpoles. They'll turn into whistling tree frogs. And those mottled brown ones with the darker bands? They're Booroolong frog tadpoles – a critically endangered species.'

Pippa looked at him with renewed admiration. 'Charlie must be clever to know that stuff. Did she go to university?' She felt a little daunted. Scholarly people made Pippa all too aware of her own inadequate education.

'Who, Charlie?' Levi snorted. 'Not a chance. She's completely self-taught, but I tell you what – she could give those zoology professors a run for their money.'

Pippa grinned. She was going to like this Charlie. 'Tell me about my brother.'

'Drew? What do you want to know?'

'What does he look like?'

'Well, he's about my height. Brown hair. Pretty fit.' Levi scooped a wayward tadpole from a bucket, returned it to the creek and started off towards the yards.

'What colour are his eyes?' said Pippa, chasing after him.

'Wouldn't have a clue,' laughed Levi. 'I haven't spent much time staring into them.'

They emptied their buckets at the trough and Pippa gave him a playful punch. 'I'm serious. I want to know what he's like.'

Levi dragged his gaze away from Thowra and studied Pippa's hopeful expression. 'This is important to you, isn't it?' Her mouth formed a tight smile. 'Righto. Let's go check on lunch and I'll tell you what I can.'

Levi stoked the fire and put on the kettle. Then he beckoned Pippa outside and they sat together on the porch bench. She turned an expectant face to him.

'Drew Chandler is the nicest bloke you could meet. Generous to a fault. Keeps his temper. Looks for the best in people. I don't mean he's a pushover – far from it. He'll always give you the benefit of the doubt, but if he's proved wrong? If someone hurts his friends or family? Watch out.'

Pippa listened with rapt attention.

'Oh, and he's the finest horseman this side of the Murray.'

Pippa shook her head. 'No,' she said, firmly. 'That would be you.'

Levi shot her a wry smile. 'I haven't won five King of the Mountain stockman challenge titles in a row. Drew had to stop entering to give other people a chance. And his wife, Sam? She rides just as well in her own way. Dressage. You know, classical equitation. Those two are quite a team.'

'Tell me about their wedding.'

'Now that was truly something! A double act. Sam and Drew. Charlie and Karl. Did you know that Sam and Charlie are twin sisters? Identical twins. Drew joked that he hoped he was getting the right one.' Levi chuckled. 'They got hitched up on Maroong Mountain. The whole ceremony happened on horseback. Karl wasn't too keen, but Charlie talked him round. Even the celebrant was mounted. Here. I'll show you.'

Drew sat up and found his phone. He scrolled through the photos and handed it over. 'Your brother's on the right.' Pippa took a sharp breath. Two pairs of riders faced a woman mounted on a snow-white horse. Drew, riding a gleaming black stallion, looked dashing in a blazer, moleskin trousers and Akubra hat. And that must be Sam beside him, riding Phoenix. The palomino's silver mane was braided with ruby ribbons, and Sam wore an elegant burgundy riding coat over her cream lace wedding dress. The wild Balleroo Ranges formed a dramatic backdrop to the astonishingly romantic scene. Pippa couldn't stop staring at the picture.

'Now tell me,' said Levi. 'Should they have married in a church instead?'

'No,' she whispered, gesturing to the timeless view laid out before them. 'These mountains are holier than any church. If God is anywhere, he's here.'

CHAPTER 24

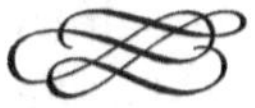

After a hearty lunch of corned beef, carrots and mash, they sat side-by-side on a patch of sunlit snowgrass, nursing mugs of tea.

'Levi, about our deal …'

He held out his hand and shook his head. 'No going back, Miss Pippa. A deal's a deal.'

'You'll like what I'm going to say.'

'Go on then, try me.'

'So, the new deal is this. You don't tell anyone I'm here. In return, I use my real name and—' She hesitated.

'And what?' he said. 'The suspense is killing me.'

'And I turn myself in once Drew gets back from his honeymoon. You're right, I can't run forever and I do need to clear my name. Just give me time to talk to Drew first.'

Levi swept her up in a warm embrace, knocking off her hat and kissing her until her heart raced and her knees went weak. 'Pippa Sullivan, you're something else.'

It took her some time to compose herself. 'And you'll come with me to the police station?'

His face crinkled with pride, and the warmth of his smile echoed in his voice. 'Like I said, I'll be with you every step of the way.'

'Why is this so important to you?' she asked, puzzled by how excited he was by her decision. She'd probably go to jail, at least to start with. Was he looking forward to getting rid of her?

His smile faded to an expression of disbelief. 'Don't you know?'

'Know what?'

'I've fallen for you. Maybe I'm already in love, I don't know. But I do know that I think of you all the time. I was devastated when you left.'

'But you're the one who fired me.'

'I know, right! But I still missed you like crazy.' He tucked a loose strand of hair behind her ear as she listened. 'You're a beautiful person, inside and out, despite what you've gone through, all the shit the world has thrown your way. You still have the kindest, bravest heart of anyone I know, and I love you for it.'

Her heart sang to hear him. She felt the same way.

'Listen, I hate the idea of leaving you here alone tomorrow,' he said. 'Come home with me.'

'No. Then you'd be harbouring a fugitive.'

Levi rolled his eyes skywards. 'Give me strength. What happens if Cade comes, or some other lowlife?'

'The rifle—'

'What if he surprises you? Come on.' He took Pippa's hand and pulled her to her feet. 'Time for some basic self-defence tips.'

Pippa was all for the lesson if it meant getting up close and personal with Levi. They went outside to a patch of soft snowgrass. He showed her how to escape a wrist grab and a bear hug. He taught her the leg trip, the eye gouge and how to deliver a kick or a knee to the groin.

Pippa began to understand the power she had, even when faced with a heavier, stronger attacker. What a revelation! If only she'd known this stuff when she was back with Cade. But then it wouldn't have done her any good. She'd have been too scared to challenge him. Well, she wasn't scared any more.

'Don't panic if he knocks you down,' said Levi. 'The eye poke works well on the ground. It's a good idea to have a few kicks that work there as well. Lie down and I'll show you.'

Pippa stretched out on the grass, looking up at him.

'If you're prone, and your assailant is standing, it gives you an advantage because your legs are longer than his arms. That means he'll have to expose his body to your kick if he wants to reach you.' Levi slowly lowered his body over hers. 'If he gets down and dirty, use your knee. Once you see an opening strike upward into his crotch, the harder the better.'

'Like this?' She swiftly raised her good knee, then gasped an apology as Levi fell on his back, groaning.

After his eyes stopped watering, Levi managed a wan smile. 'Yes, exactly like that.'

When night fell, Levi pushed two mattresses together on the floor in front of the fire. He'd caught and cooked a brace of plump rainbow trout, serving them for dinner along with fresh warrigal greens, foil-wrapped potatoes baked in the coals and leftover corned beef from lunch. Afterwards they lay together beneath a blanket, eating chocolate and sharing the rest of the brandy, while Duke snoozed at the foot of their makeshift bed.

Pippa couldn't ever remember being so happy, and it was all because of Levi. Thanks to him she'd soon have her life back. No, that wasn't right. She couldn't have back what she'd never had. What she really meant was that thanks to Levi, she'd finally have a life. Cade would never again control her. There'd be no more miserable days and weeks, staring out the kitchen window at dusty paddocks and dying sheep. No more figuring out how to keep Cade happy and failing. No more running. No more guilt, and best of all – there'd be Levi.

He popped a piece of caramel-filled chocolate into her mouth, and she savoured the creamy sweetness. Another sip of brandy and she was ready to ask some questions of her own. Levi knew a lot about her life, but she knew next to nothing about his.

'You say you've never been married,' she said. 'But what about girl-friends? Anyone special?'

It took him a while to answer. 'Yes, but it didn't work out.'

'Why?'

'Hannah and I were childhood sweethearts. Our families came to Australia from South Africa when we were babies. Her mother and my mother were best friends, and everyone loved it when at sixteen we fell for each other. It was like a fairy tale.' He paused, as if remembering. 'She really did have the prettiest hair, like spun gold.'

'So, what happened?'

'We grew apart, I guess. She left school and studied accounting. I studied Equine Management at Marcus Oldham and did my practical placement here at Brumby's Run. Drew offered me a job when I graduated. Meanwhile, Hannah had found work in Melbourne, and we wound up at loggerheads. She wouldn't live in the bush, and I wouldn't live in the city.'

'Didn't she like horses?'

'She adored them. That's one of the reasons I loved her. Hannah's a champion when it comes to dressage. I used to drive her round to competitions just to watch her ride. Put that girl on a horse and it's pure poetry in motion.'

Pippa was beginning to wish she'd never asked. 'Do you still see her, this Hannah?'

Levi gently lifted her chin. 'Why Miss Pippa, I do believe you're jealous.'

She batted his hand away and sat up. 'Well, can you blame me, with you going on about your perfect Hannah? Beautiful, well-educated, a champion rider—'

Levi sat up too. 'Woah, hang on a minute. You asked, and she's not *my* Hannah,' he said. 'I see her maybe twice a year – at Passover, for instance. It's not my fault our families are close.'

'So she's Jewish too?'

Levi pressed his palm to his forehead and groaned. 'What's that got to do with anything?' He sculled the last of the brandy. 'You asked about any special ex-girlfriends, so I told you. Maybe I shouldn't have.'

He looked endearingly bewildered. Pippa sighed. She was being unreasonable, and she knew it. 'I'm sorry,' she said. 'If I ever ask you about ex-girlfriends again – run.'

Levi laughed and swung her into the circle of his arms. They kissed, relishing the taste of each other. Her hand ran down his torso. It felt lean and lightly muscled beneath the fabric of his shirt. Pippa explored further, reaching down to his groin, astonished at her boldness. Levi unbuttoned her top. His hand cupped her breast, stroking it before lowering his mouth to her taut nipple. She gasped and ran her fingers through his hair. But he didn't go further, even though her senses were spinning. Instead Levi kissed her lips briefly, got up and tossed the blanket over her. The effort that decision caused him was etched into his face.

'I'll put the kettle on, shall I?' he said in a voice hoarse with frustrated desire.

'No.' Pippa took a steadying breath, fighting disappointment. 'Come back.'

He didn't want to rush things, that was plain. But she longed to be close to him, to feel his touch once more on her skin. An unexpected thought took her way, way back. This was how she'd expected to feel on her wedding night, all those naive, foolish years ago. But sex with Cade was a completely different animal from intimacy with Levi. One was about violence and power. The other was about tenderness and love. Her newfound passion had almost made her forget Cade and his cruelty. Almost.

Pippa called him back to bed again, but Levi would not be persuaded. Instead he produced a deck of cards. 'Can you play two-handed 500?'

Pippa sighed and smiled. 'You're looking at the 500 queen.'

Levi dealt the cards. The two of them played long into the night, while the moon made its silent journey across the shadowy Balleroo Range.

· · ·

Seven-thirty the next morning and Levi was preparing to return to Brumby's Run. He put some spare batteries for the radio on the table. 'Make sure you listen to the news. I'll try to get back on Wednesday, but there's a few mares due to foal soon. It's hard to make promises.'

'Don't worry,' she said. 'I'm safer here than anywhere, and surely Cade will be picked up soon.' Pippa and Levi had caught the morning bulletin. The radio reception was terrible, and it was hard to hear through the static, but there'd been no mention of an arrest in the bombing case. Disappointing, to say the least. She'd handed Cade to them on a plate. How hard was it for an entire national police force to catch one man?

Pippa watched as Drew packed his things. 'I wish you didn't have to go.'

'So do I, but it's Monday and I'll already be hours late for work. Why not come back with me?' said Levi, as he laced up his rucksack. 'I don't like leaving you up here by yourself.'

'It's only until Drew comes home. And I'm not by myself. Duke is here to protect me, aren't you boy?' Duke barked on cue. 'And anyway, I want to be here to monitor the yards. I lost Thowra, so it's my job to help get him back.'

The prospect of capturing the stallion was looking more and more promising. The mob had eaten the hay in the yards again last night under cover of darkness.

'Well, I can't make you leave,' Levi said with a frown. 'I'd feel a helluva lot better if you had a two-way, but this hut's out of range.'

Before Levi left he chopped wood and left a good supply of it on the porch. He built up the fire and added a stout back log. He also cleaned, oiled and reloaded Pippa's rifle.

'Isn't it illegal to leave a gun loaded?' she said.

Levi shot her a wry smile. 'Isn't it a bit rich you lecturing me about the law?' He handed her the rifle. 'I can't see how Cade could find you here, but even so, take this with you whenever you go outside, even if it's just to the loo. Promise me.'

Pippa felt a creeping fear at his words. They kissed goodbye and he patted Duke. 'Look after her for me, buddy.' She watched his Jeep travel down the track and vanish into the trees. For a moment she wanted to run after it. Despite her bravado, staying at the hut would feel very different without having Levi there.

CHAPTER 25

Cade scratched his chin. The growing beard was bloody itchy. He was sitting in a folding chair on the back deck of the Penrith safe house, staring at the factory car park beyond. He lit another cigarette, although he'd just finished his last one. The afternoon sun was beating down on the straggly grapevine clinging to the pergola overhead. It provided little shade and droplets of sweat ran down his face.

What was it with this run of stinking hot days in September? Cade was in a foul mood. He'd been chain-smoking ever since he'd watched the morning news bulletin and seen his face up there, large as life, on the television screen.

'Breaking news. After a tip-off from the public, police have identified thirty-four-year-old Cade Bradley Black as a person of interest in the Millburn Synagogue bombing. Black was last seen in Cobar on the night of September 18th. They ask that Mr Black come forward to assist them with their enquiries. Anybody with information as to the whereabouts of Cade Bradley Black should call Crime Stoppers.'

George's car pulled into the cracked concrete driveway. He was head honcho of the Renegade's West Sydney branch and Cade didn't like him. He acted all buddy-buddy, but Cade wasn't fooled. George was as fake as they came. Plus the bloke had tickets on himself. George hadn't carried out the greatest patriot attack that the state of Victoria had ever seen. He'd had no involvement in the bombing whatsoever, but to hear him tell it, he'd masterminded the whole thing.

Cade ground his cigarette butt into the deck with his heel. He didn't fit here in Sydney the way he had in Millburn. He was treated somewhere between an unapproachable hero and a country hick. The Millburn Renegades had disbanded, for now at least, melting back into their communities. Cade hated knowing that he'd never be one of them again. He missed their camaraderie and companionship. He especially missed Dylan, who'd been moved north to Brisbane. Without his friend's steadying influence, Cade was finding it harder and harder to cope. He wished he'd never bombed the synagogue at all, and that things could go back to how they were before.

George plonked a six-pack of beer down on the plastic outdoor table. Didn't anybody buy food around here? The fridge was full of nothing but booze. Cade's mouth watered to think of Pippa's delicious breakfasts: eggs, bacon, grilled tomato and beans on homemade sourdough bread. George offered Cade a stubby. 'Get that into you.' Cade ignored him. George shrugged, pulled up a chair and swigged his beer.

'Don't stress about the news this morning,' said George. 'They were bound to put a name to you sometime.' He sounded both philosophical and drunk. 'Nathan Jones will start at the tannery next week with shining references and a clean slate.' George burped loudly. 'Dye your hair, grow your beard and nobody will pick you for that Cade feller. Once you're settled at work, we'll start planning our next job. How about we hit a mosque this time, teach those towelheads a lesson, eh?'

Cade bristled at the use of the word *we*. He stood up and stared at George with undisguised loathing. 'You can stick your stinking tannery job.' Then he stormed into the house, shouldering roughly past one of his housemates who stank of marijuana. He went to his room with its lumpy mattress and torn curtains. Someone had punched a hole in the wall and the carpet was sticky with filth. What a dump.

Cade's head pounded. He swallowed four Panadol along with the cold dregs from a coffee mug. Then he lit another cigarette and lay down with one arm behind his head. The words of the news announcer echoed in his brain. '*A tip off from the public ...*' Cade knew exactly who *the public* was. Pippa. She'd put two and two together. Not only had his wife abandoned him and run off with another man, but she'd also given him up to the coppers. Who else could it have been?

He should never have listened to Dylan. He should have gone back for Pippa when he had the chance. Up until now he'd been torn between wanting her dead and wanting her back. Thinking that maybe, if she begged him hard enough, he'd forgive her. But this betrayal was the final straw.

Not knowing Pippa's whereabouts was eating him up inside. Not knowing who she was with was the worst of it. He couldn't sleep. At night he'd imagine her there beside him, with her high breasts, soft skin and long, lean thighs. He'd smell the peppermint oil from her homemade shampoo and instinctively reach for her, longing to entwine his fingers in her silky, blonde hair. But the bed was always empty, and then he'd remember. It killed him to know that some other man held her now.

Cade made his decision. He couldn't allow Pippa to make a damn fool of him for one more day. He packed his things, including the items he'd stolen from George's room: tobacco, a little weed, and two guns – a pistol and a rifle. Plenty of ammunition as well. He picked up the pistol. It felt good to have a gun in his hands again. Its cold steel gave him a comforting sense of power. He stowed his gear in the old silver Barina that George had given him. A piece of junk, but it ran.

George was still sitting out on the deck, drinking and listening to some stupid radio talk show. 'Calmed down have you, Nate?' he said. 'Want that beer now?'

'Nah, mate. Look, could you stand me some more cash?'

George rose unsteadily to his feet, went into the house and came back with a wad of cash. 'This should tide you over until your first pay.'

Cade counted the notes. Two hundred dollars. Together with the cash he already had on hand, and what the Renegades had put on a debit card for him, he had plenty of money for a road trip. Cade helped himself to two of the stubbies, went around the side of the house and got into his car, careful not to be seen. Then he headed for Fairview.

CHAPTER 26

Cade approached the back gate of his farm. The sun sat on the horizon in a fiery ring, preparing to launch itself into the sky. He parked behind a stand of tea-tree and sat for a while, watching. It had taken him ten hours to get here from Penrith. He'd pulled over once and slept for a bit in the car. Damn George and his midget Barina. The crick in Cade's neck seemed to be permanent.

He checked the time – just after five o'clock. How strange. Everything looked the same, but nothing was. Skinny sheep still grazed on paddocks of dust and stubbly wheat. Ragged crows still perched atop fence posts, on the watch for an easy feed. Surely he could simply drive to the house and find Pippa baking bread or hanging out washing. She'd cook him a big breakfast and he'd take her to bed. A vain yearning for his wife brought tears to his eyes. Cade knuckled them away. Pippa had a lot to answer for.

He got out of the car and tucked the loaded pistol into his gun belt, making sure to pack plenty of clips. Cade drew the pistol a few times, just to get the feel of it. He loved how it nestled in the palm of his hand like it belonged there. He stared at the farmhouse. Would Pippa have been foolish enough to come back? Had she spilled her guts to the cops, and then returned to shack up with her new man? Cade smiled at the thought. God, he hoped so. The problem was the police could just as well be at the farm instead of his wife. If only he'd acted before he'd been identified. It would have been so much easier to track Pippa down.

There was no vantage point in this dead-flat landscape from which to observe the house. Instead he was forced into the open, creeping sideways across the adjacent paddock with his gun drawn until he could see the front driveway. No vehicles, police or otherwise, were parked at the house. A mixture of relief and disappointment coursed through him. Still on high alert, he drew nearer until he found cover in the empty hay shed.

Rats were nesting in his tractor. They'd chewed through the hydraulic hose on his hay spike. Bloody vermin. What if they'd got into the engine bay? For a split second he wanted to check the wiring, then realised with an unpleasant jolt that it didn't matter. The rats could have the damn tractor. He'd never drive it again.

The wind had whipped up. Loose roofing iron clanked and rattled forlornly. Each random bang made him jump. From the front of the shed he could see the rear of the house. The yard looked deserted. Adrenaline made him bold. He approached the back porch, half expecting Duke to rush around the corner, barking. He'd never liked that dog or the way it defended Pippa. He smiled at the thought of giving it a bullet.

But Duke wasn't there. Cade realised with a wrench that Pippa wasn't there either. He tried to push through the screen door, but it was locked, as was the front door. Cade kicked it in. The house was empty. He wandered from room to room, opening and shutting cupboards, picking up objects and putting them down again.

It was clear that someone had been in the house. Cade had rushed Pippa off that fateful morning ten days ago without letting her take her bag, phone or charger. All were now missing. But had the police or Pippa taken them? He had no way of knowing.

A dried lump of dough lay on the kitchen bench, along with a packet of flour and yeast. The pantry still held cans of soup and corn. A spider web covered one corner of the oven and a trail of ants led to the sugar bowl. Pippa's apron lay on the floor where she'd discarded it. Dead flies littered the windowsill. Cade grimaced. He couldn't imagine Pippa leaving the kitchen in such a mess if she'd been back. His wife was an excellent housekeeper.

He opened the fridge and helped himself to a beer. The cheese was going mouldy, and the lettuce was wilted. Was anything missing? He couldn't tell. He sniffed at an open carton of milk and wrinkled his nose in distaste. No, it didn't look like Pippa had been back.

Cade finished his beer. Coming here had been a long shot. The farm was the first place that he'd look for her, after all. She'd be mad to return. But how was he supposed to find her without any clues? She could be anywhere, with anyone. And then it struck him – the dead flies on the empty sill, the sill where Pippa's pot plants had been. She'd been back after all. He picked up the little tin watering can by the sink. A scribbled note fluttered to the floor. *Mum, I'm okay. I'll call xo.* Cade felt the muscles cord in his neck, and he hurled a kitchen chair against the wall. He didn't want Pippa to be okay. The very idea enraged him.

He ran back to the car and drove it up to the house. If the coppers happened to come by, he'd be a sitting duck, but it was a risk he had to take. Cade packed as much camping gear as he could, along with some cans of food, cursing the tiny Barina and its limited space. Then he checked the time, took a last look around the sad kitchen and took off into the Hattah-Kulkyne scrub.

He drove deep into the park, searching for a deserted spot to have a feed and a kip. It was too early to visit Pippa's mother. Her husband would still be home at this time of the morning, but Jay always made a trip into Ouyen on Tuesdays to buy farm supplies. Cade knew from first-hand experience that these trips ended up at the pub; a boozy afternoon with friends, talking politics, religion and generally complaining about the godless state of the world. Pastor Jay wouldn't normally be back until dinnertime.

That would suit Cade just fine. He needed to talk to Ruby Sullivan alone.

. . .

Cade drove in the back gate to the Sullivan farm, parking in the big shearing shed and throwing an old tarp over the car to conceal it. The compound was large and sprawling with lots of outbuildings and lots of cover. After a swift surveillance, he chose the stand of ancient pine trees behind the house as the perfect place to keep watch on the house.

Even if Pastor Jay had left for Ouyen, there was still the horde of kids to contend with. Pippa said that Ron didn't live at home any more, and with any luck the two older boys would be out in the paddocks somewhere. Ruby had her job cut out trying to keep those two in a school room. That only left the ten-year-old twins. They probably wouldn't know that he was a wanted man, but it would still be safest to get Ruby alone. When she visited the chook shed or went to feed the bobby calves perhaps. Or if she went to clean the chapel. That would be perfect.

He'd have to stop Ruby from calling the police once he left. Cade didn't want to kill her. He'd immediately become the prime suspect. Best to terrify Ruby with promises to kill her children. She was a weak and sentimental woman like her daughter, and would respond well to threats.

Cade took up his position in the trees and waited. He noted with satisfaction that Pastor Jay's vehicle was gone; however, the family station wagon seemed to be gone too. And the two elderly heelers were chained, dozing in the shade of the woodshed. Ruby never chained the dogs when someone was home. The heelers either recognised him, or else were too lazy to bark. Duke wasn't there though, confirming that Pippa had taken the kelpie with her. She wouldn't trust that mongrel with anybody but her mum.

After half an hour Cade grew impatient. He edged past the trees towards the house, reaching the back porch without seeing or hearing anyone. He tried the door and it opened. It was unlocked, but that didn't mean the family was home. Almost nobody locked their doors out this way.

Cade stepped into the laundry, past the concrete double-bay laundry sink and the washing machine – an old top-loader circa 1960.

Jay was such a miser. It would be a miracle if it worked. Pippa didn't have to put up with a piece of junk like that. He'd bought her a late-model front-loader, Fisher and Paykel, just like she wanted. Not new, but as good as. Ungrateful bitch.

He pushed past the collection of coats hanging on the wall. All was quiet in the hall, save for the ticking longcase clock. Cade had been here plenty of times and knew the layout. He checked the kids' rooms and Pastor Jay's study. He checked the other bedrooms, the lounge, the kitchen. All empty. Cade cursed and kicked the wall. Ruby barely went anywhere. Just his damn luck that the whole family would be away at once.

Well, since he was here, he might as well have a good look around. Cade helped himself to some biscuits from a tin in the pantry and opened the kitchen dresser drawers. He pocketed the fifty-dollar note he found in an old jam jar, then reluctantly put it back. He couldn't let people know that he'd been here.

Cade poked around in the study, hoping to find some clue to Pippa's whereabouts. A letter or postcard. An address on the back of an envelope. Nothing. Someone had been sleeping in Ron's old bedroom. He smelt pipe smoke and snorted with contempt. So Ruby had kicked Jay out of the marital bed. So much for him preaching about wifely obedience. If Pippa ever tried anything like that … and then he remembered. He was hunting his wife and yet her leaving still didn't seem real.

Cade went into the main bedroom. It smelt of roses and lavender. A pink satin heart-shaped cushion sat on the chair. An oversized teddy bear lay on the bed with its head on the pillow. There was no sense of Jay here at all. Cade opened the wardrobe and pushed the hanging clothes aside. Nothing behind them but spare blankets and two empty bottles of McWilliams sherry. You never really knew people, did you? He hadn't figured Ruby for a closet drinker.

He looked through two shoeboxes on a shelf. One was full of photos and the other was full of household receipts. He found a photo of Pippa on her horse. She was laughing and leaning down to stroke its mane. Cade could see the swell of her breasts through the neck of her checked shirt. He tucked the photo into his pocket, his longing for her so powerful that it turned his knees to jelly.

Cade pulled out a dressing table drawer, then another. What a mess. Bras and knickers all jumbled together. Some sexy ones as well. He held them up, aroused by imagining Pippa in skimpy red lace. Her slender waist, jutting hip bones and small, high breasts. The multitonal bruises mottling her body. He liked seeing them there. They were like brands, signifying his ownership of a beautiful girl, a girl other men lusted after but could never have. Except now they could. Those bruises would be fading, growing fainter and fainter until they disappeared altogether. All trace of him gone from her skin.

Aargh! He hurled the underwear away, yanked out the bottom drawer and tipped it out on the bed. Assorted bric-a-brac: a half-empty perfume bottle, lavender bags, a mother-of-pearl box filled with cheap jewellery and what looked like an old metal cash tin. It was locked. So Ruby was squirrelling away money behind her husband's back. You just couldn't trust women. The upside was that she wouldn't dare report the money missing. He could steal it with impunity.

Cade shook the tin. He couldn't hear anything, but bank notes wouldn't make a sound. In the study he found two jumbo paper clips. He straightened them out, made a ninety-degree bend in one of them and pressed it into the bottom of the keyhole. Then he inserted the other clip into the top of the keyhole and jiggled it around until he felt the lock give.

But when Cade lifted the lid he didn't find money, just some old documents and a pile of letters. He flipped through them. There was nothing from Pippa. Cade flattened out a creased piece of paper – a birth certificate for one Andrew Clive Cooper. And the mother was listed as none other than Ruby Lee Cooper, occupation: student, age: fifteen years, place of birth: Mildura, Victoria. What – Ruby had a kid when she was fifteen? The name of the father had been left blank.

Cade was shocked. And to think that slut played at being a virtuous clergyman's wife, respected by the community. Pippa was a slut too, he knew that now. The apple didn't fall far from the tree. No wonder Ruby had kept this little secret locked away from her husband.

Cade checked the date of the birth certificate. Andrew Clive Cooper had been born to Ruby twenty-nine years ago, five years before Pippa was born. So where was he – dead, or had he been adopted out? That would make sense, considering Ruby's age. Did Pippa know she had a half-brother somewhere? She'd never said, but that meant nothing, because he knew what a liar she was.

Cade went through the rest of the box. Love letters from Jay to Ruby. That was a surprise. The stern pastor had been quite the romantic back in the day. Letters from her parents who'd passed away, and from her sister in Queensland. And seven letters from a Drew Chandler, the first dated fourteen years ago when Pippa had been just ten years old.

Cade sat on the bed and began to read. The letter writer said that he understood why Ruby had given him away as a baby. Bingo. This Drew was Andrew Clive Cooper, Ruby's illegitimate son, and he'd put an address at the top of the letter – Kilmarnock, Currajong. Drew wrote that he knew Ruby was married with a family, and said that he didn't want to cause any trouble for her. But he also wrote that he was open to getting to know her and his half-siblings if and when she thought the time was right. Is that what had happened? Had Pippa been secretly in contact all along with this half-brother? Cade knew how much family meant to Pippa. He guessed that she hadn't told him for fear that he'd expose Ruby, and she was right. Jay deserved to know that his wife was no virgin on their wedding night.

Cade looked at the address on that first letter. Kilmarnock – the name of a property? He googled it and came up with nothing. Cade kept reading. Drew didn't reveal much about his life, but it was clear he lived on a farm. In one letter he wrote of bumper cattle sales, and in another he bragged about his stallion winning some championship at the Sydney Royal Easter Show. What a wanker.

The letters, spaced roughly two years apart, indicated that this hadn't been a one-way correspondence. Drew referred to the fire in the Sullivan hay shed ten years ago, and sent get-well-soon wishes for

Luke, who'd had his tonsils out six years ago. And look – a congratulation message for Pippa's own wedding in a letter dated four years ago. Ruby had been in regular, if infrequent, contact with Drew for years. Pippa probably had too.

Then Cade noticed something. The last few letters had a different address at the top. Not Kilmarnock, but Brumby's Run. He googled it and the website for Brumby's Run Heritage Horses & High-Country Trails came up. Pippa loved horses. This was an excellent lead, and if it didn't pan out he could always come back and ask Ruby in person where her daughter was. Cade's face cracked into a malicious grin. He'd like that.

Cade took Pippa's photo from his pocket and kissed it. He'd find her eventually. The idea that she'd escape her just punishment forever was inconceivable. He made a final check of the tin box, placed it at the rear of the drawer, then put the dressing table back the way he'd found it. Time to go.

It was a relief to be in the car, a relief to put some distance between him and the Sullivan farm. Google maps showed a six-hour trip from Manangatang to Currajong. Even with a kip in the car, he'd be there by nightfall.

CHAPTER 27

It was a glorious spring day up at Dead Man's Hut: warm but not hot, breezy but not windy, and with a cornflower-blue sky overhead. Pippa peered down the track, wishing that Levi's returning Jeep would magically appear. Wishful thinking. He wouldn't be back until Wednesday, at the earliest. That was tomorrow, wasn't it? For a moment she wasn't sure what day it was. Days of the week didn't much matter any more. Was this how it was for the mysterious Maid of the Mountains – losing track and perhaps marking time by the passing seasons instead of by a man-made calendar?

After a lunch of bread, cheese and hot, sweet tea, Pippa lay down and slept for a few hours. She wanted to be wide awake tonight. When she woke, Duke brought her a rabbit. He proudly laid it at her feet. How sweet. 'Why don't you have it?' she said. 'I'll have the next one.' And she meant it. Fresh rabbit would be a nice change from tinned food.

Afternoon shadows were growing long when Pippa fed out bales of hay and refilled the salt tubs in the yards. She tested the trapping mechanism and watched the gate swing shut with considerable satisfaction. Night fell early in the mountains and she wanted to make sure everything was ready.

Levi had left yesterday morning which meant today was Tuesday. They hadn't talked about her setting the trap while he was away. The assumption was that they'd do it when Drew came back from his honeymoon. But Pippa was determined to catch Thowra before then, to atone for losing him in the first place, to protect him from the coming cull – and to satisfy her longing to connect with him again.

Pippa had camped out on the hill last night to see if it was truly Thowra's mob coming into the yards, staying downwind so the brumbies couldn't smell her. She'd almost drifted off in her swag before she heard the soft thud of approaching hooves on mountain clay. It must have been one or two in the morning. She'd put a finger to Duke's lips. The dog cocked his head but stayed quiet.

Dark shapes emerged into the grassy clearing, illuminated by a full moon that almost turned night to day. Her skin tingled as she picked out mares, foals and yearlings, seven in all. Then Thowra stepped out from the pool of shadow under a spreading candlebark. There was no mistaking the stallion, his mane glittering with moonshine, his golden coat turned to burnished silver.

And there it was, the same electric, hair-prickling thrill that she'd felt the first time she'd seen him. A sense of mystery – and of danger. Something about Thowra called to her, making her forget about Levi and Drew and her coming confession. Making her forget about Cade and the deadly threat he posed. Making her forget everything but the enigmatic horse standing before her. Duke whined softly. The stallion turned and seemed to stare straight at her. A connection passed between them, she was sure of it. Then Thowra moved off and the feeling was lost.

He followed his herd into the yard, neat ears flicking back and forth, listening for danger. The other horses seemed relaxed, clearly accustomed to the high post and rail fence that was reinforced with steel panels. Pippa sensed that they'd been in that space many times before. They spent hours feeding and licking salt. One creamy mare lay down after filling her belly with sweet lucerne hay. Her pale foal folded up its long legs and slept beside her. Even Thowra appeared to doze, resting a back foot and letting his head droop.

Pippa was sleepy too, but dared not go inside for fear of spooking the horses. Instead, she'd snuggled down in her swag, with Duke's warm body a shield against the cold night air. Pippa had woken with the sun to find the hay eaten and the herd gone. A hollow sense of loneliness came over her. What if the brumbies didn't come back? It was unthinkable. She needed to see Thowra again.

Pippa wouldn't wait any longer to set the trap. It was more than a desire to fix her mistake, although that was part of it. A creeping unease was adding to her impatience, a sense of approaching menace, though she couldn't say whether the threat was to Thowra or to herself.

Pippa shared her dinner that night with Duke – baked beans and slabs of bread toasted by the heat of the coals. Time slipped by too slowly. She built the flames back up and heaved a great back log on, one that would burn most of the night. It would be good to return to the warmth of the fire after she had Thowra safe.

As twilight faded to black, Pippa set up her swag on the hill above the stockyards. It was very dark. The moon wouldn't rise for hours, though stars were pricking through the black velvet sky. She tested her torch and took a swig from her thermos of coffee. It was going to be a long night.

A cut-off shriek came from the forest, making her freeze with alarm. Not a rabbit. She knew the cry of a rabbit taken by a fox. This sound had been altogether different – louder and eerily human. A possum perhaps, snatched from the treetops by some predator. Levi had pointed out a powerful owl to her one sunset at Brumby's Run, roosting in the candlebark by the dam. The bird had massive talons and a hawk-like beak designed for tearing its prey apart. She shivered, imagining the big owl soaring over the trees on silent wings, invisible in the dark, plucking unsuspecting victims from the canopy. The forest was a dangerous place for some.

Pippa climbed into her swag and cuddled Duke close. Where was Thowra? When would he come? She lay down to wait.

. . .

Cade had slept in the car for longer than he'd meant to and arrived at the gate to Brumby's Run around midnight. He parked off the road and, armed with a torch and his pistol, slipped into the paddock alongside the drive where a row of gum trees gave him cover. His main fear was that dogs would alert the residents, and he was ready to run when he heard barking. If Pippa was here, Duke would be here too. Cade almost hoped to hear the kelpie's high-pitched guard bark, but the place remained swathed in silence.

The moon hadn't yet risen, but he could make out the shadow of a house at the top of the rise, with yards and outbuildings beyond. He dared to leave the trees. A Jeep was parked by the house. Cade slipped past it towards the buildings further up the hill. Suddenly his blood pumped harder – a station wagon was parked by a small bungalow. Would it really be this easy? He couldn't pick the colour in the dark.

He moved closer. Dammit, the car was a Commodore all right, but a later model than the one Pippa had stolen from him, and it was green, not blue. Could it belong to her new feller? Was she in bed with another man mere metres away? This ugly thought almost had him rushing into the bungalow then and there to confront them. He struggled to get a grip. No, in order to keep the upper hand he had to be smarter than that.

Cade returned to his vehicle and drove down the road until he found a turn off about three hundred metres on the right. A short track led to an old quarry. He parked his car behind a tumbledown site office, packed some snacks and a water bottle in his rucksack and made his way back to Brumby's Run on foot, armed with both handgun and rifle.

Cade walked boldly up the drive this time. These guys really should get a dog. He explored the stables and sheds with impunity, disturbing groups of yarded horses along the way. They milled about, snorting and restless. Mares rounded up their young foals, keeping them away from Cade as he made a mental map of the buildings and grounds.

As he passed close to a stockyard, a big chestnut stallion reared and rushed the rail. Cade didn't like horses. No, it was worse than that. He hated them. He'd been badly thrown by a sour ex-racehorse years ago while mustering. The fall had buggered his right shoulder, and it had never been quite right since. When he'd tried to catch his mount it had turned on him and double-barrelled him in the guts with shod hind hooves. The kick had ruptured his spleen and he'd wound up in hospital requiring an operation. Cade knew horses to be treacherous, dangerous creatures, and he could never understand the passion Pippa felt for them.

The chestnut stallion stood by the rails, snorting and pawing. Cade scowled and shone the torch into the animal's face. It didn't back off, although its eyes glowed eerily in the dark. A pulse throbbed in Cade's temple. He'd show the big bastard. Cade checked that the fence between them was solid and secure. It seemed safe enough. He picked up a fallen branch in both hands and, using it like a club, struck at the horse with all his might.

The blow missed its mark, glancing off the animal's sensitive muzzle. The stallion grunted, then snaked out its head in one swift movement to seize Cade's right bicep in its jaws. Cade stifled a scream as the horse clamped down harder and jerked backwards, dragging him off his feet. When the stallion finally dropped him, Cade fell hard, writhing in pain. It felt like his arm had been torn off.

When the pain waned sufficiently, Cade pulled off his coat one-handed to inspect the damage. The sleeve was torn, the skin lacerated and the whole area was red and inflamed. It reminded him of the crush injury he'd once received while setting a leg-hold trap for dingoes. The thick fabric of his jacket had gone some way to protect him. Without it, he'd be missing a fair chunk of flesh.

Perhaps the worst thing about the attack was the wrench caused to his bad shoulder. It ached alarmingly. When he scrambled to his feet, his right arm was weak as a kitten. He struggled to raise it past his shoulder. Damn. His first instinct was to shoot the bloody horse, but of course he couldn't do that. The noise would wake people. So instead he staggered off, transferring his rifle sling to his left shoulder.

The moon was finally rising, casting the scene in a pearly light. Cade climbed through a fence into the paddock adjacent to the drive. He found a sheltering thicket of tea-tree halfway up the hill which would offer a clear view of the house and bungalow come daybreak. If Pippa emerged from either building, he'd spot her. His trigger finger twitched at the thought. After making a rough hide, Cade lay down to wait for morning, shifting around, trying to get comfortable. What was the use – the ground was flinty and hard and poked through the mattress of his swag. To top it off, he'd forgotten his cigarettes. Cade's upper arm and shoulder throbbed with pain. God, how he hated horses.

CHAPTER 28

As night wore on Pippa cast off her sense of doom. When she next heard a shriek from the dark, she was philosophical. Owls took possums, so what? Owls had to eat, had to feed their fluffy fledglings hidden somewhere deep inside their tree hollow.

The moon rose behind the ranges, casting the ridgetops in silver, like shining battlements. The unseasonably warm breeze was fragrant with eucalyptus and sassafras. It was the most beautiful mountain night she'd seen. All seemed set for a triumphant outcome. Pippa imagined Levi's astonishment and delight when she showed him the captured brumbies.

She sat alert in her swag, bursting with excitement and expectation. Half-a-dozen times she thought she heard muffled hoof beats approaching. She held her breath, expecting any moment to see shadowy brumbies shifting through the clearing – mares and foals, followed by high-stepping Thowra. But the horses didn't come. Apart from some skittish sambar deer and a family of wallabies, the clearing remained empty.

She lay awake all night, hopes collapsing as a wash of dawn light crept over the mountains. Pippa stretched her cramped limbs and stood up, shivering. It was colder now than it had been at midnight.

Duke yawned and stood beside her. She went down to the yards. They were just as she'd left them the night before, the piles of hay untouched, the tripwire still set. Pippa felt as empty as the yards. Where was Thowra? Had the mob moved on, abandoning Maroong Mountain for richer but more dangerous lowland pastures? Had they fallen victim to the government cull, or encountered brumby hunters? She imagined Thowra's bloodied body lying prone on ground ploughed up by his death throes.

She trudged back to the hut with hunched shoulders. The place no longer felt like a safe haven. It felt like the end of the earth, a place of lonely banishment. The fire had died overnight and it was freezing inside. She couldn't be bothered lighting it again, so she crawled into her bunk, inviting Duke to join her as a canine hot water bottle. She dozed fitfully, sometimes dreaming of Thowra and his mob standing safe in the yards. Sometimes dreaming of them galloping for their lives from men with rifles. She woke and slept, woke and slept. Now it was Cade hunting the horses. Now it was Cade hunting her.

Duke whined and pawed at her arm. Pippa half-woke to see a man's figure looming in the doorway. She froze, too frightened even to scream. Instead a strangled sound came from her throat.

'Pip?' came a familiar voice. 'It's me.'

Pippa woke up properly. She exhaled as she recognised Levi. But instead of relief and excitement at his arrival, she felt a profound sense of failure. There was no yard of horses to proudly show him. She feared that she'd driven the brumbies away by her presence last night above the yards.

Levi hung his hat on the wall and sat beside her on the bunk. When he reached for her, she pulled away. Levi searched her face. 'Why so glum?'

Pippa took a deep breath and told him about her time at the hut.

Levi frowned. 'What were you thinking, camping up above the yards like that – and with Duke too? Brumbies hate dogs.'

'I wanted to see if it was truly Thowra's mob coming in. I stayed downwind of them.' Her words sounded naive and foolish, even to her.

'Well, your curiosity has cost us dearly,' he said, his voice sharp. 'Domestic horses might not have noticed you, but brumbies are wild animals. They can sense danger. Of course they knew you were there.'

Pippa didn't argue. Levi was right. With a stab of guilt she recalled the connection she'd felt with Thowra when he'd stared at her in the dark.

Levi ran a hand over his head. He was glaring at her, his eyes narrowed into copper-coloured slits. 'If you've spooked those horses they may never come back.'

There was nothing sensible to say. How could she explain the powerful pull the wild stallion had on her? She could no more have resisted seeing him than she could resist gravity. And now her weakness had put Thowra in jeopardy once more. What must Levi think of her? She'd lost his horse twice.

Levi shook his head in – what, disgust? He marched outside and returned with bags of groceries, which he dumped unceremoniously on the table without a word. The set of his jaw and each angle of his body expressed irritation. He glanced across to where Pippa sat slumped on the bunk. Duke laid a sympathetic paw on her knee.

'Come on,' said Levi. 'Let's have a look at the yards.'

Pippa trailed out the door after him. According to the sun it was about two o'clock in the afternoon. She must have slept for hours, yet she didn't feel rested.

Levi paced along the empty stockyard like an impatient horse, inspecting the posts and rails for any weakness. He examined the trap mechanism and seemed satisfied. 'Well at least you set it right,' he said as he checked the counterweight and trip wire. 'We'll try again tonight, eh? Maybe it was something else that scared them off.'

He didn't sound convinced. Pippa gave him a miserable nod.

'But we stay in the hut,' said Levi. 'You don't go anywhere near the yards until morning. Do we have a deal?'

Pippa nodded again. He was speaking to her like she was a naughty child. Cade used to speak to her like that sometimes. It made her sick to think of it.

Storm clouds were rolling in from the west as they returned to the hut. Levi set about lighting the fire, chopping wood and making lunch. Was he deliberately keeping busy in order to avoid her? She started packing away the supplies that he'd brought.

'Here, let me do that.' He took a packet of flour from her hand. 'Rest. You've had a long night.'

What did he think she was – useless? And what was that jibe about her having a long night? What he'd meant was: you've had a long night frightening off my horses. Pippa retreated to the bunk while Levi buttered bread. Should she make a pot of tea? No, he'd only take that job off her as well. Seems like Levi didn't trust her to do anything any more.

He presented her with a plate of sandwiches, a mug of boiling water and a tea bag. 'I bought you some books.' He put a bag down beside her. Pippa idly jiggled her tea bag as the silence yawned between them. 'How are things back at Brumby's?' she asked at last.

Levi told her about two new foals and about Comet and little Prince. He told her about how the youngsters were going. 'I took Zorro to bring in some Kilmarnock cattle and he loved it. He'll make someone a terrific campdraft horse one day.'

'And what about Mist?'

'She's really taken to Nullah. He has a way with the shy ones.'

Pippa felt a surge of jealousy and took a savage bite of her sandwich. She didn't much like the idea of Mist taking to anyone else. She'd hoped to be the one to help the filly gain confidence in humans.

Levi finished his account and Pippa didn't ask any more questions. He sat at the table eating his lunch. She wished he'd come over, sit close, put his arm around her shoulders. But he seemed to be lost in thought.

Pippa looked in the bag of books he'd given her. One particularly appealed to her – *Absolution Creek*. Apparently the author was born and raised on the black soil plains north-west of Moree. The book featured a dark-haired young woman on the cover, along with three riders splashing through a creek. Pippa read the blurb – a family saga set on a sheep station. She could relate to that. Before long Pippa was absorbed in the story. The act of reading calmed her and provided a soothing distraction from her current problems. Soon her eyes grew heavy, the book slipped from her grasp and she slept.

Pippa woke hours later to discover that she was alone. Levi was gone, along with Duke. She prayed that they were together. The fire blazed cheerily, giving her hope that Levi hadn't been gone for long. Pippa grabbed her loaded rifle and went outside. Levi's Jeep was still parked nearby, but there was no sign of either him or Duke. It seemed that even her dog had deserted her.

It was a bleak view looking up the mountain, nothing but a pall of grey. Pippa couldn't tell what time it was and her insides tangled into knots. At the back of her mind lay a fear that Cade was somehow responsible for Levi's disappearance. Pippa knew from the latest news reports that he was still at large, although how he'd find her in this remote place, she couldn't tell.

The clouds that had been brewing earlier were now on top of the hut, reducing visibility to a few metres and producing an icy mizzle so fine that it soaked straight through to her skin. Pippa called for Levi and Duke, but the sound was swallowed by the fog. She dared not go looking for them. She could just imagine what Levi would say if she became lost in the forest. *More trouble than she's worth.*

Pippa wandered about, looking for footprints or anything that might indicate which way they'd gone. After ten minutes of fruitless searching, a muffled sound came to her out of the void. A boot striking stone perhaps. She swung to face the sound and raised her rifle.

A shadow darker than the rest loomed from the fog – Levi, carrying a brace of rainbow trout. Duke followed at his heel. 'Steady on.' He stopped short when faced with the raised rifle. 'You do know that's loaded.'

Pippa lowered the weapon. Pleased as she was to see him, his words still irritated her. She'd been around rifles all her life. Of course she knew it was loaded.

'Dinner.' Levi held up his catch. 'The best fishing is in the rain.'

'You could have said you were going.'

'I didn't want to wake you.'

He was making perfect sense. She had been asleep, and he hadn't gone far. The creek was a stone's throw away from the hut. So why did she feel abandoned? Well, abandoned might be too strong a word, but Levi had certainly withdrawn. When he'd last been at the hut he couldn't bear to be apart from her. He found excuses to sit close, to touch her, to kiss her. They'd shared a powerful bond that was entirely new to her. It had been a revelation, a promise that romantic love between a man and woman could truly exist. She hadn't believed in love for such a long time.

And now that precious connection was unravelling. Levi was holding back. It hurt, and she didn't know how to fix it. The hut would be a lonely place tonight, even with him there. Please God, let the horses come back. If she'd driven Thowra away for good, Levi may never forgive her. And how could she blame him?

CHAPTER 29

At five o'clock that afternoon Cade abandoned his tea-tree hide on the hillside above Brumby's Run. He gritted his teeth at the pain in his injured arm as he packed up his swag and shouldered his weapons.

He'd been watching the house all day, but there'd been no sign of Pippa. He'd seen two blokes, that was all. One was a tall man who seemed to be in charge. Could that be Drew, Pippa's half-brother? The other one was a blackfella.

The tall man had packed his Jeep and left before lunch, leaving the other bloke alone. Nobody else had come or gone. Cade amused himself by aiming his rifle and catching the man in the crosshairs of his scope as he went about his day. Bang, you're dead. The bugger wouldn't know what hit him.

Then the weather had turned. A cloud came down, obscuring his view, rendering his surveillance pointless. It brought with it a freezing drizzle that soaked right through him. Damn these claustro-phobic mountains. He never thought he'd say it, but he'd swap them in a minute for the Mallee's endless days of sunshine. Cade swal-lowed some Panadol and made his way down the paddock to the road. The cloud may have put a stop to him watching the house, but it also helped him escape detection. Nobody would see him in this fog.

It seemed to take him forever to reach his car concealed at the old quarry. He found the whisky bottle in the back and took several swigs. Lord, he needed that. His shoulder throbbed like a demon, making it hard to think. He wished Pippa was there. He imagined her tenderly washing the wound, applying some healing balm and a bandage. But, of course, that was a fantasy. Pippa wasn't the kind, loving person of his imagination. She was a faithless, treacherous bitch.

Cade came to a decision. He needed information. Perhaps the best way to get it was to simply ask for it.

The black man saw Cade park the car outside the house at Brumby's Run and came down from the yards. 'G'day. Can I help you?'

'That depends on who you are.'

'Nullah Nelson.' The man offered his hand.

After a moment's hesitation Cade shook it, trying not to wince at the pain in his arm. Would Nullah recognise him from the wanted photograph? Probably not. Cade wore sunglasses. He had longer hair now, and a light beard. Cade pulled his hat down a little further over his eyes and put on the most nonchalant voice he could muster. 'I'm looking for the man in charge. Would that be Drew Chandler?'

'Ordinarily,' said Nullah. 'But Drew's on holiday right now.'

'Well that's a real shame.' Cade scratched at his beard. 'I was wanting to buy a horse for my wife.' A piercing neigh came from the yards above the house, making Cade jump. Could that killer stallion smell him from here?

'Our manager, Levi Goldstein, should be able to help you. He's not here right now, but he'll be back tomorrow afternoon. What exactly are you looking for?'

'A nice little mare for trail riding. But there's one thing. I reckon women have a gentler way about them than us ham-fisted blokes. And since the horse is meant for my wife, I was wondering ...'

'Yes?'

'Do you have any females training horses here at Brumby's Run?'

'We did have a girl,' said Nullah. 'But she left on Saturday.'

Bugger. Today was Wednesday. If it was Pippa, she had a four-day head start on him. And then it struck him. What if this Levi character was her new bloke? What if he'd squirrelled her away somewhere until her brother came back?

'I'd like to talk to Levi.' Cade plucked a grass stem and ground it between his teeth to distract from his aching shoulder.

'Sorry, mate. Like I said, he won't be back until tomorrow.'

'I've come a long way,' said Cade, his voice rising. 'Made a special trip.' He was hungry, tired and his shoulder was throbbing like buggery. It took all his self-control not to seize Nullah's throat and choke the information out of him.

As if Nullah could read Cade's mind, his friendly expression became more guarded. 'Levi's away in the high country overnight. No mobile reception.'

Cade forced himself to relax and put on an interested smile. 'Rotten weather for camping.'

'It would be,' agreed Nullah. 'But he's at a hut.'

Cade's ears pricked up. 'Where is this hut? Maybe I could talk to him there.'

Nullah cast a disparaging glance at the Barina. 'The road is four-wheel drive access only, and it's closed to the public right now in any case. If you come back tomorrow I'm sure Levi can find the perfect horse for your wife.' He drew a business card from his pocket and handed it to Cade.

Cade smiled and tipped his hat. 'Thanks, mate. Much obliged.' His thank you was genuine. Nullah had given him a strong lead. In addition, the icy cold air was numbing his shoulder, tempering the pain. Things were looking up.

Cade headed back along the road towards Currajong. He'd seen Levi's Jeep leave before lunch and had noted which direction it went. Visibility was still poor. He drove slowly, searching for any turnoff on his right that would lead him uphill. And there it was, smack bang between Kilmarnock Station and Brumby's Run – a broad track leading into the mountains. A rusty gate, off its hinges, leant against the fence. It bore a sign reading, *Road Closed. No Public Access.* Cade grinned with satisfaction. It suddenly seemed too easy. Although he wouldn't visit the hut tonight. He'd wait until Levi returned to Brumby's Run in the morning. If Pippa was indeed hiding out up there, Cade would prefer it to be a private reunion.

Cade noticed a gaping pothole in the road ahead, but was too late to dodge it. He hit it fair and square. It felt like the suspension had been ripped out, and a shaft of pain speared through his shoulder. He cursed and slammed the steering wheel. Nullah was right about the bloody Barina. It would never make it up the mountain track. He needed to swap the piece of junk for a four-wheel drive, and he had to get it from a place where his abandoned Barina wouldn't turn heads. Cade knew small country towns. A stranger's car left parked on the street would rouse curiosity after a few hours, let alone overnight.

No, he couldn't steal his new four-wheel drive from Currajong. But the much larger town of Wodonga was only two hundred kilometres away, and it had a train station. The Renegades often stole cars and numberplates from railway car parks. Owners off on their daily commute took a long time to report the theft. And there was the added advantage that Cade could leave the Barina parked there without causing suspicion.

It seemed like a plan. He'd return to Brumby's Run by morning and keep a watch out for Levi to get back. Then Cade would make his own trip up to that high-country hut Nullah had spoken of. He swallowed four more Panadol, turned on the radio and settled in for the drive.

CHAPTER 30

Levi and Pippa spent a sleepless night, waiting and hoping for the horses to return. Levi was perfectly kind, perfectly attentive – a perfect gentleman. But this time their evening was filled with none of the romantic intimacy that Pippa craved. He kept the fire burning, but he didn't push the two mattresses together on the floor in front of the flames. He cooked a delicious trout dinner. But afterwards they didn't lie side by side, eating chocolate and drinking brandy – sharing stories and kissing. Instead they lay on separate bunks, reading and thinking private thoughts.

When dawn tiptoed down the mountain, the yards were empty and the hay lay untouched. Their shared disappointment was profound.

Levi was ready to leave by noon. The fog had remained overnight, hemming them in, like a fat grey toad squatting on the mountainside.

Pippa stood outside the hut watching Levi pack the last of his things in the Jeep. She stiffened when he bent to kiss her goodbye. The wall between them was too high. His handsome features softened. 'It's all right, Pip. I know you didn't mean to spook the horses.'

She couldn't meet his eyes. 'You hate me.'

Levi's dark eyebrows arched in surprise. 'Hate you? Come here.' She allowed him to gather her into his arms. 'I love you, Pippa Sullivan. You're all I've been able to think about these past few days.'

'Apart from Thowra,' she said.

'Apart from Thowra,' he agreed, coaxing a smile from her. 'I love you for caring so much about the brumbies, about keeping them safe. Don't you think I know that you're as disappointed as I am?'

A warm glow of relief flowed through her. 'We'll catch Thowra,' she said, her mood lifting. 'I'll feed out hay in the yards every day until we do. Even if it takes weeks.'

Levi pushed a strand of hair behind her ear. 'You can't.' His voice was gentle, but resolute. 'Drew and the others will be back on Tuesday.'

It took Pippa a few moments to work it out. 'That's only a few days from now.'

Pippa had known intellectually that her days at the hut were numbered. But time had lost its meaning here on Maroong Mountain, a place where she didn't even have a clock. The ancient rocks and forests, the unique animals and birds of these wild ranges – all seemed to exist as much in the future and past as they did in the present.

Levi's words were a bitter reminder of what she was about to lose – what was at stake.

The chance to catch Thowra, for one thing. They couldn't leave the trap set with nobody at the hut. When she left, Levi would go back to salting the yards every two weeks and staying the odd night when he could. Hoping that between the government cull and the brumby hunters Thowra might somehow survive.

Her liberty, for another. After meeting Drew, Pippa had promised to turn herself in, and she intended to. What would happen then? Would she be dragged away in handcuffs? The thought terrified her. She'd already lived years of her life in a prison with Cade, being told where to go and what to do. How could she now endure a jail cell, especially after knowing these precious weeks of freedom?

And last, but most definitely not least, there was Levi – a man who'd utterly changed her life. A man who'd made her believe in the value of truth and kindness and tolerance. A man who'd made her believe in herself. He said he loved her. Would he stand by her if she went to jail? Would she lose him too?

Levi took her chin in his hand and tipped her face towards him. 'A penny for them.'

His touch was almost unbearable in its tenderness. 'You said I had a brave heart,' she said. 'But you're wrong. I'm scared.'

His face creased with concern. 'Scared to stay here alone? Come back with me then.'

'No, it's not that. I want to stay here while there's still a chance to catch the brumbies. I'm scared of … of something else.'

Levi took her hand and led her to the slab bench on the porch. They sat down, and he kept hold of her hand. 'I won't let you down, Pip, no matter hard things get. And as far as the police go, you never did anything wrong. They can't charge you. You're Cade's victim, not his accomplice.'

'You don't know him,' she said. 'He'll turn it all around.'

'The law will see right through a man like that,' he said. 'If I were you, I'd be itching to tell the cops my story to clear my name.'

'I guess you're right ...'

'What do you mean, *you guess*? Of course I'm right.'

He kissed her then, the first proper kiss of his visit. Levi's questing lips asked for an answer. She responded, kissing him back, feeling his solid arms around her. Pippa absorbed strength and courage from his faith in her. And suddenly she felt incredibly selfish. She had Levi. She had Duke. She had a chance to catch the brumbies. She had a long-lost brother who she'd soon get to meet – and she was alive, safe from Cade. Not like Zadie. The young woman's death still haunted Pippa each night before she slept.

Levi kissed her again, this time chastely on the cheek. 'Are we good?'

'We're good.' She could tell he was reluctant to leave, and she loved him for it.

'Don't go anywhere,' he said. 'I'll be back on Monday to collect you.'

'That means I have four more nights to catch Thowra.'

'So you'll keep the trap set?'

'If it's okay with you.'

'Of course it's okay, but curb your curiosity. Don't camp out above the yards. And if by some miracle you should catch the brumbies, don't go near them. Throw them hay from a safe distance. They may be beautiful, but they're also wild. Wild animals can be dangerous, especially when they're trapped. And remember to take your rifle whenever you leave the hut.'

'You can be bossy, you know that?'

Levi frowned. 'I'm serious. This Cade character is still on the loose. Until you're safely ensconced in the Currajong Police Station, pouring your heart out to some copper, he's a threat.'

'To be honest, I've never felt safer from Cade in my life. How on earth could he find me way up here?'

'He probably can't. But probably isn't the same as definitely, so stay on your guard and keep the fire stoked. I don't want you freezing to death. There's plenty of wood.' Levi tossed her his coat and patted Duke. 'Look after her for me, mate. I'm counting on you.' Duke creased his brows and whined.

She threw her arms around Levi one last time, eyes glistening 'Be careful driving. It's hard to see in this fog.' He touched her face gently in farewell. Pippa watched his Jeep bump off down the track, her optimism restored. She'd make Levi proud, she knew she would.

CHAPTER 31

Lunchtime saw Cade on watch again in his hide above Brumby's Run. He'd made it back from Wodonga by mid-morning, but had waited for the fog to lift before resuming his spying.

It was easier than he thought to steal some new wheels. It had taken less than a minute to access the four-wheel drive and be gone. The owner had made two classic mistakes. The first was leaving the window slightly down. To Cade, a car with a window down a crack was the same as an unlocked car. He simply grabbed the top of the glass and rocked it back and forth until it came off its tracks. Then he pried the window down far enough so he could get his arm in and unlock the door. The second mistake was leaving a spare key under the sun visor.

Dylan said that a full ninety per cent of cars that the Renegades stole came from simply scoping out the vehicles and finding the keys. Apparently a car was stolen every ten minutes in Australia. People should be more careful.

Cade's new vehicle was parked back at the old quarry. Well, it wasn't new exactly. It was a white 1997 Land Rover Discovery, but the old 4WD drove well and had sufficient room for him to sleep in the back. As a bonus it was fitted with a long-range fuel tank – a tank that was almost full. He'd packed a few spare jerry cans of diesel anyway, just in case. He had no idea exactly how far this high-country hut was from the road.

Pity getting his hands on some decent painkillers wasn't as easy as nicking a car. Cade swigged some whisky, along with four more Panadol, and rolled a joint. Smoking weed was the only thing that seemed to help his shoulder. It was growing more painful. Probably infected. Who knew what filthy germs lived in the mouth of that crazy nag?

Cade changed his position, trying to get comfortable. A boring job, this watching, but when it came to finding Pippa he could be patient. The day at Brumby's Run wore on at a snail's pace, punctuated by the occasional visitor. His hopes soared when a young woman arrived, but it wasn't Pippa. Too short and stout. Nullah showed her the stallions and they talked for a while before she left. An empty float came and departed with a mare and foal. A man dropped off his young daughter for what appeared to be a riding lesson. Cade was disgusted. What sort of father would leave his girl alone with a blackfella?

Nullah mucked out some stables, fed out some hay, rode a few horses. Every now and then he'd stop what he was doing and look around – up the mountain, across the paddocks, down to the road – as if he could feel Cade watching him. Then he'd shake his head and get on with his work, no doubt feeling foolish. After all, there was no good reason for him to think that he wasn't alone. More fool him.

It was after four o'clock before Cade sat up and paid attention. Levi's Jeep was bumping back up the drive to the house. Cade held his breath. Would Pippa be with him? Blood rushed in his ears, but no – Levi emerged from the vehicle alone.

Cade watched for a while longer as Levi talked with Nullah and unpacked a few things from his car. Good, it looked like he was staying put. Cade waited until the two men walked up the hill and vanished into the stables. Then he rose stiffly and dodged across the paddock, keeping low until he reached the trees. A cloud was descending again, bleeding colours, shrouding the world in the softest white. Why was this bloody mountain weather so changeable?

Cade stumbled into a runoff ditch when he reached the road, falling heavily on his sore shoulder. Damn – too much whisky. But it wasn't just the whisky. A combination of marijuana, pills and hunger were also taking their toll. He scrambled to stand, the earth spinning and his lids heavy, closing against his will. It took all his determination to reach the Land Rover without falling asleep on his feet. When was the last time he'd slept? Cade couldn't remember. Despite his crushing desire to find Pippa, his body was pulling rank. There was nothing else for it but to lie down in the back of the car, pull a blanket over him and shut his eyes. He'd catch a few winks, that was all. Then he'd head for the hut …

Levi stood on the verandah, staring into the swirling white void. He disliked this kind of evening: when the mist closed in like walls, cutting him off from the nocturnal world.

He said goodbye to Nullah, who was heading out for a counter meal and a few drinks at the Currajong Hotel.

'Come with me,' said Nullah. 'We'll have a good night. Better than staying home and mooning around over that girl.'

'Nah, mate. Reena's foal isn't suckling as well as I'd like. Might stay here and keep an eye on him.'

Nullah shrugged. 'Suit yourself. I'll be in the front bar with Spike Morgan if you change your mind.'

'What are you two scoundrels up to?'

'The King of the Mountain Festival committee is sponsoring an Indigenous competition to be held here at Currajong – kind of like a stockman's challenge for top Koori jackaroos. They want me and Spike to organise it.'

Levi laughed. 'You two couldn't organise a piss-up in a brewery.'

'Thanks for the vote of confidence, brother.' Nullah pulled a comb from his pocket and dragged it through his thick, wavy hair. 'Don't wait up.'

. . .

Levi stayed out on the verandah long after Nullah's car had been swallowed by fog. How was Pippa, he wondered? He felt the space between them like a physical pain. And where was Thowra? Had he really taken his mob off the mountain, or did Pippa still have a chance to catch them? How he longed to be back at the hut. His mind was a kaleidoscope of unanswered questions rearranging themselves in endless variety.

And what about Cade? Levi had scoured news websites, checking hourly for updates. The man, if that's what you could call him, still hadn't been arrested. The sight of Pippa's terrible bruises and the horror of Zadie's murder were never far from Levi's thoughts. He almost wished Cade would come so he could get his hands on him.

Pippa should be safe up at Dead Man's Hut. Cade had no way to track her there. But Levi remained worried, unable to shake a sense of unease. He'd had it on and off for days now as he moved around Brumby's Run – a feeling that he and Nullah weren't alone. He wished Duke was there. You couldn't fool dogs. Levi had gone so far as to search the outbuildings for intruders, but found nothing amiss. His imagination was playing tricks on him, that was it. He was letting this bizarre situation get to him. In a few more days the danger would pass. Drew would be home. Pippa could talk to her brother and then turn herself in as promised. That was the plan, but who was he kidding? His attempt to reassure himself sounded hollow. Things rarely went according to plan where Pippa was concerned.

Levi sighed and walked up to the stable to check on the new foal. It was doing better, on its feet and feeding while its mother nickered encouragement. Sam would be thrilled to see the colt's snowy mane, silver tail and honey-coloured coat. Her registered brumby stallion, Phoenix, had done it again. Brumby's Run was gaining a reputation for breeding quality palomino foals.

Phoenix was a lovely horse, no doubt about it, but he was a born-and-bred brumby, compact and sturdy, no more than fourteen-two hands high. Thowra, on the other hand, was descended from the famous Champagne Charlie who stood at almost sixteen hands. His mother was even taller, an elegant thoroughbred mare who traced her pedigree back to Carbine himself. Levi could see Thowra when he closed his eyes, rearing in defiance, framed against the sky. Beautifully bred, beautifully conformed and with a flawless golden coat. The vision left Levi weak with both excitement and dread. It would be a dream come true to own such a horse. It would break his heart to lose Thowra to a bullet.

The little colt collapsed back to the straw with a full tummy and milk dripping from the corner of his cream muzzle. Reena promptly set about licking her baby all over, occasionally glancing at Levi as if to say, 'I've got this. You can go.'

He finished checking the rest of the horses and returned to the house. He had a big day tomorrow. Three visiting mares had come into season. The stallions – Jarrang, Phoenix and Phantom – were all up for stud duties in the morning. Add to that several buyers coming to look at youngsters and a two-hour group campdraft lesson in the afternoon. He and Nullah would be busy all day – one of them at least should get an early night.

Levi went to bed, but sleep was beyond him. He missed Pippa. He was edgy and irritable, tired physically, but not mentally. Levi got up, made a cup of coffee and took it to the lounge room. He flipped through the latest *Australian Stock Horse Journal* with its motto, *The breed for every need*, emblazoned on the cover. September was the stallion feature edition. Usually Levi could lose himself in the news of what horse was standing where, and who'd won what championship or futurity. But tonight, even an article on equine artificial insemination breakthroughs couldn't distract him. Levi tossed the magazine onto the coffee table and went back to bed.

He lay staring at the bedroom ceiling. Fog crawled through the open window, deepening the gloom. He sniffed. A rat must have perished inside the wall and its faint, cloying odour lingered in the air. The smell of death was in his nose as sleep claimed him.

CHAPTER 32

Pippa lay in her bunk, watching dust motes drift in rays of morning light, loath to leave the warmth of her blankets. She'd honoured her promise to Levi: she hadn't camped last night above the yards. Instead, she'd spent a sleepless night in the hut. She hadn't sneaked out at midnight for a quick look, although she'd dearly wanted to, and she hadn't even risen at the crack of dawn and rushed out to check. She'd stayed snuggled under the covers with Duke instead until the sun was well and truly up. Not that it was easy to tell. A cloud still sat on the mountain, muting the sunshine to shades of grey.

The longer she put it off, the harder it was to face the likely disappointment. Pippa strained her ears as if she'd somehow be able to hear if horses were in the yards. But all she heard was the occasional magpie and a kookaburra chorus. The birds seemed to be laughing at her. Was Levi right? Had her presence above the yards that night scared the brumbies off for good?

The fire hadn't lasted. It was no more than a glowing bed of coals and the hut was freezing. Pippa had gone to bed fully clothed but still shivered when she threw back the blankets. She craved a cup of hot, sweet tea and set about rekindling the flames. It would have been quicker to heat the kettle on the butane camp stove, but rebuilding the fire served as meditation. A time to take stock.

Today was the first day of October; a new month and a new start. Pippa counted back the days in her mind. It had been two weeks since that momentous morning when Cade kidnapped her from their farm. A mere two weeks, and yet now she could wake up in the morning and not think about him first thing – after thinking about him first thing every morning for four years. Terrible, fearful thoughts that had cast a pall over every waking moment. But that was all over.

Her first thought that morning had been of Levi, of his copper-gold eyes, filled with honesty and kindness. Of his handsome face, square-jawed and strong, and with that adorable dimple. The character and strength shown on his face came from somewhere deep within him. It made her want to feel his lips move on her skin. It made her want to feel his hands follow the curves of her body. It made her flush with desire.

Her second thought had been of Thowra and his mob. Was it possible that Levi was wrong? That at this very minute, the brumbies were restlessly walking the stockyard rails, trapped by the stout five-bar gate, safe at last from those who would kill them?

The kettle boiled and she made her tea, sipping it slowly, making it last. It wouldn't be the end of the world if the horses hadn't come. She had three more nights to try. Pippa finished her tea and set the mug down on the table. No more putting it off. She pulled on Levi's coat, tied up Duke, grabbed the rifle and went outside.

An eerie mist blanketed the mountain, sucking green from the trees and blue from the sky, leaving everything a ghostly grey. The brumbies could be standing a few metres away from her and she'd never see them in this fog. Pippa rounded the corner of the hut and made her way surely to the yards. She didn't need to see far ahead. After five days of exploring, she knew the mountain well.

Pippa heard them before she saw them: soft whinnies and muffled hoof beats. And then, there they were – the elusive brumby stallion and his mob. The horses' shadowy figures shifted away, presenting her with a solid row of rumps ranged against the farthest rails. All except for Thowra.

Pippa held her breath as the horse moved towards her in a succession of small rears. No longer a golden stallion, his coat now shone like he'd been dipped in liquid silver, seeming to draw colour from the swirling mist. A magical horse dancing out of a dream.

'Hello, boy.'

She could see the Dandalong Station brand on his near shoulder – proof of his first-class heritage. Pippa stretched out her hand and advanced on the yard. The connection she'd always felt with the horse grew stronger with each step.

When she reached the rail Thowra arched his neck, then extended his muzzle to touch Pippa's hand – as gentle a gesture as she'd ever known. A charge of electricity passed between them. He was a wild stallion weighing half a tonne, and capable of all the ferocity that wildness implied, yet Pippa understood in that moment he posed no danger. He felt more like an old friend, and Pippa was sorely short of friends.

She climbed the fence, perched on the top rail and told Thowra her life story. He listened with twitching ears and the occasional nicker. She told him about how she was born loving horses. She told him about Pepper and her childhood on the farm. She told him about her stern father and her devoted but deferential mother. And she told him about Cade.

Something in Pippa's tone of voice must have changed when she talked of her husband, because Thowra became agitated, snorting and tossing his lovely head.

'Levi's not like Cade,' she said. 'He's the kindest man. He'll protect us both.'

Duke chose this moment to burst from the tea-tree, yelping excitedly and making a beeline for his mistress. The stallion's ears snapped backwards and he rolled his eyes. Pippa remembered Levi saying that the mob had been hunted by dogs. Thowra reared and rushed the fence, lunging for the kelpie at her feet.

Startled, Pippa lost her balance and toppled off the rail. She hit the ground, bundled Duke into her arms and rolled out of harm's way. Thowra raged on the other side of the fence, rearing and stamping, swishing his tail and baring his teeth – a truly terrifying sight. It was hard to believe he was the same horse who'd been calmly listening to Pippa's stories a few moments before. Only then did she think of Levi's warning: *If by some miracle you should catch the brumbies, don't go near them ... Wild animals can be dangerous, especially when they're trapped.*

Thowra swung around and slammed a double-barrelled kick into the gate, a kick so powerful that it made the earth shake. She could see now why Levi had reinforced the yards with steel panels. Thowra snorted in disgust and returned to his mares, melting into the mist.

Pippa gave Duke a baleful look. 'Thanks for that.' He whined an apology. She climbed to her feet, dusted herself off and retrieved her rifle. 'Come on, mate. We'll feed the horses and then feed ourselves breakfast, eh? After that I could use a nap. You might have snored all night, but I barely slept a wink.'

Pippa burped and shared the last of her toast with Duke. Delicious. Everything tasted better up here in the high country. She threw an extra log on the fire, then crawled into bed with a mug of hot tea. Duke curled up on a blanket by the fire, and Pippa watched him fondly. How she loved that dog. However, he had some serious rivals for her affection these days, and she wasn't just thinking about Levi. A neigh rang out from the yards, and a pang of missing Thowra hit her hard. She'd lost him and now she'd found him. She couldn't wait to tell Levi and get Thowra safely home to Brumby's Run.

Unexpected tears flooded Pippa's cheeks as her mother's smiling face came to her. Duke was by her side in an instant, licking her face. Pippa patted the dog absentmindedly. According to Levi, once Cade was behind bars she'd be able to clear her name. And then she'd be free to see her mother and siblings – free to put their minds at rest.

'I'm sorry, Mum,' she whispered, 'for putting you through this. But I'll make it up to you. Maybe even help you stand up to Dad.'

Pippa made herself a promise. In the past two weeks she'd gained an astonishing amount of confidence and courage. She'd love to see Mum make similar strides. During her time on the run, Pippa had spent a lot of time pondering her parents' relationship. Dad wasn't an evil man, not like Cade. He was bombastic and bossy and manipulative – used to having his own way. It wasn't hard with someone as amenable and uncomplaining as her mother. But Pippa knew her father, and believed that he'd mellow pretty quickly if challenged by the woman he loved. Mum was his rock. He relied on her to work tirelessly behind the scenes, supporting the hold he had on his congregation. He'd never jeopardise that. Her mother had a great deal of power in their marriage – she just didn't realise it. With some encouragement, Pippa was sure Mum could become more assertive.

Pippa finished her tea, stretched luxuriously and sighed with pleasure. The brumbies were safe and so was she – safe in the most beautiful place on earth. Thowra and his mob still had plenty of hay and water. She could sleep until lunchtime if she wanted to. She could do whatever she liked. Pippa's lids grew heavy and her mind drifted. So much to look forward to. Could life possibly get any better?

Cade woke with a crick in the neck, stiff limbs and a bladder fit to burst. It was still light outside. Good, that meant he hadn't slept for too long. But when he checked his phone, he realised his mistake. Dammit – it was the next day. He'd lain down in the back of the car yesterday and hadn't woken until seven o'clock this morning. What if Levi had headed back up to the hut overnight? That would throw a spanner in the works, but it wouldn't stop Cade. He intended to kill them both anyway. He'd simply prefer to have some time alone with his wife first. The last thing he needed was her jewboy Romeo getting in the way, trying to play the hero.

Cade opened his last can of Coke and gulped the entire contents, feeling strength return to his dehydrated muscles. He burped and tossed the can out the window. His hangover wasn't too bad, considering how much he'd drunk yesterday. Today he'd stick to water. He wanted a clear head when he found Pippa. His shoulder still hurt, but the pain had ebbed to a dull throb, and he felt more rested than he had in days. Cade found the esky, slapped some ham between slices of bread and set off, eating breakfast as he drove.

Cade's Land Rover bumped through the gateway leading to the stock route. Damn this fog. He could barely make out the track in front of him. It would make for a slow trip. Not that it mattered. He'd reach the hut sooner or later, and then ... A rush of adrenaline killed the pain in his shoulder and he suddenly felt like Superman. The prospect of coming face to face with his wife made him tremble with anticipation. He refused to countenance the idea that he wouldn't find her. Cade didn't care about what happened later. He only cared about dealing with Pippa and her boyfriend. Whether he got away afterwards or not was of no consequence. It was simpler to think that way.

Cade made his painstaking way uphill, one stretch of narrow rutted road at a time. He wasn't a man prone to imagining things, but sometimes monstrous forms seemed to loom out of the claustrophobic pall blanketing the mountain.

The track became more and more treacherous: punctuated with hairpin bends and washaways, hemmed in by trees. Often his progress slowed to a crawl. He cursed the fog, cursed the fringing forest, cursed the rocky earth itself. During some climbs his wheels spun so hard on the loose shale that he was sure his tyres would be ripped to shreds.

He passed a rickety sign reading *Balleroo National Park*. He was on track. As the morning wore on a gusty wind picked up. It occasionally cleared the fog, revealing incomparable views across the range. Then the whiteness came swirling back. Cade didn't appreciate the scenery. He and Dylan had often discussed the pointlessness of locking up vast tracts of productive land in national parks. When he saw virgin forests stretching to the horizon, all he saw was waste. 'Bloody greenies,' he muttered in disgust.

Cade came to a fork in the road and got out to look for tyre tracks. There they were, leading right. Intriguing to think who might have been behind the wheel. He drove for more than an hour, hemmed in by cloud, until a particularly strong gust of wind rattled his Land Rover and cleared the fog.

Ahead he could see another hand-painted sign: – *Hut 8 km* → His foot found the throttle with a mind of its own. Cade struggled to restrain himself from surging forward. That would be suicide. A serious washaway lay ahead, far more dangerous than any he'd encountered previously. He'd better get out and take a look before the cloud closed in again.

Half the track had collapsed, but there was probably room to squeeze past, as long as he stayed hard against the bank. Tyre tracks showed that another vehicle had successfully taken that same path within the last day or two. Cade walked to the edge of the road, trying to judge how solid the ground was. Stepping carefully to the brink, he peered over. What the hell? Below him, ten metres or so down the cliff, was a dark blue station wagon. *His* dark blue station wagon! The one that Pippa had stolen from him two weeks ago.

Cade shook his head in amazement and let the implications of his discovery sink in. Pippa must have been travelling this very road when the car was caught in a landslip. Had she been driving? Of course she had. He peered at the car more closely. It was wedged in trees and the front passenger door gaped open. He couldn't see a body in the car. Perhaps she'd tried to escape and instead plummeted down the escarpment. The cliff was so high that he couldn't see the bottom. It would have been a fatal fall.

The thought that Pippa might have escaped her final reckoning with him filled Cade with misery. He needed to see her again. He needed to talk to her, to make love to her one last time. And he needed to be the one to kill her. That right belonged to him, as her husband. It certainly didn't belong to this wild, indifferent mountainside.

No, he had to stay positive and believe that Pippa was alive. Finding the car was a blessing, confirming he was on the right track.

His wife was somewhere ahead, holed up in some damn hut. Cade had to admit he was impressed by her choice of hiding places, although it was probably her boyfriend's idea. Those high-country shacks were as remote as could be. If he hadn't explored Ruby's bedroom, he would never have found her. But then, Pippa had always underestimated him.

Cade glanced at the time – one o'clock. He'd be at the hut in time for lunch. Maybe he'd have Pippa rustle him up some tucker before the fun began. He started the car, hugged the bank and set off to find his wife.

CHAPTER 33

Duke's barking interrupted Pippa's dream. The noise dragged her from a heavy sleep, and for a few seconds she didn't know where she was, or why her pulse was racing so. A thud came from outside and Duke redoubled his barking. Not Levi. Duke never warned her about Levi. But it seemed inconceivable that Cade could be here in this peaceful place. Cade and Maroong Mountain did not compute. A wandering hiker perhaps, or a park ranger? But her gut told her otherwise.

Someone bashed at the door, sending Duke into a frenzy. It was bolted shut, but the timber jamb was full of woodworm. Pippa fumbled for her rifle, limbs clumsy with sleep. Too late. With a terrifying crash Cade burst inside, leaving the door swinging off one hinge. Pippa heard herself scream. She prayed this was a nightmare, prayed he wasn't real, but she could already smell the foul stink of him.

A bellow erupted from Cade's throat – a cry barely human. Halfway between a snarl and a roar, full of rage and madness. He reached her in a single bound. For a few seconds they played tug of war with the rifle, but Pippa didn't have a proper grip on it. He snatched it from her and delivered her a blow with the butt that rattled her teeth and made her ears ring.

Duke clamped his teeth onto Cade's leg. Cade howled with pain and turned on the furious dog. To Pippa's horror he pulled a pistol from his pocket and aimed it at Duke.

Cade's thin lips parted in a malicious smile. 'I should have finished you off years ago.'

'No, Duke,' she yelled. 'Leave off!'

Duke merely changed legs, but it was enough to throw Cade off balance. When he fired, the bullet whizzed past the dog's head. Duke yelped in fear and took off out the door.

Pippa exhaled. Cade was a crack shot. It was a miracle that he'd missed. Now that Duke was safe, she could think. And that's what she needed to do if she had any chance to survive this. Use her brain.

Cade snorted. 'I'll deal with him later.' He reached out to touch her cheek, an absurdly tender gesture. 'You look good, Pip, except for the hair. Did you miss me?'

She stayed silent, eyeing him like she'd eye a dangerous snake.

Cade slapped her face. 'I said, did you miss me?'

He wore a strange expression – half angry, half hopeful. Perhaps if she played along …

'I missed you as soon as I left,' she said. 'But I couldn't go back. You would have killed me.'

Her directness seemed to throw him off track. 'Maybe. Or maybe it was your boyfriend who didn't want you to go back?'

'Boyfriend?' Her blood ran cold.

'You know, the cowboy who stashed you up here. Or did your brother put you up to it? Clever plan, but not clever enough, eh?'

My God, he knew about Levi. He knew about Drew. Cade was right. Not clever enough by half. What a fool. Why had she ever thought she could get away from him? And now she'd put both Levi and her brother in terrible danger.

'I know about the bombing,' she said. 'You should have told me. Then I would have understood why we went on the run.' Pippa put a hand on his arm, even though her flesh crawled to touch him. 'Let's just jump in your car and head off down the mountain. Put all this behind us and make a fresh start somewhere.'

'You'd like that, would you?' His face twisted in a hideous grin. 'Where's your wedding ring?'

'I … I lost it,' she stammered, noting that Cade still wore his.

He pulled her to a standing position and delivered a blow to her stomach that left her doubled over.

'Stand up straight.' His voice was terrifyingly calm. 'Here, let me help you.'

He dragged Pippa upright by her hair. Needles of pain pierced her scalp and time stood still. Memories of a hundred similar scenes flared in her mind. She knew what was coming, and some all too familiar feelings began to take hold. First she'd find where she'd put her shell and retreat inside it. Then she'd dissolve in a puddle of fear, trembling and crying and begging him to stop – struggling to detach from the pain. She'd apologise for whatever misdemeanour she had or hadn't committed: undercooking the roast, forgetting to buy his cigarettes, visiting Mum without permission. And eventually he'd stop, always with one last kick to the kidneys. She'd slink off to lick her wounds until next time. That's how it normally went.

But there was nothing normal about what was happening here. Cade wouldn't stop this time. He was different: crazier, desperate, out of control. And she was different too. It took her a few moments to realise how exactly. And then it struck her – she wasn't afraid of him. She was scared of what he would do, scared of the pain, even scared that she might die. But she wasn't scared of Cade.

He yanked her head back and kissed her, forcing her lips open with his thrusting tongue. His mouth stank of cigarettes, stale whisky and unbrushed teeth.

Pippa endured the kiss and then, despite a surge of bile rising in her throat, she kissed him back, hugging him round his neck like she had when they'd first married. Cade grunted and his right shoulder flinched from the weight of her arm. Instinctively she pressed harder. He pulled away and, astonishingly, let her go.

The last few minutes played through Pippa's mind on fast forward, and certain details suddenly stood out. Cade was right-handed, yet he'd taken that potshot at Duke with his left hand. He'd wrestled the rifle away from her with his left hand. He stood a step away from her, anger unaccountably on pause, his right arm flexed in an unnatural way. A thrill of understanding ran through her. Cade was hurt. He had a weakness.

'Are you hungry?' she asked.

Cade burst out laughing, a strange, humourless sound. 'Aren't I always? What have you got for me? How about bacon, beans and eggs?'

For an absurd moment Pippa could have been back at the farm cooking breakfast for her husband. 'Bacon, beans and eggs it is.'

She studied him, keeping her tone deliberately light, though her mind was working furiously, and her mouth was so dry that she thought she'd choke. He seemed to have relaxed somewhat. Well why not? In his mind she was just where he wanted her, with the odds all in his favour. He was armed and she wasn't. Violence was his comfort zone, not hers. But Pippa had one big advantage, apart from his injured shoulder. Cade still knew her as his craven wife – she could tell by the contempt in his eyes. Her husband had no idea who he was dealing with.

Cade stepped closer. 'I missed you, Pip. You're my life, you know that, right?'

He kissed her again, more gently this time. Pippa yielded her lips, pressing her body against him in a sensuous curve. His body tensed momentarily, as if in confusion. How many years had it been since she'd responded to him like that? No wonder he was surprised.

'Hey, what's your game?' He shoved her away, a bewildered look on his hard face. 'Is that some trick Romeo taught you?'

She feigned a hurt look. 'Remember our honeymoon? Sex on the balcony overlooking the beach? I was so hot for you then ...'

Cade raised his left arm. It took all her strength not to cringe, but he didn't hit her. Instead he dragged his hand over his tangled hair. Then, quite slowly, Pippa undid the buttons of her shirt. 'It's hot in here with that fire, don't you think?' She wasn't wearing a bra.

Cade's expression changed from bewilderment to open hunger. He reached for her exposed breast and twisted the nipple painfully. She slapped his hand away in what she hoped was a playful way. 'Naughty boy. Now sit down. We'll eat first and make love for dessert.'

She held her breath, thinking on her feet, edging closer to the table where the bread knife lay under the newspaper. Pippa steeled herself, ready to fight if she had to. But to her utter astonishment, Cade sat down on the bunk, just as she'd told him to.

'I'll have my eggs sunny-side up,' he said, unable to take his eyes off her.

How extraordinary! During their entire marriage she'd never given Cade a single command – until now. Her husband's fascination with the new Pippa currently gave her the upper hand. But it wouldn't last. Cade was too vengeful, too full of hate. He wouldn't let her leave the hut alive.

Levi made a face and pushed his plate away. 'I'm done.'

Nullah pouted. 'Way to hurt a feller's feelings. I slaved over a hot stove for hours.'

Levi grinned. 'When I said we'd take turns making lunch during the week, I didn't mean stale Vegemite sandwiches. Where are your standards?'

Nullah shrugged. 'Fair enough, boss. I'll have medium-rare roast beef sangers and homemade lamingtons on Monday when it's your turn.'

Levi stood up, pushed back the kitchen chair and tossed the half-eaten sandwich at Nullah. 'Make us a cuppa, will you mate? I'll find us some fruit cake.'

The two friends sat on the front verandah finishing their lunch. The vantage point usually offered a stunning view of the Balleroo Ranges, but not today. The fog hemmed them in.

Nullah helped himself to his third slice of fruit cake. 'Did that bloke get back to you about a horse for his wife?'

'What bloke?'

'Tall feller with a scruffy beard. A little wild looking. Came by late Wednesday arvo.'

'Did this bloke have a name?'

'Didn't say. He wanted to know if we had any female trainers here at Brumby's Run. Said he thought women had a gentler way with horses.'

A worm of concern turned in Levi's stomach. 'What did you tell him?'

'That we did have a girl, but she left last week. I'm surprised he hasn't been in touch. That man was deadset keen to talk to you. When I said you wouldn't be back till Thursday, he wanted to go find you then and there. But I said his little car would never make it up to the hut, and the road was closed anyway.'

The worm turned into an eel slithering inside him. 'Something's come up,' said Levi. 'I'm taking an early Friday knock off.'

Nullah snorted with laughter. 'You mean something's come up between now and your last slice of fruit cake?'

'You got it.' Levi grabbed his hat from a hook by the door.

'No way, mate.' Nullah looked bewildered. 'Brandy's back in season and she's going home on Sunday. You said yourself if we don't get her served, we'll lose the stud fee. I don't fancy introducing Phantom to a mare without you there to hold him.'

Levi thought about letting Nullah in on his fears. No, he'd promised Pippa to keep her secret until Drew came back, and he was probably worrying about nothing. It was uncommon for buyers to want horses trained by women, but not unheard of. Still, he'd rather be sure than sorry. His gut told him to go, and his gut didn't lie. 'It can't be helped,' said Levi. 'This can't wait.'

Nullah narrowed his eyes in a searching look. 'If you say so, boss.' He did not sound convinced. 'Where will you be? Tell me that at least.'

Levi stared into the enveloping cloud. 'Dead Man's Hut.'

Surreal, seeing Cade sitting across from her in that previously safe space – like the troll she used to imagine hiding under her bed when she was little. Except this monster was real. The sight of him unnerved her so much that she couldn't think straight. And she had to think straight, had to turn the tables on Cade before … No, she refused to go there. Cade would not win this time.

She slipped the bread knife from under the newspaper. There was no hiding it. Cade's eyes were on her like a hunting hawk's. He stiffened, his jaw set in a cruel line. The longer she could normalise things, the better. This calm before the storm could end at any time.

Pippa offered the knife to him with a smile, handle first. She pointed to the loaf. 'Cut us a few slices, hun. And can you toast them for me? There are green sticks by the fire.'

Her luck held. Cade cracked his knuckles, then took the knife and visibly relaxed as he ran a finger along its blade. He began slicing the bread, casting distracted glances her way as Pippa's open shirt revealed the occasional glimpse of breast.

Pippa lit the camp stove, poured a generous amount of canola oil into the cast iron skillet and added eggs, bacon, beans and thick slabs of tomato – the thicker the better. Then she frowned and sloshed in some more oil. Cade nodded approval. He always liked his food drowned in fat. Minutes passed in silence. The food began to sizzle and spit in the pan as Cade crouched by the fire.

Pippa could feel the throb of her own heartbeat. 'How's that toast going?'

Cade turned to show off a golden-brown slice of bread on a stick. 'Got any booze to go with—'

Pippa smashed the upturned pan over his head. Boiling oil scalded his face and neck. She was momentarily frozen by the horror of what she'd done.

Cade clasped his face and a bestial scream of pain and rage escaped him. He lunged for her, and Pippa came to her senses. She raised the heavy skillet above her head with both hands and brought it down with crushing force on Cade's right shoulder. He howled, losing his balance and hitting the floor. She kicked his shoulder, laying her boot in so hard that it made her gasp with the effort. All the while his left arm roamed around with a clutching hand, blindly searching for her.

Pippa stomped on his fingers with the heel of her boot.

'You bloody bitch!' yelled Cade, his left eye swollen shut. Stumbling to his feet, he grabbed for the pistol at his belt.

But he wasn't quick enough, wasn't used to using his left hand, wasn't used to seeing with only one eye. Pippa shoved him backwards and swept her leg behind his ankles as Levi had taught her. Cade crashed back to the floor. With trembling fingers she plucked the pistol from him and bolted out the door.

Pippa escaped into a swirling, protective cloud, half-laughing and half-crying. She'd done it – she'd defeated Cade. Pippa knew the mountain well and Cade was no bushman. He could hunt her for days without success, especially in this fog. Once she found Duke she'd head up into the forest to put as much distance between herself and Cade as possible.

Pippa didn't dare call for the dog. Cade would hear. She covered her ears as he roared out her name and what he intended to do when he caught her – a string of the most dire threats any person could imagine. Any normal person, that was. She knew Cade too well. He meant every one of those threats and he was just getting started.

Pippa wasn't too worried about Duke. If she didn't find him, he'd find her, though it might take him some time to calm down. Duke was especially scared of guns after having been winged as a pup when Cade and his mates were hunting rabbits. Pippa suspected that someone had shot at the dog deliberately. Since then Duke always took off at the sound of gunfire.

Cade's screaming stopped and Pippa moved a little higher up the hill. It was more unsettling now that he'd gone quiet. At least before she'd had a rough idea of where he was. Every instinct told her to run up the mountain and keep running, but she had to stay close to the hut so that Duke could find her. If Cade found him first? Well, it didn't bear thinking about. She strained her ears, hoping to hear a welcoming whine, willing the dog to come bounding out of the fog. But there was no sign of him.

Time passed, maybe an hour, maybe more. As the adrenaline waned, Pippa began to hurt. Her tongue explored her mouth and there was a metallic taste on the inside of her bruised cheek. She felt dried blood on her temple where he'd struck her with the butt of her own rifle. Her stomach ached. She ran a finger down the barrel of Cade's pistol, felt the weight of cold steel in her hand. She'd kill him if she had to.

Twice Pippa heard the sounds of Cade moving through the bush: twigs cracking, leaves rustling and faint footfalls. She retreated into a thicket of sheltering snow gums, their twisted branches like enfolding, protective arms. Pippa stamped her feet impatiently, rubbing her hands together to keep them warm. A gusty wind was clearing the cloud and she wanted to get going up the mountain. She didn't fancy being anywhere near the hut when the fog lifted. Where the hell was Duke?

A neigh rang out, then the sound of Cade shouting. Pippa's fear took a horrifying new turn. Thowra and the mares. Cade didn't like horses. If he wanted to hurt them, the mob was at his mercy. Nightmarish thoughts tumbled in. She was a fool. It wasn't just her who was in danger.

What would happen when Levi arrived at the hut on Monday? His handsome face swam into vision, his warm smile and kind, copper-brown eyes. Levi loved her. He'd shown her who she could be, helped her reclaim her life. A silent wail came from deep inside and echoed around her brain. She knew all too well what would happen if Cade confronted him. Levi's death would be on her head.

Cade shouted again, calling her name. Pippa looked down at the pistol. She was clutching it so tightly that her hand ached. What had she been thinking? She hadn't defeated Cade, far from it, and hiding out here in the bush like a scared rabbit wasn't a plan. It was a cowardly act, based on the primal instinct for self-preservation, nothing more. It left Cade free to visit whatever atrocities he wanted upon those she loved. Levi. The brumbies. And what about her family? She wouldn't put anything past Cade, especially if he failed to exact the vengeance that he craved. His anger would know no bounds.

Pippa felt her teeth grind together. Never mind his anger. What about hers? She'd buried it for so long, but now the rage was rising, turning her mouth to sawdust and making the blood pound in her temples. Stupid, lazy, cold-blooded Cade, whose callous violence had killed her unborn child, and almost killed her as well. Being married to him was a kind of living death. Pippa imagined Cade standing before her. The hairs on the back of her neck stood up, like the hackles on a fierce dog. She raised the gun and aimed at where his heart would be – if he had a heart. 'Bang.'

The cloud was clearing fast. Colour was returning to the washed-out world as she made her way down the mountain towards the hut. It was further than she thought. Pippa hadn't realised how far her fear had taken her.

She stopped within the forest margin at a place with a view of the yards. There he was, wandering around with a bottle in his right hand and a rifle held awkwardly in his left. Pippa smiled in grim satisfaction. Cade would never normally hold a gun that way. It meant his right shoulder still pained him. And if he was getting drunk, so much the better.

Pippa examined the pistol – a .38 revolver. She'd never handled one before, but had read about them while browsing through Cade's extensive gun magazine collection. The firearm seemed pretty straightforward. There didn't seem to be a safety device, so she was super careful about opening the cylinder lock and checking the chamber. Five bullets. That would do.

Pippa looked for Cade. He was straying close to the yards. She took a deep breath as Thowra tossed his head and laid back his ears, but Cade ignored him. He swigged from the bottle and looked up the mountainside, yelling her name. It seemed his fixation on her was working in the brumbies' favour – for now.

Duke chose that moment to bound from the bushes, wagging his tail and whining with excitement. Pippa crouched down and clasped her hand over his muzzle. 'I'm glad to see you too,' she whispered, hugging his neck and kissing his nose. 'But shush now, okay?'

Pippa glanced at Cade. He stood staring in her direction. Dammit, he'd heard them. Cade started up the hill.

She gestured for Duke to follow her. They needed to move, and fast. Pippa took a few steps, then stopped. She turned to aim the gun at Cade. She was a good shot, and he wasn't more than a hundred metres away. Well within range. Her trigger finger stiffened.

Duke whined softly, releasing Pippa from her trance. She didn't intend to kill Cade. Her plan was to capture him and bring him to justice, have him betray his murderous terrorist gang to the authorities and bring them all down.

But however thrilled she was at the prospect, it would take some doing, especially now that Duke was back. How could she ambush Cade with Duke trailing after her, barking and whining – inevitably giving her away? She had to have the most vocal dog on earth.

As Pippa racked her brains for a solution, her gaze landed on the small hay shed behind the hut. If she could get to it without being seen, she could use baling twine to tie Duke up safely out of the way.

She could even fashion a makeshift muzzle from the same material to stop him barking.

She melted into the trees, moving downhill in a wide arc, heading for the creek. Using its tree-ferned banks as cover, she managed to get close to the hut. Then one well-timed dash across the clearing brought her to the hay shed. Cade had undoubtedly searched there already, and wouldn't expect her to double back into danger. She barely believed it herself.

Pippa finished knotting Duke's new muzzle and fitted it over the outraged dog's head. Then she attached twine to his collar and triple-tied it to the shed wall. Duke lay down in the hay looking thoroughly miserable.

'It's for your own good,' she whispered. 'Now, for once in your life – stay!'

She stood back to assess her handiwork. Duke's snout was firmly trussed. He'd have trouble barking or howling, but he'd still be able to whine. Pippa hoped he'd be feeling too sorry for himself to complain. She sighed and tried not to lose heart. She'd done her best, and Duke was a lot safer hidden here behind the bales than running around outside with Cade taking pot shots at him.

The fog had lifted, and patches of blue showed through the cloudy sky. A family of magpies carolled a welcome to the sun. Pippa could hear Cade swearing and crashing around up the hill, near to the place where Duke had found her. She had time; she could do this.

Pippa steeled herself, then broke cover and raced for Cade's car to look for his keys. If worst came to worst she could release the horses, grab Duke and drive away. She reached the Land Rover, opened the driver's door quietly, and glanced at the ignition. Damn, they weren't there.' If only she knew how to hot-wire a car. One of Cade's many skills, no doubt. She couldn't believe how naive she'd once been, thinking that Cade wasn't a criminal. But then she'd been wrong about so many things.

She softly shut the car door. What now? Try the hut. The keys could be there. She ran inside and searched the obvious places: table, bunk, by the fireplace. Nothing. But her rifle was there. Operating on the assumption that two guns were better than one, Pippa jammed the pistol into the pocket of her jeans, grabbed the rifle and checked that it was loaded.

Up until now she'd only ever seen guns as a practical tool; useful for humanely putting down stock or for harvesting rabbits to supplement the table. But she was starting to realise why Cade liked firearms so much. The sense of power and confidence they gave her in this situation was exhilarating. She was as well armed as a commando. But she couldn't use two guns at once, so she hid the rifle in the woodpile on the porch. The pistol would be more useful in a close encounter.

Pippa ducked behind the water tank when she saw Cade making his way downhill. There was something odd about his gait – halting and hesitant. Suddenly he tripped, fell to his knees and dropped his rifle. Why didn't he pick it up? He was swearing and groping around with his left hand, peering down. He only retrieved it when it was right under his nose. And then she realised – Cade was nearly blind. She could barely restrain herself from laughing out loud.

Cade was slowly heading towards the creek, perhaps to bathe his burnt face. Pippa dared to test her theory. She stepped out from behind the tank, raised her pistol and made her cautious way towards him. Cade took absolutely no notice. She could shoot him right now and he wouldn't even see it coming.

Pippa moved nearer, near enough to see his scalded face with blisters erupting over splotchy red skin. His left eye was closed completely. His right eye was buried in an inflamed mass of weeping tissue. He could see with it, but only just.

How did the old saying go? The best defence is offence. She circled, closing in. Her foot kicked a stone, and she froze. Cade froze too, swinging his head to and fro like a radar dish. Then he shuffled forward, using the rifle to prod the ground ahead of him like a blind man with a cane.

Pippa followed him until he reached the creek. Then she crept up close behind him, her pulse racing, ready to smash his injured shoulder with the pistol and snatch his weapon. Thrilled and terrified all at once.

Maybe she was overconfident. Maybe he heard her heart pounding out of her chest, but for whatever reason her plan failed. Cade swung round and struck her with the rifle before she'd even raised her arm. Then she was fighting for her life.

Cade may have been injured, but he was tall and powerful and fuelled by a manic intensity. Pippa didn't have room to attack his injured shoulder, or even poke him in the eyes. He hugged her arms close, trying to wrestle the pistol from her grasp.

Strange, how life could turn in an instant. Pippa twisted and squirmed, struggling to gain control, but it was no use. He had her, and now he'd made her drop the gun into the creek. It was over. Pippa closed her eyes and braced herself for what was to come. She just hoped Cade wouldn't drag it out for too long.

And then, miraculously, she was free. Pippa's joy turned to horror as she saw why he'd let her go – Duke. The dog's teeth were clamped onto Cade's leg.

Cade roared with rage and clubbed the dog with his rifle. The force of the blow sent Duke flying into the air. He landed in a patch of reeds and lay still.

'No!' screamed Pippa, her heart breaking.

Cade lunged for her. She dodged and sprinted away, cursing herself, her vision cloudy with tears. If she'd shot Cade when she had the chance, Duke would still be alive. Pippa raced for the woodpile on the hut's back porch. She wouldn't make the same mistake twice.

Pippa glanced back. He was coming after her across the clearing with his rifle raised. It cracked, then cracked again and suddenly her knees collapsed under her. What a time to lose her balance! But when Pippa tried to stand, she couldn't. Her left leg wouldn't bear her weight. Then she saw the blood, and a searing pain kicked in, like a red-hot poker spearing her thigh. Cade had hit her with a lucky shot and all she could do was crawl.

Pippa's tears were no longer just for Duke. They were for herself as well. Tears of grief for the life she might have had. Tears of anger, guilt and despair. Even with limited sight Cade would find her eventually. Duke had sacrificed himself for nothing. Damn Cade Black!

Waves of pain broke over her. Pippa vomited. She watched the blood seep from her thigh, staining the snowgrass red. But it didn't spray in time with her heartbeat. The bullet hadn't severed an artery. With a sudden surge of determination, she took off her shirt and ripped it into strips. She tied them around her injured thigh to stem the bleeding. Why make this easy for Cade? She wouldn't be able to reach the woodpile for the second rifle now, but perhaps she could drag herself to the closest cover and hide. If he was going to kill her, she would damn well make him work for it.

Cade was lurching in her direction, stopping every few metres to peer around with his half-open eye. He looked like the monster he was. Maybe she could crawl along the yards and hide in the hay shed.

Pippa raised herself on all threes and tried to move. Her leg hurt – a lot. Every shift of position was an agony. After five minutes she'd only moved a few metres nearer to the yards, and Cade was getting closer. She stopped to rest, dismayed at how weak she was. Her leg had started bleeding again. Reaching the hay shed was seeming more and more impossible.

Thowra was watching her with a singular intensity. In her grief over Duke, Pippa hadn't considered the brumbies' plight. It was only Friday. How would they manage until Monday without her there to provide feed and water? It would be an ordeal for them. She could see their trough was already empty. At the very least the mares' milk would dry up, and an injured Cade was likely to take out his frustrations on any living things within his power.

Pippa made up her mind. She'd caused Duke's death and was resigned to her own. She couldn't let Cade harm the horses as well. Her last task would be to release them. Taking their chance with the brumby hunters was preferable to being sitting ducks for Cade.

'I'm sorry, Levi,' she whispered, as she dragged herself closer and closer to the slip rails. 'You did so much for me and all I've done is let you down.' She consoled herself with the thought that there'd be nothing to keep Cade at the hut once she was dead. Levi should be safe enough when he returned on Monday, and he'd be better off without her anyway.

Pippa moved in slow motion. It seemed to take forever, but finally she was almost at the gateway. Cade paused a mere ten metres away, turning his head to and fro. He was moving inexorably towards the yards and his eye looked a little more open. Thowra sensed that something was up. He paced the fence, arched neck damp with sweat, watching Pippa draw nearer and nearer. She still felt their connection, felt Thowra silently urging her on. How magnificent he was. If the golden stallion was the last thing Pippa ever saw, she'd die happy.

Thowra stood at the slip rails and nickered loudly, nostrils flared and eyes wide. The mares answered with whinnies of their own. She willed him to be quiet, but Cade heard. He moved towards the yards, stepping faster and more confidently than before. The bastard thought he had her.

Pippa crawled faster too, closing her mind to the pain, determined to accomplish this final thing. She reached the gateway and yanked the bottom sliprail out of its wire loop – first one end, then the other. The rail dropped to the earth, clouting her injured leg as it fell. She grunted involuntarily as a river of agony shot through her thigh. Fresh blood flooded her leg and soaked her filthy, makeshift bandages.

Cade was moving up on her quickly, now. Pippa hauled herself upright by using the gatepost. She tried to take down the top sliprail, but it was heavy – and then Cade was right there, glaring at her with his one mad eye. Time seemed to stop. Pippa had always loved the stories from the old *Myths of Greece and Rome* book that lived in her parents' hall. She'd scared herself silly when reading about the Cyclopes – an uncivilised race of murderous one-eyed brutes. She'd thought the stories weren't real. She'd been wrong.

Wearily she turned from him and tried to crawl beneath the top rail. Thowra stamped and reared on the other side, but Pippa wasn't frightened. Compared to what was behind her, the stallion seemed like a familiar friend. Cade seized her, hauled her back and slammed her into the gatepost. The dizzying burst of pain seemed to come from somewhere far away. Idly she wondered if her ribs were broken. Cade pinned her against the post, mauling her bare breasts and fumbling with the buttons of her jeans. In order to attack her he'd dropped the rifle. She should fight back, target his injured shoulder and face, but she was so very weak and it didn't seem to matter any more.

A menacing growl cut through Pippa's confused thinking. Duke! The dog launched himself at Cade with savage power, seizing him by the leg. The surprise assault caught Cade completely off guard. He stumbled and Pippa saw her chance. She jammed her thumbs into his eyes and clawed with all her strength.

Cade let out an inhuman howl. Lurching backwards, he tripped over Duke and fell heavily. Duke renewed his attack, tearing though Cade's jeans and ripping into the flesh of his calf. Cade screamed. He felt around for something to defend himself with and his hand chanced on a thick stick. He waved it around wildly and tried to drag himself away. Pippa's eyes widened in amazement. In his blind desperation to escape the dog's slashing teeth, Cade had crawled under the sliprail into the brumbies' yard.

Duke started to follow him. 'Leave off,' said Pippa, before slumping to the ground. Duke limped over, whining and wagging his tail. She hugged him, wondering if she was dreaming, mesmerised by the scene playing out before her.

Cade lay huddled inside the yard, stick in hand, curled into a fetal position. Did he know where he was? Pippa doubted it. He moaned and dabbed at his blistered face with a tentative hand, his bleeding eyes squeezed shut. The horses stood bunched together along the farthest fence, refusing to face the commotion unfolding behind them – all except Thowra.

The stallion stood at attention a few metres from the man, tension evident in every line of his shining body. Cade raised himself onto one elbow. 'Pippa,' he called in a strangled voice. 'I can't see. Help me, babe!'

Was he kidding? But then the Pippa Black he knew might indeed have helped him. How often had the old Pippa escaped from a beating only to cook his dinner or wash his clothes?

Thowra tossed his head at the sound of Cade's voice and laid back his ears. He circled Cade in a slow, high-stepping walk, as if making up his mind about something. A curious foal detached itself from the herd, walked up to the man and nuzzled his hair.

Cade swore and exploded into action, landing a vicious blow on the foal's nose with his stick. The little colt bolted for his mother and Thowra made his decision. With a soft snort he approached the intruder in a series of half-rears.

'Who's there?' called Cade.

Thowra answered the question with a loud, trumpeting neigh. Cade's blotchy face blanched with fear. He could be in no doubt now of the danger confronting him. Scrambling to his feet, he roared out a challenge. 'Where are you, you bastard?'

Cade swung his stick blindly. The stallion bared his teeth, stamped a contemptuous forefoot and snaked out his neck with lightning speed. Pippa watched in horrified fascination as Thowra seized Cade by his injured shoulder. He shook the man like a terrier with a rat, then dropped him to the ground. Cade shrieked and tried to stand, but Thowra had other ideas. He struck Cade with a foreleg, leaving him screaming and squirming. Then Thowra reared high and brought his iron-hard hooves down on Cade's skull.

The screaming stopped. Pippa's stomach turned over. She trembled with horror, and cried with astonishment and relief. Duke was alive. Thowra was safe. The man who'd terrorised her for years was nothing more than a crumpled heap of filthy clothing lying in a patch of bloodstained mud.

Duke licked her face. 'You saved my life,' she whispered, stroking the dog's ears the way he liked.

Thowra nickered and trotted to the fence, as if to say, 'What about me?'

Pippa smiled. 'You saved my life too. You and Duke are my heroes.'

Thowra seemed satisfied. With a final toss of the head he returned to guard his herd.

Pippa took a cursory look at her injured thigh. It still hurt like hell, but it looked like the bleeding had stopped. She should get up to feed and water the brumbies. She should examine Duke's sore leg. He was limping badly and for all she knew it might be broken. She should search Cade's body for the car keys. Duke would need to visit the vet. But each breath hurt and she was getting awfully sleepy. Cold was creeping deep into her bones, and she could barely keep her eyes open. She hugged Duke to her. He was so warm, just like the hot water bottles Mum used to give her on winter nights. Maybe she'd just …

Pippa lapsed into blissful unconsciousness.

CHAPTER 35

An icicle formed in Levi's stomach as he rounded the final bend in the track. An unfamiliar Land Rover was parked at the hut. It could belong to out-of-season hunters. It could belong to four-wheel drive enthusiasts who hadn't realised the track was closed. Or it could belong to Cade Black.

Levi grabbed his rifle from the front seat and cautiously climbed from the car. Should he call for Pippa? No, he didn't want to squander the element of surprise. The hut door hung open. Why would Pippa leave it that way on such a chilly day? As he drew nearer he realised something ominous. The front door wasn't just open. It swung off one hinge.

Levi edged inside. The fire was almost out. An oily mess of bacon, beans and eggs lay strewn over the floor beside the upturned cast-iron skillet, and a packet of cigarettes sat on the table. Levi blinked at them stupidly. Winfield Blues. Where the hell was Pippa?

Levi ran his tongue over lips that felt like sandpaper. He glanced at the bunk. Her rifle was missing from its place beside it. That could be good, or it could be bad. He raised his own rifle. Time to find out.

Levi crept out the back door and froze. Horses milled about in the yard beside the hay shed. Not just any horses – Thowra's mob. He

"

recognised the piebald mare with her chestnut filly. The creamy mare and her palomino colt. A shock of joy coursed through him. Pippa had done it; she'd damn well done it!

Thowra stalked from the mob and stood staring at Levi, pawing and snorting. The horse was even more beautiful than he remembered, but his golden coat was dark with sweat and his pale forelegs were stained red with blood. He'd been hurt somehow. Levi approached the yard with calm, deliberate steps. He'd never forgive himself if his capture plan had caused Thowra to be injured.

A dog whined. Duke? Levi turned towards the sound. Pippa lay slumped by the gatepost, naked above the waist. A rifle lay on the ground nearby. Her shirt had been torn into strips and wrapped around her filthy, bloodstained thigh. Duke lay beside her, clutched tightly in her arms. Levi cast a horrified glance from Pippa to Thowra and back again. Her face was battered, and her breasts were scratched and bruised. Had the stallion done this? Levi took a final look around for Cade, then ran to the collapsed girl.

'Pippa – Pip, can you hear me?' No response. Levi pressed two fingers to her neck and let out a deep breath. She had a pulse, but her skin was icy. 'Pippa.' He gently shook her shoulders. 'Pip, wake up!'

She stirred, then opened her eyes. 'It's you.' Her smile was ghostly white.

'Tell me what happened.'

She pointed to the yard and Levi's heart broke.

'Come on.' He slung his rifle round his shoulder, then scooped Pippa into his arms and carried her to the hut.

She wrapped her arms around his neck and murmured in a drowsy voice. 'Well-aimed thumb jabs to the eyes can temporarily or even permanently incapacitate an attacker.'

What was she talking about? 'Hush now – save your strength.'

'It's what you told me,' she whispered. 'And I did it too. After that Cade couldn't see at all.'

'Cade?' Levi tensed and quickened his pace. 'So Cade's here?'

Pippa gazed up at him, eyes like clear blue pools. 'In a way.'

What was that supposed to mean? There was that wan smile again.

He stared at her bloodied, swollen face. What in the world did she have to smile about?

Levi laid her on the bunk under a pile of blankets. 'Wait here.' The advice was moot. She was already asleep – or unconscious. She needed medical attention, but he couldn't afford to be ambushed by Cade on the way to the car.

He stepped outside and circled the hut with his rifle raised. No sign of anyone. It didn't make any sense. According to Pippa, Cade was a jealous, violent man, determined to track her down and kill her. So if he was here, why didn't he show himself? Maybe the four-wheel drive and cigarettes had an innocent explanation, and the spilled food likewise. Pippa was injured, dazed and rambling. She was also terrified of her husband and could easily have imagined him in her confusion.

As he turned to go inside, Duke came limping towards him on three legs. Had Thowra attacked him too? Levi knew the stallion hated dogs. Perhaps Pippa had gone into the yard to rescue Duke and been attacked herself. Tears welled up as Levi realised the heavy responsibility that lay ahead of him.

He picked up the kelpie and was about to put him in the car when he remembered the rifle lying near the yards. Pippa must have dropped it. Levi couldn't leave a loaded firearm lying around, especially if Cade was somewhere near. He carried Duke to the hut and tucked him in beside his sleeping mistress. 'Keep her warm,' he whispered.

Levi averted his eyes as he approached the yards, trying not to look at the brumbies. Thowra wouldn't have it. He cantered to the fence and demanded acknowledgement, his wild neigh ringing round the ranges. A surge of energy seemed to pulse between them, and Levi wondered if shooting the stallion was beyond him. Maybe he should simply release the horses, let them take their chances with the government shooters and brumby hunters. At least Thowra would have a chance that way, and who would know?

But he couldn't cast the image of Pippa's battered body from his mind. She could have died. She almost certainly would have if he hadn't found her. Hypothermia and blood loss were a deadly combination. Levi knew how dangerous stallions could be. He'd once worked at a breeding farm where a stud stallion had attacked a boy mucking out his box. The horse had seized the stable hand by the back of the neck, hurled him to the straw and knelt on him, breaking five ribs and puncturing his lung. The boy had barely survived. Levi couldn't in good conscience allow Thowra to be caught by someone else and inflict that sort of damage. He made up his mind. After Pippa was safely in hospital, he'd return to the hut and deal with the golden stallion himself. At least he'd be sure to carry out the grim task humanely and with respect. Thowra deserved that.

Levi retrieved the rifle lying by the gate, then paused to take a second look. Wait, it wasn't Pippa's weapon. Hers was an old Remington .22. The rifle he held in his hands was longer, heavier and of a higher calibre – a .303 at least.

Levi glanced warily around him, then examined the ground where he'd found Pippa. The springy snowgrass didn't hold footprints, but it revealed something else – a gory trail leading away from the yards. He followed it across the clearing. The trail grew bloodier as it went, then ended abruptly in a slurry of disturbed soil and pink mud. Levi spent a few moments making sense of what he saw. There was no other explanation. This was the place where Pippa had sustained her bleeding leg injury – not up at the yards.

Thowra wasn't responsible for the attack on Pippa after all. But someone was. What on earth had happened here? Levi checked that the rifle was loaded and ran for the hut.

Pippa was still asleep, cold but not freezing thanks to Duke's warm body, and with a little more colour to her pallid skin. He gently shook her awake, gave her a few sips of water and asked the question.

Levi gazed at what had once been Cade Black. No wonder he hadn't noticed the man earlier. His trampled body buzzed with flies like a big pile of manure and was the same dull brown colour as the ground. Levi entered the yard, ducking under the sliprail. The bottom rail had been dislodged somehow, so he slid it back into position to stop the foals escaping.

He stood looking down at Cade. The bloodied corpse was a terrible sight. What remained of the man's face was hideously disfigured and his skull was crushed. Levi stared at the stallion while Pippa's words echoed through his brain.

'Thowra?' she'd said, wonderingly. 'Of course he didn't hurt me. He saved me.'

That was apparently so. Levi was struggling to comprehend Cade's sheer brutality. He'd murdered Zadie, then tracked his wife down and shot her. He would have murdered Pippa too, if not for her courage and defiance. Oh … and a little help from her friends.

There was no doubt that Cade roundly deserved to die, but it still made Thowra a man killer. Not everyone might understand how justified the stallion's attack had been. Once the police found out, they'd swarm this place. He and Pippa had better get their stories straight.

When Levi returned to the hut, Pippa was sitting up with a blanket wrapped around her, propped up by pillows and her sleeping bag. He made cups of coffee with lots of sugar on the camp stove and watched her wrap her long, slim fingers around the warm mug.

She stroked Duke's ears, causing him to whine with pleasure. 'Cade knocked Duke out with his rifle. I thought he was dead. His front leg might be broken.'

Levi pushed back the blankets and gently probed the leg. Duke wagged his tail and put up with the examination. 'I think badly sprained, not fractured, but he'll need an x-ray to be sure. So will you for that matter, to make sure there's no bullet in your leg, Either way, you'll both be out of commission for quite a while.'

Pippa crooned some soothing words and hugged the happy dog. 'Can you believe how brave Duke was? He was on three legs when he attacked Cade the second time, and he's terrified of guns. I said that

Thowra saved me, but it was Duke too. He grabbed Cade's leg, I jabbed his eyes and Thowra finished him off.'

Levi looked with wonder and admiration at the skinny young woman lying on the bunk, as if seeing her for the first time. 'Sounds like you guys were quite a team.'

Pippa's swollen face split into the proudest of grins.

Levi held up his hand. 'That said, it will be safer for people to believe that Cade was accidentally trampled by the mob, rather than deliberately attacked by Thowra.'

Pippa seemed confused. 'Surely nobody could blame Thowra after what Cade did?'

Levi sighed. It was time he told her a story. 'You know Whirlwind, that big dapple-grey in the broodmare paddock with a dark foal?'

'You mean Mist's dam?'

'That's right. Years ago, she spent a few weeks as a saddle bronc. They named her The Demon and not one man made his eight-second ride on her. She was the star of the show.'

Pippa shook her head. 'Not sweet Whirlwind?'

'She wasn't so sweet back then. Wild-caught off Maroong Mountain and thrown straight into the rodeo circuit. It was enough to send a high-spirited mare like her a little mad. One day she threw a rough-as-guts cowboy named Rowdy Clarke, and then she turned on him. Stamped his skull in according to all accounts, a bit like Thowra did to Cade. It put Whirlwind on death row.'

'So ... how come she's eating her head off back at Brumby's Run with a gorgeous new filly foal at foot?'

'Your brother.' Levi leaned in close as if someone else might be listening. 'Drew stole that mare from the showgrounds the night before they planned to shoot her, hid her out at Brumby's Run and altered her brand. The Demon became Whirlwind, with a new career in dressage. Sam went on to win some serious titles with her.'

Pippa was delighted with the story. 'Bravo, Drew. I love my brother already.'

Levi smiled. 'Yes, I thought you'd approve. But it shows how seriously they take dangerous horses around here. You don't want to put Thowra at risk, do you?'

Pippa shook her head, looking horrified.

'Right, let's get you to a doctor. It will be a bumpy ride, I'm afraid.' He found some Panadol on a shelf. 'It won't help much, but it's better than nothing.'

'You'll have to feed and water the brumbies first. And throw me a shirt from my bag, will you? I don't want the police to take me to jail half-naked.'

'For the last time, you won't go to jail,' he said. 'After what happened here, they're more likely to give you a medal!'

CHAPTER 36

To Pippa's utter astonishment Levi was right. Well, not about the medal, but about the police believing her story. They interviewed her at Albury Base Hospital on the following afternoon. It wasn't quite the ordeal that she'd imagined. Two detectives – a rather formal middle-aged woman and a pleasant young man – asked her questions for half an hour before taking her statement. She told them about being kidnapped by Cade, escaping from the motel and how she came to be at Dead Man's Hut.

'That place has earned its name, then,' joked the male detective.

His half smile quickly faded when his senior colleague shot him a filthy look. 'You should have come to us right from the start,' she said to Pippa. 'We could have protected you from Black and saved ourselves a hell of a lot of investigative hours at the same time.'

'I truly am sorry. I was scared.'

She patted Pippa's hand. 'Well, at least you had the decency to call Crime Stoppers. That lead was gold. We'd like to interview you again in the next few days, once you're feeling better.'

'About the bombing?'

'Specifically about the morning after. We want to trace your husband's movements, and those of Dylan Moore.' She must have sensed Pippa's apprehension. 'Relax, you're no longer a suspect in relation to any terrorist attack.'

'What about Cade?' she said. 'His death?'

The male detective gave her a reassuring smile. 'That bastard broke your ribs, smashed your face and shot you. Even if you'd killed him, you could legitimately claim self-defence. But your story matches the evidence. Black stumbled into the brumby yard during a struggle. The frightened horses stampeded around the perimeter, accidentally trampling him. Odds on the Coroner will find death by misadventure.'

A motherly looking nurse came in, plump as a peach, and frowned at the detectives. 'Let the poor girl get some rest.' She read the chart at the end of the bed and checked her watch. 'Are you comfortable, love?' She took Pippa's pulse and blood pressure. 'I'll give you some more pain relief.'

The detectives excused themselves. Pippa murmured the words *death by misadventure* as they left. She felt drowsy and warm and blissfully happy. Life seemed too good to be true. Cade was gone. She'd been cleared of suspicion in the bombing. Duke was recovering from a sprained shoulder back at Brumby's Run. Thowra and his mob were safe. Even her pot plants were fine, having been rescued from the hut by Levi and given over to Nullah's tender care. Her brother would be home on Tuesday … and Levi loved her.

Pippa's leg barely ached as she drifted off to sleep, dreaming of eagles.

She woke some hours later to find Levi sitting beside her bed. He still wore his hat and seemed too big for the low chair, adjusting his long legs and trying unsuccessfully to fold them beneath him. Levi was a man who didn't belong indoors.

'I'm still getting used to seeing you without a scarf,' he said.

She put her hand on her heart and let out a great sigh. 'I never want to see one again.'

Levi took hold of her hand. 'I bought you a few things.' He put a plastic shopping bag on the bed.

Pippa looked through it: two pairs of horse-print pyjamas, a hairbrush, toiletries and a purple paisley bag to keep them in. It felt like Christmas.

'And these are for you too.' From behind his back he produced the biggest bunch of flowers she'd ever seen.

'Lucky you,' said the young woman from the next bed. She eyed Levi appreciatively. 'Is he your boyfriend?' She spoke as if Levi wasn't in the room.

Pippa was taken aback by the question. She could suddenly hear her father's disapproving voice. *You're a married woman, Phillipa. Married in the eyes of God.* And then it struck her. Since Cade was dead she wasn't married any more. Pippa felt suddenly light, as if even her injured leg and broken ribs wouldn't stop her from dancing.

The nosy next-door woman rolled her eyes. 'I said, is he your boyfriend? Cause if he's not …' She winked. 'I'll have him.'

A chuckle came from the patient in the opposite bed. All of them, including Levi, were looking at her curiously, waiting for an answer.

'Yes,' said Pippa at last. 'He's my boyfriend.'

Levi grinned approval. As if to prove the point, he stood up, took her head in his hands and kissed her – a kiss full of passion and need.

'Get a room,' called Miss Nosy.

Maybe it was the shock of it, or because she'd barely eaten, or because she was already lightheaded. Who knew – maybe it was the morphine? But for whatever reason, Pippa fainted dead away.

Pippa opened her eyes to find the curtains drawn around her bed, and both Levi and the motherly nurse bending over her.

'Oh, you did give us a fright, love. Here, sit up and sip this Lucozade.'

Levi lifted her, like she was light as a feather, and deposited her higher up in the bed. Pippa sat sipping her drink with dreamy eyes, looking like the cat that got the cream.

The nurse smiled at Levi as she adjusted the mattress. 'We could do with a few more of you around here, mate.' She picked up the flowers. 'I'll go find a vase, shall I? Give you lovebirds some privacy.'

Levi's mouth twitched with good humour. 'Are you going to faint every time I kiss you, Miss Pippa Sullivan?'

'Maybe.'

He grinned. 'You'll be unconscious a lot, then.' Levi put his hand in his pocket and pulled out an iPhone. 'This is for you.'

'Not more presents!' Pippa shook her head, but accepted the phone. 'What do I have to do for it to work?'

'Nothing. It's all set up.'

'Is it a smartphone?' She turned it over in her hands. 'Can it connect to the internet?'

'Of course.' He handed her a card. 'That's your PIN and phone number.'

Pippa read her number out loud. 'So what's your phone number?'

'It's already in there,' he said. 'Under "The Boyfriend" – just to make it official.'

A giggle came from Miss Nosy.

Pippa laughed too, although it hurt her ribs, and her heart swelled with pride. How sweet and funny he was. Levi seemed to belong to an entirely different species from her dead husband. The thought of Cade momentarily clouded her happiness, but she pushed it away. Cade had no right to haunt her. She wouldn't allow it.

'I can ring my mum, 'she said, delighted.

'You can ring whoever you like.' Levi unfolded his long legs and rose to go. 'One more thing – don't switch off your phone. You'll be getting an important call later on.'

'Who from?' Levi didn't answer. 'Well, aren't you going to tell me?'

'It's a surprise. Now, is it safe to kiss you goodbye?' He gave her a chaste peck on the cheek this time.

'Look after Duke and the horses for me,' called Pippa as Levi left. She missed him already.

Pippa rang home as soon as Levi was gone. She didn't care what time it was. She didn't care who answered the phone. She didn't have to watch her words. This new freedom was exhilarating.

'Mum, it's me.' The following conversation was both the most difficult and the sweetest one of her life. Her mother confirmed that Andrew Chandler was indeed Pippa's brother, while Pippa outlined the dramatic events of the last few days

'Oh, my poor darling daughter – what a terrible story. I never liked Cade, but to think he—' Mum dissolved into tears.

'It's okay, Mum. I'm fine, I promise. It's still a mystery how Cade found me, though. You won't believe how remote that hut is.'

Mum hesitated. 'That might have been my fault. A few days ago, I found the clothes in my dresser all mussed up. I was worried your father might have been in there and found Drew's letters and birth certificate. I keep them at the back of a drawer, you see. But Jay isn't a curious man and he's been behaving no differently … Do you think it was Cade?'

'Perhaps, but he's dead now and it doesn't matter,' said Pippa, firmly. 'How are Dad and the kids?'

'Worried sick about you, of course. I can't wait to tell them that you're all right. When will you be able to leave the hospital?'

'The doctor says Monday. I'm lucky. The bullet passed through muscle and missed bones and arteries. But I'll still be on crutches.'

'Don't you worry about a thing, my girl. We'll be there bright and early on Monday to bring you home.'

Pippa almost dropped the phone. She'd assumed that she'd go home with Levi, but could she? The two of them hadn't discussed what would happen next. And if she did go with Levi, how could she explain it to her parents?

'Sorry, Mum, I have to go.' Pippa ended the call. She felt sick. Her perfect future was crumbling. She'd need looking after for a while, help with changing dressings and outpatient appointments. Her doctor was optimistic, but concerned about possible nerve damage. She couldn't expect Levi to be running after her, especially with Brumby's Run gearing up for their busy season. And she wouldn't have a job there like she'd hoped. Levi said Drew was bound to keep her on, especially with the glowing reference he'd promised to provide. But not now. She wouldn't be able to push a broom for weeks, let alone ride. Pippa felt the prick of angry tears. Cade was still managing to ruin her life from beyond the grave.

And now that he was gone, there was no practical reason why she shouldn't go home to her parents' farm. The thought horrified her. Dad would hate Levi once he knew he was Jewish. He'd do everything he could to chase him off, and it wouldn't be long before Levi forgot all about her. She imagined sitting in the back room helping her siblings with arithmetic. Sitting in the kitchen slicing apples. Sitting on the porch mending clothes the way she had as a teenager – the clock turned back.

She couldn't return to that narrow, isolated life – a life ruled by Pastor Jay Sullivan. Not now that she'd experienced the possibilities of the outside world. It would damn near kill her.

CHAPTER 37

At five-thirty a cheerful orderly brought Pippa's dinner – a half-decent serve of shepherd's pie with cheesecake for dessert. But she'd lost her appetite. The problem of where to go after being discharged still loomed. She turned on the television, hoping for a soap opera to distract her, but it was the wrong time of day. And anyway, compared to the last few weeks of her own life, soap operas would now seem boring.

Levi said he'd downloaded some games that she could play on her phone. She picked it up, trying to remember how to find them and feeling rather stupid. She'd only ever had a dumb flip phone. It could make calls, send texts and that was it. The dizzying features of her iPhone were still very new to her. Pippa settled back on her pillow, determined to learn her way around it.

The phone rang, startling her. The ringtone was an alarming trumpet fanfare. Pippa stared at it, in two minds about what to do. If it was Levi, she wanted to answer it. If it was Mum, she didn't. Simple as that. It had to be one or the other of them. Nobody else would be ringing her. Wouldn't caller ID show up if it was Levi and tell her that 'The Boyfriend' was calling? Pippa couldn't help smiling at that.

She'd apparently taken too long to decide because the phone

stopped ringing. Pippa wished she'd answered now, convinced that it had been Levi. She was trying to remember how to call him back when the trumpets sounded again.

'Hello, Levi?'

'No … this is your brother, Drew.'

She almost dropped the phone. A mixture of emotions flashed through her brain. Would Drew want to know her? He'd never tried to seek her out, and on top of that she'd caused a great deal of trouble – brought a killer to Brumby's Run.

'Pippa, are you there?'

'Yes,' she said, a little lost for words. 'It's nice to meet you.'

'You too, little sister.'

His voice was warm, and she could hear the smile in it. It made her smile too. His weren't the sort of words you use before rejecting someone.

'Levi told me what happened,' said Drew. 'He's proud of you – said you've been very clever and brave.' A pause. 'I'm proud of you too.'

Could this be happening? Her first ever conversation with this long-lost brother and he'd praised her for being brave. Her first impulse was to correct him, to say that she wasn't brave at all, and everybody knew that. But something stopped her – that kernel of self-esteem that had sprouted and flourished ever since she'd found the courage to leave Cade. Don't put yourself down, it said. Learn how to take a compliment.

'Thank you,' she said, simply.

'How are you feeling? Can I come to see you tomorrow?'

'I thought you weren't coming home until Tuesday?'

'When we heard what happened we came home early. So … are you up for a visit?'

'I'd like that,' said Pippa, shyly.

'And can I bring my girlfriend—?'

An indignant interjection came from the sidelines.

'I mean, can I bring my wife, Sam? We're both dying to meet you, but if it's too much—'

Pippa interrupted him. 'Yes … a thousand times yes!' She felt like singing. 'I can't wait to meet you guys either.'

Sunday morning. Pippa's stomach churned with excitement, but she forced herself to eat the breakfast of cold toast, soggy Weet-Bix and an overripe banana. She stirred two extra sachets of sugar into her tea. She'd need all her energy to cope with today's meeting.

Pippa showered, wrapping plastic around the bandage on her thigh like the nurse had shown her. She put on the new blue pair of horsey pyjamas. She brushed her hair and looked at herself in the mirror, frowning. Her face was still bruised and swollen. There'd been a lipstick in the care package that Levi had given her, along with a powder compact and brush. She dusted her face. There, that was better. Then she tried the red lipstick. She'd only ever worn lipstick once before – on her wedding day. It hadn't suited her then and it didn't now. Her mouth looked like a bloody gash. She hurriedly wiped it off, got back into bed and picked up her iPhone.

Pippa felt very modern now that she was glued to her phone like the other patients. She was still exploring all the miraculous things it could do, such as tell her how long it would take to drive to anywhere, from anywhere, in the entire world. For instance, it would take fifteen hours to drive from Paris to Rome. How fascinating! But she was also obsessively checking the time. Pippa's very special visitors were due at eleven o'clock and she was counting down the minutes.

At precisely 10.55 Levi arrived in the doorway of her ward room. 'Can we come in?'

Pippa swallowed and nodded, her mouth gritty and dry.

Two people followed Levi into the room. Pippa clasped a hand to her mouth. She would have recognised Drew anywhere. He looked so much like her brothers, with the same square, regular features and strong chin. And he had Mum's smiling green eyes.

The young woman, who must be Sam, was dark-haired and slim with a pretty turned-up nose. 'I love your pyjamas,' she said in a posh voice.

They made their introductions and delivered an abundance of goodies: chocolates, toffees, flowers and a soft toy Palomino pony. Pippa, who'd been so excited to meet them a few moments earlier, now turned painfully shy, barely able to speak. Levi saved the day by fielding questions and expanding on Pippa's monosyllabic replies.

The visitors didn't seem perturbed by Pippa's reticence, and they chatted away happily to her anyway. Sam, her sister Charlie, Drew, and Charlie's husband, Karl, were all good friends, so the four of them had decided to extend the double wedding into a double honeymoon.

Pippa's curiosity got the better of her. 'Where did you go?'

'Lord Howe Island,' said Drew.

'Is that one of those luxury resort islands on the Great Barrier Reef?'

'Not exactly. Lord Howe is a tiny speck in the Tasman Sea between Australia and New Zealand with less than four hundred permanent residents. And its main claim to fame? It's home to a giant stick insect, so large that it's known as a tree lobster. It's the rarest insect in the world. Until recently they were believed to be extinct.'

Pippa was nonplussed. 'You went there on your honeymoon to see a big bug?'

Sam chuckled. 'My sister Charlie picked the place. She and Karl wore us down, didn't they Drew? They're both nature nuts, but I must admit it was a great choice. Lord Howe is actually a paradise of rainforests, reefs and beaches. I've never seen such wonderful snorkelling.'

It didn't take long for Pippa to feel at home with the new members of her family. She asked a lot of questions. How had Drew and Sam met? What made them decide to start a brumby sanctuary? Where did the foundation stallions came from?

Sam answered that last question. It was clear that she was as deeply involved with Brumby's Run as Drew was. 'Our two brumby sires, Jarrang and Phoenix, were wild caught off Maroong Mountain,' she said.

'And what about the stockhorse stallion?' asked Pippa. 'Where did Phantom come from?'

'I bred him myself.' Drew's voice rang with pride.

'You should have seen your brother when Phantom was born,' laughed Sam. 'He spent every damn moment with that little colt: bonding with him, training him, following him around. Drew would disappear up to the yards for hours. I'd go looking and find him sitting on the rails, just admiring Phantom. To tell you the truth, I was a little jealous.'

Pippa could understand Drew's actions completely. It was the same with her and Thowra. She could watch the golden stallion all day long.

'Guilty as charged.' Drew put his hand up. 'Breeding quality stockhorses has been my passion for as long as I can remember.' He moved closer to the bed and held Pippa's gaze. 'That's why I have a proposition for you, little sister.'

Pippa didn't even have to hear it. She was bursting to say yes, whatever it was, but she had the good grace to listen first.

'I suppose Levi told you Thowra's story – about him not being a true brumby?'

Pippa nodded. 'A wild stallion stole his mother from a station when Thowra was a foal at foot, and he has the brand to prove it.'

'That's right. Thowra has a pedigree reaching back to the legendary palomino stockhorse, Champagne Charlie. I'd love to have Thowra stand at stud at Brumby's Run. That's if you'll agree, of course.'

Pippa didn't understand. 'It's a wonderful idea,' she said. 'But what do I have to do with it?'

'Thowra belongs to you,' said Drew.

Pippa's mouth fell open in amazement. She glanced at Levi, who grinned. 'Don't you remember me telling you about old Stan Grant, the man who bred Thowra? He said it's finders keepers to whoever catches him.'

'Yes, and that would be you,' said Drew.

'No,' protested Pippa. 'Levi trained the horses to enter the yards. He bought the salt and hay. He showed me how to operate the gate mechanism. It was sheer luck that Thowra came when Levi wasn't there.'

'Don't argue.' Drew held up his hand. 'The three of us have discussed this and come to a mutual decision. You were the one who set the trap that night.' He picked up the toy palomino pony from the foot of the bed and tossed it to Pippa. 'Thowra's all yours.'

Pippa wondered if she was dreaming. She'd wanted a horse for so very long, and now the most beautiful stallion in the world belonged to her. It was hard to get her head around it. She was on cloud nine for the remainder of the visit, so much so that she forgot about the small problem of where she would go upon discharge. It wasn't until her visitors were about to leave that she had a reminder.

'Your mum must be happy,' said Levi. 'Your whole family.'

Pippa's joyful mood deflated like a pricked balloon. 'Mum wants me to go home with her tomorrow.'

'That's a good idea,' said Levi, apparently oblivious to her misgivings. 'How long did the doctor say you'll be on crutches?

'Four weeks,' said Pippa, miserably. 'Maybe a bit longer.'

'You'll get looked after a lot better at your mum's than at Brumby's, what with the busy season coming up.'

Pippa had never felt more useless. It was just as she feared. She'd be fobbed off onto her parents and it wouldn't be long before Levi forgot all about her.

'But I'll miss Thowra – and you.'

Sam glanced at Drew, then stepped forward and squeezed Pippa's hand. 'Whatever you decide will be fine with us. And remember, you have a standing offer of employment at Brumby's once you're well. Now, come on Drew, let's give Levi and Pippa some private time.'

Drew gently hugged his sister, kissed her cheek and followed his wife from the room.

'What's up, Pip?' Levi asked once they'd gone.

Paranoia was setting in. It was all she could do not to say, *Are you trying to get rid of me?* 'Don't you want me to go home with you?' she managed, instead.

'Of course I do.' Levi pulled up a chair. 'I'm just worried you won't get enough attention. You said yourself that your mum loves looking after people.'

Pippa couldn't look at him. 'Kilpa is a long way from Currajong.' She bit her lip and stroked the toy pony. 'You'll forget about me.'

There, she'd said it. Now Levi knew just exactly how insecure and desperate she was. Pippa hadn't known quite what to expect, but it wasn't a great burst of laughter.

'Forget about you?' gasped Levi. 'Now that would be difficult. I've known you, what, two or three weeks?'

'Two weeks and three days.'

'In that short space of time you've lost the valuable stallion that I'd been chasing for years, caught him again, and then claimed him for yourself.'

'I didn't—'

Levi shook his head. 'Let me finish. I've fired you, rehired you, hidden you from the law, kept a major secret from my boss, been insulted by you, gone on a wild, rescue dash to save you from a killer, discovered a dead body, been interviewed by the Major Crimes squad—'

A strangled shriek came from Miss Nosy next door.

'... rushed you to hospital when you were shot – all the while falling head over heels in love. Now tell me – do you think you're that easy to forget?'

Pippa had been attempting to interject while Levi recited this laundry list of extraordinary happenings, but she couldn't get a word in. When he'd finally finished, she tried one last time. 'It's not like I—'

'Oh, and you stole my favourite saucepan from the bungalow. I want it back.'

Pippa suddenly saw the funny side. She erupted into peals of giggles. Levi joined in and they laughed so hard they both lost their breath. She'd almost recovered when his mouth swooped down to capture hers and she locked her arms around his neck, reeling from her own aching need. When he let her go she felt wet tears on her cheeks.

Pippa leaned into Levi, who sat beside her on the bed and offered her tissues.

'That young sister of yours,' he said, softly. 'Joan or Joanne? How old did you say she was?'

'It's Janie,' said Pippa. 'And she's almost eleven. Why do you ask?'

He gave her a long, searching look. 'I bet that little girl misses you.'

Levi spoke the words slowly, with a certain gravity that gave Pippa pause. And then it struck her. She couldn't abandon her sister – couldn't let Dad convince Janie that women weren't as good as men, and that they should obey their husbands no matter what. That was one reason why Pippa had put up with Cade for so long. Because she believed he had a God-given right to abuse her. But Pippa could open Janie's eyes to different ways of seeing the world, show her new options.

Pippa squeezed Levi's hand. 'Well, maybe I *could* go home for a while, seeing as I'm so unforgettable ...'

'Now there's an understatement. But seriously, I can't think of anyone better to set the cat among the pigeons. Shake up that family of yours.'

Pippa's smile was tinged with sadness when she thought of what a little tomboy Janie was. Dirty overalls. Out in the paddocks with her twin brother looking for lizards and tadpoles, climbing trees and collecting stones to build castles.

But Janie was growing up, and it wouldn't be long before Dad drew the reins in. She'd have to wear dresses all the time and not go rambling with Luke. She'd only go mustering if they were short-handed. When her brothers helped with the harvest she'd be confined to the house, cooking and cleaning and sewing. Pippa knew firsthand how Janie's already narrow world would shrink. Until what – she married the first man who came along in order to escape the loneliness and boredom of her life?

Pippa would make it her mission to ensure Janie had a better adolescence than she'd had; to ensure that she grew into the independent young woman she was meant to be. An enforced recuperation at Utopia would be the perfect way to begin. Pippa looked into Levi's concerned face. Sometimes all it took to find your strength was for someone to stand with you. Nobody knew that better than she did.

Pippa suddenly felt ashamed to have doubted Levi's loyalty and commitment. He'd never given her the slightest reason to. 'I'll go home with Mum tomorrow,' she said.

Levi swept her into his arms, raining kisses on her face and neck, causing her to laugh aloud with pride and joy. Her ribs hurt, but she didn't care. 'I'll visit whenever I can,' he said. 'I'll ring you every day.'

'I can imagine Dad's expression when he finds out that you're Jewish.'

Levi made a face. 'Do me a favour. While you're busy empowering Janie and your mum, can you teach your dad not to be such a bigoted bastard?

CHAPTER 38

Pippa woke up in the same bed that she'd slept in for the first twenty years of her life, under the same fringed candlewick bedspread. She looked at the same 1950s floral pattern wallpaper and the sun streamed in through the same pony-print curtains. The cut-out calendar picture of Mist's look-alike was still on the wall.

Pippa could see the remains of a Mallee sunrise through the window – rosy skies stretching to infinity. A pair of willy wagtails sang sweet short melodies and magpies carolled a greeting to the new day.

Pippa stretched and reached for her phone. It was on a different corner of the nightstand from where she'd left it. Someone, most likely Ian, had borrowed it overnight. Her new iPhone had caused quite a stir among Janie and her brothers.

She smiled to think of how frustrated the thief must have been when they realised the phone required a passcode. Like Pippa at their age, her siblings weren't computer literate. This put them at a massive disadvantage in the age of technology. That would have to change.

Levi had joked that she'd lived an Amish childhood. Pippa had no idea what he'd meant and had googled it. Levi was wrong. The Amish were Christians who lived an even more basic lifestyle than her own family. They used horses instead of tractors, hooks and eyes instead of buttons and zippers and they washed their clothes by hand. However, the most important thing that set Amish life apart from her own family was the high value they placed on humility. There was no way that her father, so full of arrogance and pride, could ever be part of their church.

When Pippa had first arrived home, her parents had been shocked by the extent of Cade's abuse. 'Why didn't you tell us, love, and come home?' her father had asked, genuinely puzzled.

'Are you serious? After listening to hundreds of sermons about how husbands are head of the house? After telling me what a catch Cade was? You'd have given me a lecture and sent me back.'

Jay didn't deny it, and had the good grace to look abashed. 'How could I have been so wrong about that man? I should have known when he stopped going to church.'

'You should have known long before that, and so should I,' said Ruby. 'We're so sorry, darling. I'll never forgive myself for putting you through that.'

'You didn't hurt me, Mum. Cade did, and I went out of my way to hide it from you. Please don't blame yourself.' What was done, was done. She meant to put the past behind her and wanted her parents to do the same.

Pippa yawned and checked the time. Eight o'clock. Mum was spoiling her again with a sleep-in. This was Pippa's third full day back at the farm. Being here wasn't nearly as difficult as she'd imagined. It wasn't winding back the clock after all. She was too different a person for that. It was turning the clock forward and bringing her family into the twenty-first century.

A knock came at the door and then her mother's voice. 'Breakfast's ready, Pip. Do you need some help?' Mum poked her head round the door. 'Don't worry about getting dressed, love.'

A few minutes later Pippa clunked into the breakfast room on her crutches. She'd become rather good at using them and quickly found herself a place at the enormous timber table that could seat ten people. She'd expected to receive a stern word from Dad about coming to breakfast in her pyjamas. Instead he simply said, 'Good morning, Phillipa.'

Pippa had forgotten how ample a meal breakfast was at the farm: homemade lamb sausages, scrambled eggs, grilled tomatoes, mushrooms and thick buttered slices of Mum's famous sourdough bread.

The inevitable barrage of questions started from her siblings. They knew better than to ask about Cade's death. They'd learnt on the first day that was a no-no, but it barely put a brake on their curiosity. How did it feel to be shot? How had she escaped? Why had she fled to Currajong in the first place? This last awkward question was being asked more and more, although Dad had been strangely silent about it. In fact, since she'd come home, Dad had been strangely silent full stop.

Ian was the most relentless interrogator. Somehow, he smelled a rat. 'But of all the places in Australia, why did you drive straight to Currajong? Do you know someone there?'

Pippa didn't want to lie about why she'd chosen Brumby's Run, but she didn't want to tell the truth either. Drew wasn't her secret to tell. So instead she deflected and avoided and obfuscated, while her mother looked more and more uncomfortable.

Finally, Ruby could bear it no longer. And right there at the breakfast table, Ruby stood up and confessed to bearing a child at fifteen and placing him up for adoption. Pippa held her breath. This could tear her family apart.

The ten-year-old twins, Luke and Janey, were too young to realise the significance of their mother's bombshell. 'Yay, I have a new big brother!' said Luke. 'When can we meet him? I bet he's nicer than Ian.'

Fred and Ian were more circumspect about the news. They kept looking to their father, waiting for the explosion. Pippa half-expected him to bellow and scream, proclaim their mother a fallen woman in the eyes of God and order her from their home. But that was unthinkable. Mum *was* their home, its very heart and soul.

To everyone's amazement, Jay said nothing. He sat, stony-faced, and continued eating breakfast as if nothing had happened. Afterwards, he asked Pippa and Ruby to meet him in the chapel. Ruby was shaky as they approached the little timber church. She looked like she was going to an execution. The other children were strategically hidden around the yard, watching.

Pippa wished she could squeeze her mother's hand, but was scared she'd drop her crutch. Instead she said, 'I'm so proud of you, Mum. Dad will be unhappy to start with, but he'll forgive you.' Ruby turned anxious eyes on her daughter and did not look convinced. 'Think of it this way. Now you and Drew can have the sort of open, honest relationship that you both deserve. His adoptive mother died years ago. I reckon he could really use your special brand of unconditional love.'

This last comment seemed to embolden Ruby. She set her chin as they entered the chapel together. Pippa expected Jay to be standing cross-armed on the pulpit, or pacing about in anger, but instead he was sitting on one of the rough-hewn pews with his head in his hands.

Ruby drew in a swift breath and her determined face softened. She hurried to her husband and put a consoling hand on his shoulder. To Pippa's utter astonishment, Jay wrapped his arms around Ruby's waist and buried his face in her skirts.

'I'm sorry love,' crooned Ruby, stroking his hair.

Pippa had never seen such tenderness, intimacy even, between her parents. It reminded her that once upon a time they'd been young and in love the way she and Levi were.

Pippa turned to leave, but Jay called her back. 'I have something to say to both of you.' He indicated the seat beside him. 'Sit. You too Ruby.' So there he sat, flanked by his wife and daughter, summoning the courage for – what?

'My own confession.' Jay linked his arm through his wife's, and she leaned into him as he spoke. 'Ruby, I already knew about your boy, Andrew. I found his birth certificate in your dresser drawer twenty years ago.'

Ruby pulled away and stared at him. 'All this time and you never said?'

'I had to protect you. God would have made me cast you aside.' He hung his head. 'I couldn't live with that.'

Ruby looked at him askance. 'You weren't keeping my secret from God. God already knew.' Jay couldn't look at her. 'You were keeping it from your followers. How could you judge and condemn them when your own wife was a sinner, right?' Jay's lower lip trembled. 'Do you know what you could have done instead?' said Ruby. 'You could have forgiven me. I was a child when Drew was born.'

'I have forgiven you,' said Jay, a note of desperation creeping into his voice. 'How else could I have lived with you all these years?'

Ruby snorted. 'If you'd forgiven me you'd have told me so. You wouldn't have left me living with the shame and fear of you finding out. You wouldn't have made me hide Andrew's letters and write to him in secret. You would have allowed him to know his brothers and sisters.'

Pippa was astonished in several ways, not least of which was the passionate way that Mum was standing up to Dad.

'And do you know what else you could have done?' said Ruby. 'You could have used our marriage as a model of forgiveness. Maybe then Ron would be speaking to us.'

'What's this got to do with Ron?' asked Pippa.

Ruby glared at her husband. 'Tell her, Jay.'

Dad's chin quivered. 'Ron didn't leave to work at a garage in Swan Hill,' he said, his voice cracking. 'I threw him out.'

Pippa couldn't believe it. Among the siblings it was generally agreed that Ron was Dad's favourite.

'Your father discovered that Ron was sleeping with his girlfriend. You know Tammy Howard from Rush Creek Station? He quoted some stupid scripture, promised Ron misery in this life, hell in the next, and thundered that his only chance of salvation was to break it off with Tammy and never see her again. Ron refused, so Dad told him to leave and not come back. Told Ron that he was no longer his son.' Ruby stopped to catch her breath. 'That was three months ago and we haven't seen or heard from Ron since.'

Pippa glared at her father with reproachful eyes. 'Oh, Dad, you didn't ... you couldn't!'

'It was wicked of me.' He wrung his hands as if trying to wash off the guilt. 'I miss Ron so much I could weep. I pray every day—'

'Pray, shmay,' said Ruby, standing with hands on hips. 'You need to apologise to that boy. In case you haven't noticed, you're not perfect and you're not God. Stop being so damned high and mighty. I'm warning you, Jay, at this rate you'll drive all the kids away – and maybe me as well. Don't make me choose.'

Pippa felt like clapping. Bravo Mum! She thought back to the promise she'd made herself – the promise to help Mum assert herself and recognise the power she held in her marriage. She seemed to have succeeded without even trying. Mum hadn't needed help standing up to Dad after all. In the end she'd made that decision for herself, and Pippa felt a sense of deep pride in her mother because of it.

Pippa watched Janey urge Pepper into a canter and jump the low poles. The old horse had never looked better, his thick black mane lying neatly along his neck, his dark bay coat brushed and shining in the sun. She'd forgotten that her little sister was almost as horse-mad as she was.

Pippa relaxed on a picnic chair under the shade of an ancient peppercorn tree. Her crutches lay beside her, but she barely needed them any more. She gazed about in admiration at the well-kept fences, weed-free pastures and leafy windbreaks protected by star pickets and sheep netting. Dad was a hard man, but he knew what his land needed. By contrast, Cade had been a lazy, stupid farmer. He'd let his fences fall into disrepair. He'd cut down every tree and shelter belt, hoping to cadge an extra hectare or two of crops. In return the topsoil had blown away. Pippa wondered how hard it would be to rehabilitate Fairview.

The spring break had finally come, and come as a deluge. Beyond the small riding paddock, sheep grazed on freshly green pastures. A troop of tiny emu-wrens foraged in the red mallee gums along the fence. On the dam – almost a lake really after such heavy rains – wood ducks and teal guided fluffy ducklings through the reeds. Manangatang wasn't the high country, but it possessed its own special beauty. Pippa was recovering her childhood love of these unique Mallee plains.

Janey waved to her and cantered a figure of eight, legs moving like windmills to keep Pepper going. 'Well done,' Pippa called. Reconnecting with her little sister had been a joy. So much so that Pippa was almost grateful that she'd been shot. She'd never have come back otherwise, except for a passing visit. Janey needed more than that.

Pippa realised that during her marriage she'd been oblivious to everyone's needs except for Cade's. This extended time at the family farm was a revelation in so many ways. Seeing how her very presence sparked a curiosity and thirst for knowledge about the outside world in her family. Seeing Mum take back her power. Seeing Dad admit he was wrong. That was a first.

Pippa had watched *The Wizard of Oz* last night with Janey and Luke. They'd sat on the couch, one twin on either side of her, and watched the movie on her iPhone, thanks to a Netflix subscription provided by Levi. Pippa had loved the book as a child, but watching the movie was a first for all of them. She could still see herself as the Cowardly Lion, underestimating her own courage, but she found another connection with a character close to home. Dad was the Wizard of Oz: a self-absorbed charlatan who held people in thrall, convincing them that he was great and powerful. When challenged, he was revealed as an ordinary person, filled with ordinary human frailties. He'd never be able to fool them again.

Pippa called Janey over. 'It's getting too hot for an old horse like Pepper. Go brush him down and turn him out. I need to go inside and pack.'

Janey pouted. 'I wish you weren't going.' She hopped off. 'Can I see the pictures of Thowra again?' Pippa found them on her phone. 'He's sooo beautiful! Tell me about how you caught him again. Is he really yours? When can I come to see him?'

'Soon,' said Pippa. 'Just as soon as I can drive.'

'Maybe Levi could drive me? I'll ask him when he comes. You're sooo lucky to have him as a boyfriend. He's much nicer than Cade.'

Pippa smiled at her chattering sister. Now wasn't that the understatement of the year?

'Dad didn't like Levi at first though, did he?' Janey frowned. 'I wouldn't dare bring home a boy that Dad didn't like.'

Pippa gave her sister an amused look and picked up her crutches. 'You're a bit young to be worrying about boys. But here's something I've learned; something I wished that I'd known when I was a girl. It's not your job to keep the people you love happy, Janey. Not Dad, not your brothers, not your friends. I promise, it's not. The hard truth is that you can't, in any case.'

Janey went quiet. They watched Pepper munching on the lush grass. Pippa sensed that her sister was trying to find the courage for something. She sat back down on her chair and waited.

'I'll never bring a boy home anyway,' Janey said at last. 'I'm not pretty enough.'

Pippa's heart broke to hear this echo of her own childhood insecurities. Janey's clear-eyed face was in transition. It held traces of the baby she'd been, but also hinted at the lovely young woman to come. Janey would never lack for male admirers. Yet even at the tender age of ten, society's impossible ideal of female beauty was draining her confidence.

Pippa chose her words carefully. 'You're plenty pretty enough, but you're a lot more than that. You're clever and funny and kind. You're a terrific helper and very talented at drawing. Could you draw a picture of Pepper for me before I go? I'll put it on my wall back in Currajong.'

Janey nodded, cheering up. 'I'm not beautiful though, am I – not like the girls in Mum's magazines?'

'We'd all look like models if someone spent hours doing our hair and makeup.' Pippa beckoned Janey closer and whispered low. 'I'll let you in on a secret. All those glamourous girls in Mum's magazines? They don't really look like that. Their photos are edited – changed – to give them longer legs and skinnier waists and slimmer thighs.'

'That's cheating!' exclaimed Janey.

'It is, absolutely.'

Janey's mouth formed a tight, angry line. 'Do they edit out pimples too?'

'They do.'

Janey gave an outraged gasp.

'So don't go comparing yourself to all those *perfect* magazine models, okay?'

'Okay,' said Janey with a determined nod of her head. 'They won't trick me again.'

After having spent a month at Utopia, Pippa was finally going home to Brumby's Run. Levi would be coming for her soon. He'd visited the farm each week. Her father had been outraged when he discovered her new boyfriend was Jewish and had initially banned him from the house. Ruby came to the rescue.

'I don't believe it,' she said, with that new hands-on-hips attitude of hers. 'You've only just mended fences with Ron, and now you mean to chase Pippa away?'

Jay backed down and allowed Levi to come for lunch. After an awkward start, Levi succeeded in winning Jay over – they both barracked for the Collingwood football club. Pippa was amazed at how easily Jay's hostility had crumbled, along with the inherited prejudices of the kids. Within an hour of meeting Levi, Ian had arranged a backyard cricket match and Jay had joined in.

Pippa recognised what was happening with her family. It had been the same with her. Once she'd met Levi and discovered what a wonderful person he was, her preconceived notions evaporated. He'd forgiven her because he understood where her intolerance came from. 'You grew up with such a narrow view of the world. It must have been difficult to see that your father's way wasn't the only way.' How right he was.

Pippa was proud of how her family had set aside their prejudices to embrace Levi. Fingers crossed it was the first step towards them opening their minds and hearts even further – the first step towards them fully discarding their bigoted beliefs. And although she couldn't wait to get back to Brumby's Run, she would miss them all – even her father. Who'd have thought?

CHAPTER 39

Coming back to Brumby's Run felt like coming home. Living and working beside Levi, free from the fear, secrets and lies that had ruled her. Knowing that Levi was as happy as she was. For the first time in her life, Pippa felt fully alive.

Every corner of Brumby's Run reminded Pippa of some special moment. The stables – making that first, true connection with Levi during the birth of Comet's foal. The sand arena – riding Mist and gaining Levi's respect for her horsemanship. The kitchen wall phone – tearful calls to her mother and Levi's unfailing kindness. The pot of tea he'd made, accompanied by that pretty blue-and-white milk jug and Tim Tam biscuits.

The first week was a whirlwind of meeting new people and getting to know others better. Levi did his best to explain who was who. Drew and Sam generously gave Pippa their room, even allowing Duke to sleep on the bed. Levi had told them how the dog had saved her life, and he was regarded by all as a hero. The bedroom was right next door to Levi's which raised some tantalising possibilities.

The newlywed couples moved next door to Kilmarnock Station – a property belonging to Drew's widowed father, Bill Chandler. The house was large and grand, but Bill didn't live there any more. He'd retired to the Gold Coast with his new partner, Faith, and they were currently on a world cruise.

Drew, Sam, and Charlie returned each morning for breakfast – a shared meal taken by the whole Brumby's Run team in order to plan their day.

Charlie and Sam looked uncannily alike, but their personalities were quite different. Charlie was hands on, down to earth and somewhat blunt; the sort of person who didn't suffer fools lightly.

Pippa complained to Levi after the first breakfast. 'I don't think Charlie likes me.'

Levi gave her a knowing wink. 'Ask her about frogs.'

Next morning, over golden syrup pancakes, Pippa looked at Charlie and said, 'Do you know about frogs in the Mallee where I grew up?'

It worked. Charlie's eyes lit up. 'The Mallee is the largest catchment in Victoria, covering over forty thousand square kilometres. It's home to nine species of amphibians, including the endangered growling grass frog.'

Drew groaned. 'Don't get her started.'

But Pippa was intrigued. 'What does it sound like? As a kid I used to hear a strange frog call from the bush near the dam – sort of a high-pitched cackle.'

'That's a Peron's tree frog, commonly known as the laughing tree frog. They have gorgeous, big yellow tadpoles.'

'I remember seeing tadpoles like that,' said Pippa. 'I always wondered what sort of frog they'd turn into.' From that morning on she and Charlie became friends.

Sam was more mellow – a gracious, well-spoken young woman who did her best to make everyone feel welcome. She and Charlie had the same rich cinnamon-coloured hair, but wore it differently. Sam had an elegant, shoulder-length wave and Charlie a practical bob. Most helpful for telling them apart. However, in one respect, Sam and Charlie were identical. They shared a heartfelt love of horses.

Charlie and her new husband were passionate conservationists. Karl worked as a ranger in Balleroo National Park. Charlie sometimes joined him in the field, helping to document the endangered species that lived in the park, such as spotted tree frogs, Snowy Mountain skinks and pygmy possums. Karl himself was reserved – a difficult man to know – but friendly enough in a shy sort of way.

Connecting with Drew was a joy. He always made time for Pippa. On long summer evenings they'd sit by the stockyards, talking and watching the foals play. Drinking mugs of black tea and eating Malt 'O' Milk biscuits. Catching up on their lives while the sun dipped behind the purple range.

Drew was as interested in her as she was in him. 'There's not much to say,' said Pippa when he asked questions. 'I never really lived until I came to Brumby's Run.'

'I'm sure that's not true.' Drew wouldn't be put off. 'Tell me about your family then, your mother – my mother too.'

This was easier than talking about herself and Pippa soon opened up.

'So I have a whole bunch of new family members to meet. Will you help me with that?' asked Drew. 'Truth is, I'm a bit scared.'

'You, scared?' said Pippa, thinking how nobody radiated quiet confidence like Drew. 'I don't believe it.'

He looked pensive and kicked the ground. 'Oh, you'd be surprised. An old proverb says fear and courage are brothers forged in the same fire. One can't exist without the other.' He fixed his kind green eyes on hers. 'You'd know all about that. My little sister was at the front of the queue when they dished out bravery.'

She blushed. Drew always knew how to make her feel special.

'Tell me,' he said. 'How do you find life in the high country? It must be quite a change for a Mallee girl.'

'I love it here,' she said. 'There's you, and Levi. There's the brumbies and forests and the fact that it actually rains. But it's more than that. It's the peacefulness of this place – a calm that seems to filter right through me and flow into the rocks and trees. A sense of time standing still. It's strange. Sometimes I feel that I'm part of these ranges.' Pippa offered him a shy smile. 'Do you feel it too?'

The warmth of Drew's expression said it all. 'Mountains make a person appreciate how small they are in the grand scheme of things,' he said. 'They humble us in a good way – put our lives into perspective.'

The pair sat together for a while in companionable silence. Pippa felt like she'd known Drew forever.

'Speaking of lives,' he said at last. 'What do you plan to do with yours?'

The question took Pippa by surprise. For years she'd made an art form of taking one day at a time. Now she dared to look towards the future. 'I plan to work here with you and Levi. Learn all about brumbies. Become the best horsewoman I can be.'

Drew fished a biscuit out of the tin. 'So ... you and Levi—'

'I love him,' she said, firmly, before Drew could finish. 'Can't imagine life without him.'

Drew dipped the biscuit in his tea. 'Levi says the same thing about you, little sis.' He took a bite and grinned at her. 'Well, since he's a top bloke, I'd best give you my blessing.'

'I don't need it,' said Pippa, with a wicked twinkle in her eye. 'Nobody makes decisions about my life except me.'

Nullah wandered over with a paperback under his arm. He always had a book on the go. He helped himself to a mug of tea from the big cast iron teapot, leaned against a rail and began reading.

He and Pippa worked together now, exercising youngsters or halter training the foals. She'd tried to apologise for her initial hostility, but Nullah had waved her clumsy attempt away. 'It wasn't my idea to send you packing, Pip. Like I told Levi – two days and you'd have come round.' She soon realised why Levi liked him so much. Nullah was fun, clever and blessed with a razor-sharp wit. In short, Pippa found him absolutely charming.

Drew tossed the dregs of his tea to the dust. 'How are plans going for the Deadly Jackaroo Challenge?'

'All good,' said Nullah, without taking his nose from the book. 'Me and Spike have it sorted.'

'What are you reading?' asked Pippa.

'The Brumby Wars.' Nullah held the book out for her to see. The cover featured a dramatic photo of stallions fighting. 'Drew lent it to me. This bloke Sharbrook reckons the real Man from Snowy River in the poem was a blackfella.'

'It's a fascinating read,' said Drew. 'The landscape described in the poem points to it being set around Byadbo. The rugged granite cliffs, the native pine forests. Byadbo is an area where all the stockmen were Indigenous.'

Nullah flipped through the pages. 'Here. Apparently a story was published in 1887 about a Snowy River-born Aboriginal boy named Toby who was an expert rider and a whizz at tracking brumbies. Sharwood says there's overwhelming evidence that this kid was the original Man from Snowy River.'

'Makes sense,' said Drew. 'All the best stockmen back then were Aboriginal.'

'What's this *back then* business?' said Nullah, in mock outrage. 'They still are.'

And then there was Thowra. Karl had pulled some strings at Parks Australia and they'd promptly repaired the washed-away stock route. Drew had trucked the brumbies home.

When Pippa first saw the golden stallion again, he stood in a stoutly fenced yard with one of his mares for company.

'I've added two extra top rails,' said Drew. 'Just in case. He must have been well-handled as a foal, because he's taken to training like an old hand.'

Thowra arched his neck and pranced towards them. The connection that she'd always felt with him was stronger than ever. How could it not be, after that last day at the hut? The stallion reared, boxing the air. Pippa laughed with delight, drinking him in. 'Why does he have a red ribbon tied around his neck?'

'He's gift-wrapped,' said Drew. 'For you.'

A few days later Sam called Pippa and Levi into the back room that served as an office. 'We'll be starting up trail rides in two weeks,' she said. 'Dead Man's Hut needs cleaning and maintenance.' She fixed her gaze on Pippa. 'I was wondering if you and Levi would head up there for me and do the job?'

Pippa blanched. What … return to the place where Cade had shot and almost killed her? The idea was terrifying.

'I understand that you might not want to,' said Sam. 'But I had to give you the opportunity before asking someone else.'

She looked helplessly at Levi. He didn't seem in the least bit perturbed by Sam's proposal. Pippa recalled her mother's advice to her when she was a child frightened of spiders. 'Scared of spiders? Get a spider.' Mum had given her a box containing a huntsman with only two legs. Pippa's natural compassion outweighed her fear and she'd looked after the spider for months, feeding it slaters with tweezers until it regrew its limbs.

She closed her eyes for a moment and thought of Drew. Of how he said she'd been at the front of the queue when they handed out bravery.

Levi reached out, took her hand and laced his fingers with her own. 'Are you game?'

And for some foolish reason she was.

Pippa and Levi set off for Dead Man's Hut the following morning. Why put it off? Best to get the ordeal over with.

They arrived at lunchtime. Duke jumped out of the Jeep first. It was Levi's idea to bring him. Pippa had worried that the hut could bring back all sorts of bad memories, but the wise dog knew that the danger had passed. He raced around the clearing in joyful, fearless circles.

Pippa stood beside the Jeep, her pulse racing. She knew that Cade was dead, but that didn't seem to help. She was on guard, wide awake, like she'd had way too many coffees. Alert for any sudden sound or unexplained movement in the trees.

The mountain was showing Pippa a different face today. Last time, swirling fog had obscured everything. Now her vision was laser clear. She saw a lizard exploring fissures in the rock face by the creek. Silver snow daisies growing in pockets beyond the porch. A pair of eagles soaring towards the distant peaks, wingtips upturned to catch the updraft. Looking south, a silver stream meandered through rich river flats in long, lazy loops. And above everything, set in an azure sky, the sun ruled a land little changed for thousands of years.

'Breathe,' said Levi.

Pippa gasped, unaware that her lungs were bursting. She steadied her airflow – in and out, in and out – until her breath no longer came in ragged spurts. All her senses were heightened. She could hear a yellow robin's thin piping and the buzzing of bees. The air was scented with mint bush and eucalyptus and pine needles. Levi turned Pippa's face towards him. He didn't smell like Cade. He smelled of horses and hay, soil and saddle leather. They kissed and her body ached for him. She needed to lie beside him; have her heart beat next to his. Needed to know what it was like to love a real man and banish every trace of Cade.

Pippa took Levi's hand with trembling fingers and led him to the hut. She paused in the doorway, hesitant to cross the threshold, uncertain of what she might find. But when they went inside she found it was just a hut. It held no terrors. Her main recollection of its dusty interior was of Levi saying that he loved her for the very first time. The memory brought a shiver of joy.

They sat together on the narrow bunk. Levi brushed the hair back from her face. Ruby had cut Pippa's scarecrow mane into a stylish bob. Strawberry-blonde roots showed through, creating an unusual two-tone effect.

Pippa knew what she wanted. Slowly, she unbuttoned Levi's shirt. 'Take it off.' He shrugged it from his shoulders, and she ran her fingertips across his bare torso. A light dusting of coppery-gold chest hairs matched his eyes. 'Your turn.'

He reached out tentative hands and undid Pippa's buttons. Her breasts responded to his touch, tingling with pleasure and expectation. Yet he was so hesitant, so gentle – so controlled. Pippa understood why. He was being careful because of Cade. But Pippa didn't want careful. She wanted passionate and bold. She wanted Levi's daring to inspire her own.

'It's all right,' she whispered, nibbling his ear. 'I won't break.'

He'd needed to hear it. Levi laid Pippa down and undressed her while his lips seared a path down her neck, her shoulders ... skin to skin.

Afterwards, they lay for the longest time: sharing stories, sharing hopes. Darkness had overshadowed Pippa's life for so long that she'd almost forgotten how to dream. It didn't matter. Levi was doing enough dreaming for the both of them.

'We'll work at Brumby's Run to save up and then buy our own place,' he said. 'Become an overflow sanctuary for the Balleroo brumbies. Start our own stud. Offer training and agistment. I know you've leased Thowra out to Drew, but it's only for two years. We could have him back after that. What do you think?'

Pippa lay nestled against him. What did she think? She thought Levi had looked inside her head. She couldn't imagine a finer life than the one that he proposed. And perhaps the most marvellous thing of all was that Levi simply assumed that she'd be part of his future.

Pippa kissed his bare shoulder, then raised herself on one elbow. 'This place that you propose we buy together – whereabouts are you thinking?'

Levi looked thoughtful. 'Cleared land is expensive and hard to come by up here in the mountains. We'd need to look farther afield to begin with. Maybe somewhere out your way, so you could keep an eye on young Janey and the others.'

Pippa grinned. 'We already have a place out my way. Cade died without a will. The State Trustees office sent me a letter saying his farm automatically comes to me as his widow.' She savoured Levi's dumbfounded expression. 'It's badly rundown, but it would be a start. Maybe Charlie and Karl could give us some advice on restoring the land.' Pippa surprised herself with her next remark. 'The Mallee is really quite beautiful.'

Levi wrapped his arms about her and delivered a toe-curling kiss. 'How did I ever deserve you?'

Pippa smiled and closed her eyes, certain that it was the other way around.

Later, they sat on the porch, watching day meld into night. They drank beer and waited for the herbed beef pot roast. Levi liked cooking and Pippa didn't. All she'd had to do was slice the carrots. Perfect.

Duke dozed on the doorstep. Kookaburras laughed and the sun set into a nest of purple clouds. She could hear the evening froggy chorus tuning up. Were they endangered frogs, she wondered? Charlie would know. Pippa wanted to know too.

Levi turned on the radio and found a station playing mellow jazz. 'Dance with me.'

Pippa went all shy. 'I don't know ...'

He held out his arms and the two of them swayed in time with the music. Dusk fell as peace embraced her. Like the brumbies, she and Levi belonged to this high country. Part of the mysterious mountains, part of the ancient forests – at one with the spirit of the land.

ACKNOWLEDGEMENTS

Thank you to my publisher at Penguin Random House, Ali Watts, for enthusiastically embracing this story. Thanks to my editor Grace Arlov and the rest of the publishing team. Thanks also to my agent, Clare Forster of Curtis Brown, for her wisdom and practical support.

Thank you to my literary friends, talented writers all, who encourage me and understand like nobody else the joys and pitfalls of this journey. A special thanks to Julia Carp and Toby Green for some cultural advice in the writing of this novel.

Thank you to the brave women battling and triumphing over domestic violence. I met many of you during my former life as a lawyer, and I never ceased to be amazed by your courage.

Thank you to Elyne Mitchell. Elyne inspired my love of our high country brumbies back when I was a bookworm of a child. Her magnificent writing still inspires me.

Thank you to my patient family for putting up with the time I'm locked away writing, and for believing in me. I am forever grateful.

And last but not least, thanks to my animals – my horses, dogs, cats, chooks and heritage Southdown babydoll sheep. I can't imagine life without you.

ABOUT THE AUTHOR

Bestselling Aussie Jennifer Scoullar writes page-turning fiction about the land, people and wildlife that she loves.

Scoullar is a lapsed lawyer who harbours a deep appreciation and respect for the natural world. She lives on a farm in Australia's southern Victorian ranges, and has ridden and bred horses all her life.

Her passion for animals and the bush is the catalyst for her best-selling books, which are all inspired by different landscapes.

Visit Jennifer's website to enter the monthly prize draw! If you enjoyed this book and have a moment or two, please leave an online rating or review. Reviews are of great help to authors.

www.jenniferscoullar.com

www.ingramcontent.com/pod-product-compliance
Lightning Source LLC
Chambersburg PA
CBHW060813190726
48285CB00002B/649